Orsina of Melidrie is a paladin of the Order of the Sun, sworn to drive out corruption and chaos wherever she finds it. She has been ordered to leave her home and travel around Vesolda in search of a great evil she is supposedly destined to destroy. But after two years of fighting monsters and demons and evil gods, she does not seem to be any closer to her goal—or ever returning home.

Aelia is the Goddess of Caprice, the personification of poor decision-making. The Order of the Sun has classified her as a chaos goddess, meaning that her worship has been outlawed. During a run-in with Orsina, she is trapped in a mortal body, rendering her unable to leave Inthya.

Aelia is found by Orsina again, but this time Orsina does not recognize her in her new body. So Aelia pretends to be a mortal woman who is fleeing an abusive family. Aelia plans to use Orsina as protection as she hunts down the magical relic that will free her from her mortal body.

As Aelia and Orsina grow closer to one another, Aelia wrestles with her own desire to tell Orsina the truth about who she is, and her fear that Orsina will turn on her if she does. But the decision might not be hers after all, because their actions have not gone unnoticed by Aelia's siblings.

DAUGHTER OF THE SUN

Tales of Inthya, Book Two

Effie Calvin

A NineStar Press Publication
Published by NineStar Press
P.O. Box 91792,
Albuquerque, New Mexico, 87199 USA.
www.ninestarpress.com

Daughter of the Sun

This is a work of fiction. Names, characters, places, and incidents are either the product of the author's imagination or are used fictitiously. Any resemblance to actual persons living or dead, business establishments, events, or locales is entirely coincidental.

Printed in the USA
First Edition
November, 2018

Print ISBN: 978-1-949909-36-4

Also available in eBook, ISBN: 978-1-949909-29-6

This book is dedicated to my sister's cat Fletcher because he is a chill dude.

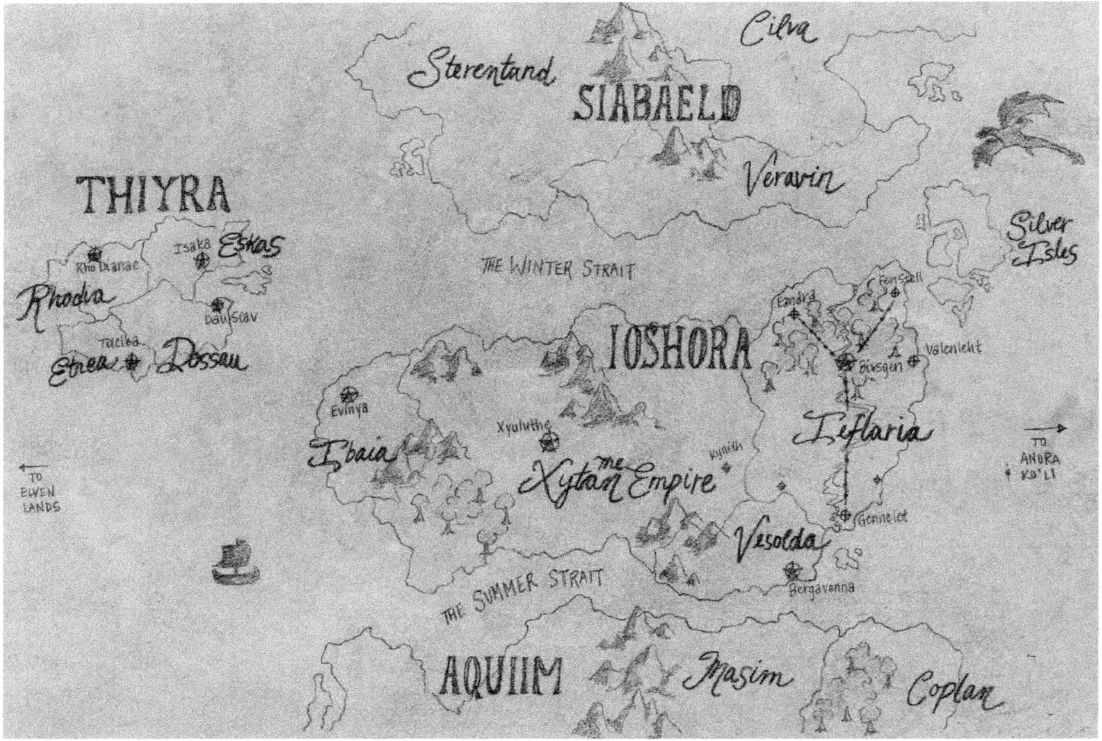
THIYRA
Rhodia
Rho Dianae
Isaka
Eskas
Daušcav
Tacíca
Etrea
Dossau
TO ELVEN LANDS
Sterentand
SIABAELD
Cilva
Veravin
Silver Isles
THE WINTER STRAIT
IOSHORA
Evinya
Ibaia
Xyuluthe
The Xytan Empire
Kynith
Eandra
Fenscell
Valenleht
Bivsgen
Ieflaria
Genneleit
Vesolda
Bergavanna
TO ANORA KO'LI
THE SUMMER STRAIT
AQUIIM
Masim
Coplan

Chapter One

ORSINA

Even from a distance, Orsina of Melidrie could tell something was wrong.

The little village of Soria appeared to be a typical Vesoldan farming community. A field of green barley stretched toward the south, almost ready for the springtime harvest, and the farmers raised their hands to Orsina in greeting as she rode past. Down in the olive groves, trees were beginning to put out tiny, cream-colored blossoms while Sorian youngsters rested beneath the branches and tended to flocks of fat sheep.

But when Orsina inspected the fields more closely, she saw the crops were choked with weeds and beginning to rot. It was as though they had been neglected for weeks, despite the presence of the farmers.

Orsina also didn't fail to notice that all Soria's sheep still wore their heavy winter coats, though all the surrounding communities had held their springtime shearing days nearly a month ago. Most passersby would probably not notice such small details, but Orsina had dealt with situations like this before. She knew the signs of a village in thrall.

According to storytellers, the correct attire for a paladin was heavy plate armor, and a matching set for her horse. Orsina supposed none of those storytellers ever visited southern Vesolda, for even in early spring it was too hot to even contemplate wearing anything heavier than her chain mail and tabard.

Still, when she rode into Soria, children dropped their toys in the dust and abandoned their games to follow her. She doubted any of them had seen a paladin before, and so she gave them warm smiles and tried her best not to look intimidating. She did not know how successful she was.

A temple of Eyvindr, God of the Harvest and Third of the Ten, stood at the center of town. But as Orsina rode past, she noted that the windows were dark and the orange trees in the garden were beginning to wither. Despite her curiosity, she did not linger there.

Orsina dismounted in front of the tavern and tied Star, the gray Vesoldan mare that had been her mount for the last four years. The children were upon her in a moment, asking thousands of questions simultaneously. Was she a paladin? Was she from the Order of the Sun? Had she ever spoken to Iolar? Or one of the other gods? Was she from Bergavenna? Had she ever killed a dragon? A demon? A chaos god?

Orsina answered the questions as best she could, but she wasn't even sure if the children heard her replies. Finally, a man stepped out onto the front steps of the tavern, drawn by the noise.

"Here, leave the poor woman alone!" he yelled to the children. "Go on, back to your chores. Get!"

The children backed away reluctantly, and Orsina gave the man a grateful smile. He smiled back, but she could see the tension in his shoulders and the fear in his eyes. He did not want her here.

"Do you have a room?" asked Orsina. "I was hoping to stay the night."

"Just the one. It's not much, though," he glanced at her armor. "Count Doriano's manor is only a day's ride from here. If you hurry, you might be there before dark, and not have to sleep on a straw mattress—and don't tell anyone I said so, but his wine is better, too."

"I have endured worse than straw mattresses," said Orsina pleasantly, wondering if the man would outright refuse to serve her. But instead, he turned back and yelled into the tavern.

"Benigo!" he called. "See to the Dame Paladin's horse, and bring her bags upstairs."

A young child, probably the man's son, rushed out to take Star's lead. Orsina let him do his work and went inside.

The tavern was nearly empty, save for a few old grandfathers sharing stories. When they saw her, their conversations ended abruptly. Orsina looked around, taking in the ancient wooden furniture and dust collecting in the corners. Open windows let in the midday sunlight, and a massive empty stone fireplace took up the entire north wall.

"It is an honor, Dame Paladin," said the tavern-keeper, speaking too loudly as he moved around the back of the bar and fumbled for a tankard. "What brings you to Soria?"

The question was innocently posed, the sort of question anyone might ask a strange traveler. But it was well known that paladins from the Order of the Sun were forbidden to tell lies. The tavern-keeper wanted to know how much she suspected, how much she knew.

The old men were all watching her as well, their filmy eyes locked on her.

"I am in search of a prophecy," said Orsina. "Two years ago, my Baron, Casmiro of Melidrie, received a vision from Iolar. I was informed that Iolar meant for me to leave

Melidrie immediately and defeat a great evil. I obeyed, of course, and have been in search of it ever since."

The tavern-keeper looked uncomfortable. "And you believe that evil is here?" he asked uneasily, his eyes darting back to the old men.

"I do not know," admitted Orsina. "Unfortunately, the Baron's vision was sparsely detailed. I have destroyed many evil creatures in Iolar's name since I left home, but never have I received a vision telling me that my quest was complete. While I am proud of all that I have accomplished, I admit I will be glad when I am finished."

"But you believe there is evil here?" the tavern-keeper pressed.

Though her vows forbade her to lie, even Iolar could understand the occasional need to be obtuse. "There is evil everywhere, sir," she said. "But we are only vulnerable to it when we tell ourselves otherwise."

The atmosphere in the room became oppressive, but Orsina was not worried. After all she had faced in the last two years, she could hold her own against a handful of villagers, even ones in thrall. The real challenge was always when she happened upon a foe clever enough to use the villagers themselves as weapons, forcing them to throw themselves at her blade until she retreated or managed to subdue them.

At her request, the tavern-keeper led her upstairs to the tiny bedroom where his son had delivered her traveling bags. His assessment of its quality had not been wholly incorrect, but after two years of constant travel, Orsina was used to uncomfortable conditions.

Orsina went to the window and looked out at the neglected temple below. Regardless of whether this village was the home to Iolar's prophesized evil, there was something amiss here. Even if she had been blind to the little signs, the protective tattoos on her arms were slowly growing warm, reacting to the presence of something *wrong*.

Men's imaginations could get the better of them, and stories became wilder after every telling, so Orsina was careful to keep an open mind whenever she first heard a new rumor. Demons and chaos gods did walk on Inthya, but it was infinitely more likely that any given problem had nothing at all to do with the forces of chaos.

For example, ten months ago some terrified villagers had begged her to come investigate the nearby forest where, at night, young women could be heard screaming. The villagers suspected murder, sacrifices, obscene rituals. Orsina had marched in, ready for a fight...only to find out that the source of the noise was a single red fox.

And last winter, she'd gone to confront a werewolf that had been taking sheep and found only ordinary gray wolves who had become hungry enough to forget their fear of men.

But the most memorable occasion was when she had received word of a manticore terrorizing the southern shore. Manticores were native to Aquiim, but they were capable of flight, so it was not impossible to believe one made it across the Summer Strait. Orsina had prepared for the fight of her life, joining with five other paladins to track the beast down. But when they finally cornered the monster, they found that their 'manticore' was actually a rabid brown bear.

The fight had not been pleasant, but it was certainly an improvement over what Orsina imagined a battle with a manticore might have been like. After it was over, the paladins had wondered to each other how anyone on Inthya could manage to confuse a brown bear with a venom-spewing winged lion.

Orsina stepped away from the window and closed the shutters. The sun was still high, and the day was fair. Tonight she would confront whatever evil had taken root here, but in the meantime, her letter to Lady Perlita was incomplete. Orsina gathered up her writing instruments and went downstairs, intending to compose her letter at the long table just in front of the tavern's sunny windows.

Lady Perlita was the daughter of the Baron of Melidrie. In childhood, they had played together when none of Perlita's noble friends or cousins were around. Perlita called for raids upon the kitchens, or the cherry trees, or the Hedoquan cactus pears that had flourished in the warm Vesoldan climate, and Orsina carried out her orders without question.

Years later, Orsina returned home from her paladin's training in Bergavenna to find that Perlita had transformed from a wild, skinny girl into an elegant, olive-skinned beauty with topaz eyes and a waist so small Orsina thought she could have encircled it completely with both her hands (she was mistaken on this last point, as it turned out, but only just).

Orsina regularly wrote letters to Perlita, detailing her adventures. She never received anything in return, but Orsina knew that Perlita was very busy learning to take her father's place. Replies were probably too much to expect.

Orsina also occasionally wrote to her parents, assuring them that she was still alive and well. They did respond, but Orsina moved around so frequently and unpredictably that it was usually months before the letters found her.

As she wrote, Orsina was struck by the sensation that she was being watched. Without looking up, she folded the letter into thirds and packed her ink and quills away.

Moving at a leisurely pace, Orsina left the tavern and walked across the town square to the abandoned temple. It was one of the only buildings in town with glass windows, and it was dark enough within that Orsina could see her reflection in them.

Orsina did not spend much time in front of mirrors, but she recognized her own face: oval, sun-darkened, with a strong nose and stubborn lips. A few wisps of dark brown hair had escaped from her braid to cradle her face.

But something was amiss with her reflection. Orsina quickly tried to divert her own gaze, but her reflection smiled broadly, and she knew she had been caught.

"Will you meet me in the village square, or shall I hunt you through the forest tonight?" Orsina asked the presence in a low voice.

"You're so pretty," breathed her reflection in a soft voice that was not her own. "Do you really wish to destroy me? We can have such fun together."

"Who are you?" demanded Orsina. Her reflection only laughed.

Orsina had not really been expecting an answer, for that would have made her job too simple, but sometimes her adversaries liked to brag. She waited, but after a few minutes, it was clear that the presence—whatever it was—had gone. Orsina turned and walked away from the glass, determined not to show any sort of reaction.

Dusk came soon enough, and the tavern filled as the people of Soria began returning from their day's work. Most were farmers or shepherds, but the village also had a carpenter, a miller, a few tailors, and a blacksmith. Orsina sat in her corner, simply watching, and most of the Sorians refused to make eye contact with her.

She could see they were not too deeply in thrall. They could still speak, and reason, and apparently retained a good deal of their own will, quite unlike the shuffling, empty-eyed thralls she had encountered in the past. But in a way, this was almost more insidious, for it gave the illusion of freedom.

Some of the younger Sorians could not resist approaching the paladin in their midst, and she was happy to oblige them with stories of her past adventures. The tale of the manticore-that-wasn't got a particularly good reception and by the time she was finished, the smiles of the young shepherds were genuine.

There had been no sign of the village priest yet. Nor had she met the administrator assigned to manage the village and send reports back to Count Doriano. Orsina knew better than to ask after them, unless she wanted every villager in the room to turn on her.

As the last traces of sunlight slipped away, the tavern-keeper's son came to light the fire. Curiously, many of the villagers were already beginning to leave. Orsina stayed seated but watched out the window as they vanished into the darkness in the direction of the olive groves.

Orsina rose to her feet, and remaining patrons fell silent.

"Benigo!" yelled the tavern-keeper. His face was bright red, and beads of sweat dripped down his nose. "Show the lady to her room."

Orsina drew her blade, and little Benigo froze mid-step. Before any of the villagers had time to react, she was already out the front door and moving in the direction of the olive groves.

The village was dark and unfamiliar. As Orsina walked, she raised her blade to her lips, murmuring a prayer. The sword began to glow with a steady golden light, enough to guide her way.

Like all paladins, Orsina was blessed by Iolar—a rare thing, for a woman, but certainly not unheard of. She had spent years memorizing the many, many Order-specific rituals and prayers that she channeled her magic through. Orsina's blessing was not terribly powerful, but she had never felt as though she was at a disadvantage. The Order of the Sun had always emphasized the importance of physical might, and the dangers of becoming overly-reliant upon magic and therefore complacent. Those with stronger blessings were usually better suited for the Temple of Iolar.

An idealist at heart, Orsina lacked the contempt for the Temple of Iolar that many of the senior paladins had. She did not see why their organizations frequently viewed themselves as rivals. Their methods might differ, but they had the same mission—to protect innocents from the forces of chaos.

Orsina was aware of the villagers leaving the tavern behind her, but she ignored them. None approached her, or even called to her, but she could hear their shuffling footsteps in the shadows.

By the time Orsina arrived at the olive grove, a mass of villagers had already gathered there between the trees, standing in a circle. She pushed her way through the crowd, and they all parted to let her by easily. None looked her in the face.

At the center of the circle was a woman. She had long, dark hair that gleamed violet and midnight and emerald in the torchlight. Her face was round, her lips stained dark, her eyes glittering amethysts. She wore a simple dress, the sort a Vesoldan peasant might, except for the fact that it was completely black.

Orsina could see no runes on her bared arms to mark her as a demon, and there seemed to be intelligence in her eyes. A goddess, then.

Most chaos gods that Orsina encountered took bodies that were tall and thin, with pronounced neckbones and cheekbones and ribs. Some displayed unnatural characteristics, like curling horns or bestial claws or leathery wings. But this goddess looked like an ordinary woman, more or less. She was only average height and had soft curves to her silhouette.

Of course, the body was merely an avatar, created to hold her spirit while she interacted with Inthya. Still, the sight of it, so unlike the other chaos gods Orsina was familiar with, was surprising.

Orsina tightened her grip on her blade. "Tell me your name, and I will tell you mine," she said.

The woman threw back her head as her lips split open in a bubbling laugh. "You think I do not know you, Orsina of Melidrie?" she asked. "My pets have spoken of nothing else since your arrival."

"If you will not tell me your name, I will have to guess," said Orsina. "Are you Issapa?"

The goddess laughed again. "I am flattered," she said. "But I do not think Issapa has to entertain herself with forgotten villagers in the Vesoldan wilderness. Guess again."

"Are you Rikilda?" asked Orsina, naming the Goddess of Alchemy who was sometimes associated with dark practices. Rikilda was extremely powerful, and this goddess, whoever she was, would enjoy the comparison.

The woman gasped and clapped her hands. "Oh!" she cried in delight. "How sweet you are. But no. Try again!"

"Cytha?" This time, Orsina's guess was genuine. Cytha was an extremely minor goddess, associated with revenge. Her worship was outlawed, but that had never been an obstacle to the sufficiently determined.

"Ah, now we are moving into the obscure," said the goddess. "How nice to speak to someone who is educated in matters of theology. These villagers are such poor conversationalists. You are incorrect, by the way."

This goddess was not powerful at all. It was likely that the village of Soria contained the entirety of her worshippers. Still, unlike demons, a god could never be fully destroyed. For the weaker ones, there were rituals to trap, to banish, to scatter. But eventually, they would return. They always did.

"A hint, then?" suggested Orsina. "Your domain?"

The goddess smiled languidly. "Caprice."

"Aelia," said Orsina immediately, years of rote memorization under the tutelage of Order scribes paying off.

The goddess strode forward.

"Two years, since you last saw your home?" Aelia's violet eyes were searching. "You must be terribly lonely."

"Enough. It is time you made your return to Aethitide." Orsina raised her glowing blade.

"Wait!" said Aelia. "There are things I can offer you. I can find out the purpose of this mysterious quest Iolar has sent you on. No more wandering around little villages, searching for monsters to slay. If you work quickly, you could be home before summer's end."

Orsina hesitated, though her grip on the sword did not weaken.

"I will make no pact with you," she said.

"No?" But Aelia's form was shifting now. She became shorter, thinner. Her hair shifted to an ordinary shade of brown and coiled itself into a coronet. Her peasant's dress transformed into a lady's crimson gown. Orsina gritted her teeth and looked away, for Aelia was now a perfect replica of Lady Perlita.

"You have done enough," said Aelia, in Perlita's voice. "More than enough. You do not deserve to spend your days wandering Inthya in hopes of stumbling upon your destiny. You have slain more monsters, destroyed more demons, banished more chaos gods than any other paladin your age. Nobody could fault you for your homesickness."

Aelia moved closer and rested one hand against Orsina's face. When Orsina did not rip away, Aelia pressed their lips together.

Orsina could taste the chaos magic in her kiss, and her protective tattoos blazed in warning. Without taking a step forward or back, Orsina raised her blade and stabbed through Aelia's chest.

Perlita's form began melting away as Aelia screamed in pain and outrage. Orsina ignored the noise and chanted the prayer that prevented her from retreating to Aethitide, her plane in Asterium. Once bound to Inthya, Orsina could destroy her form. It would take years, perhaps even decades, for Aelia's consciousness to regenerate.

"No!" snarled Aelia as she realized she was now trapped in a mortal body. She staggered backward, into the olive trees and away from the torchlight. Orsina moved to follow the weakened goddess, but hands grabbed at her, drawing her back. Orsina tried to wrench free, but the villagers were so numerous—and so horribly fragile.

Orsina twisted around to face them, bringing her sword about in a wide cleaving motion. Fortunately, the villagers still retained enough control over themselves to recoil from the gleaming edge of the blade. That moment of delay was enough for Orsina to turn on her heel and go running into the trees after Aelia.

The villagers were already pursuing her, but their movements were awkward and clumsy. She could tell Aelia's hold on their minds was waning. With only her sword lighting the way, she smashed through low-hanging branches, boots skidding downhill.

Aelia moved in an erratic, unpredictable path, swerving this way and that in hopes of losing her pursuer. She leaped ancient stone fences in a single, effortless bound, darted around trees, vanished into long shadows. Now thoroughly lost, all Orsina could do was stand still and wait to hear the goddess's footfalls.

Someone tackled her, and Orsina went sprawling across the dirt. The blade fell from her hand, and someone struck her across the face. Orsina drew her knees to her chest and kicked outward with all her strength, sending the unfortunate villager back into darkness. At the sound of rustling branches, Orsina grabbed her sword and lurched to her feet again, intent upon following the noise.

Aelia was beginning to slow, thanks to the massive wound in her midsection. An ordinary woman would have been dead ten times over, but goddesses, even obscure ones like Aelia, were significantly more resilient.

She caught up to Aelia shortly, bringing her sword's hilt down on the back of her neck. Aelia fell, crumpling as though she was made of plaster. By the light of her blade, she saw Aelia struggle to push herself back upward on her palms, and that was when Orsina struck her head off at the neck.

Slowly, slowly, her protective tattoos returned to their normal temperature. Orsina swallowed and looked around at the unfamiliar trees. She could very well be a mile away from Soria at this point.

But more shapes were moving toward her now—the villagers, now free of Aelia's manipulations. Irritation flared up in her chest. Aelia had not been a powerful goddess, and there were at least thirty of them. The goddess should not have been able to take advantage of them so easily!

"Dame Paladin?" one of them called anxiously. "Is she dead?"

"Dead enough, for now," said Orsina, pointing her sword at the now-lifeless avatar, casting enough light upon it that the villagers could see what had happened. "Are any of your people injured?"

"I don't know," he said. More shadowy figures were coming forward, but now their movement was natural and free. They gathered around in a half-circle, none approaching her directly. When she looked into their eyes, they glanced away.

"Where is your priest?" she demanded. Nobody answered immediately. *"Where is he?"*

"Alive," said one of the village men. "She told us to lock him up. We put him in the granary."

Orsina breathed a sigh of relief. "And Count Doriano's man?"

"With the priest," said another villager, this one a woman. "Please—you have to understand! She said, she said—"

"I know what she said. I will hear your excuses tomorrow, if that is what you require. Right now, I need someone to burn this avatar," she pointed at the body. "And then I need someone to lead me back to the village."

A handful of villagers were already constructing a pyre as she began the trek back to Soria.

Her first stop was the granary, since it seemed none of the villagers wanted to face the men they'd imprisoned. When she unbolted the door and threw it wide open, both the priest and the administrator flinched. But their expressions turned to relief as they caught sight of the golden sun emblazoned on Orsina's tabard.

"Oh, thank the gods!" gasped the administrator. "What day is it? I swear we've been in here for months! Did the Count send you?"

"Yes," said Orsina. "He found your letters concerning."

"I thought he might." He cast a glance at the priest of Eyvindr. "There, see, I told you he'd catch on."

"Yes, and it only took him two weeks," said the priest dryly.

The other man ignored the jibe. "We owe you our lives, Dame Paladin. I expect the villagers planned to sacrifice us sooner or later."

Orsina very much doubted that. There was more carelessness in Aelia than spite. It seemed more likely that the two men would have starved to death once the goddess forgot about them. But she did not bother to contradict him. "The villagers have been freed, and they will no longer threaten you. In fact, I believe they are all quite ashamed of their actions. And you do not have to worry about the goddess, either. Her avatar was destroyed, and it should take years for one as obscure as her to regenerate."

The administrator seemed pleased by what he heard, and set off for the tavern, declaring that *everybody* would be buying him drinks tonight if they wished to keep their names out of his report to Count Doriano. But the priest of Eyvindr stayed behind.

"I do not know how this happened," he confided to Orsina. "I have heard tales, but...I never believed my own people could be so foolish, to fall under the spell of a chaos goddess."

"I expect I will find out the answer to that tomorrow," Orsina agreed. "Nevertheless, I believe that this is a lesson your villagers will not soon forget."

The priest bid her a good night, and Orsina stood alone in the shadow of the granary. She closed her eyes and raised her face to the night sky, waiting to see if Iolar's approval filled her mind with golden light, followed by an affirmation that her work was done at last.

It did not.

To her great surprise, tears sprang to her eyes. What was this? She raised a gauntlet to her face in confusion and stared at the teardrop gleaming on the silver metal. A paladin did not fall into despair! She had never received a direct, personal acknowledgment from Iolar before, so why did its absence suddenly feel like a rejection?

Her mind flashed back to the moment that Aelia, wearing Perlita's body, had pressed their lips together.

"You must be terribly lonely," she had said.

I'm not, Orsina wanted to say, but she was forbidden to lie—even to the quiet darkness of a tiny, forgettable Vesoldan farming village.

Why had Perlita not written to her? Her heart ached at the question she'd refused to consider for two years. If Perlita missed Orsina even a fraction as much as Orsina missed her, she should have at least *one* letter!

She closed her eyes again, remembering the kiss. It had not been the real Perlita, but it had apparently been enough to awaken the longing that she'd thought she'd successfully buried.

Orsina felt her contempt for the villagers' weakness fade to something softer. It was so easy to judge them for their failings, but she had failings too. Even now, she still carried a glimmer of curiosity in her heart. What might have happened if she had accepted Aelia's offer to determine the true purpose of her quest?

Well, it hardly mattered now. Aelia was gone from Inthya and could not be expected to return anytime soon. Orsina would have to seek Iolar's destiny in the way he had intended: slowly, and with a paladin's patience.

WHEN ORSINA AWOKE the next day, the villagers had already begun the process of shearing their neglected sheep. She was pleased to see the animals would no longer suffer in the heat, though she could have done without all the bleating.

Meanwhile, out in the fields, she could see farmers ripping out weeds that had been given far too much leniency in the past weeks. Yesterday, the farmers had moved with syrupy slowness, stopping to observe every bird that flitted past, even wandering aimlessly through their green fields. Now they labored purposefully, shouting commands to one another as they wrenched the choking weeds from the earth and threw them into piles to be burned.

At the temple, the priest was doing his best to restore the orange trees using Eyvindr's green magic, and a few children were cleaning his windows. Things might be awkward for a time, but Soria would survive this. A few seasons from now, it would be regarded as little more than a curious dream, a tale to frighten children.

Triumphant as she had been, Orsina's quest was not quite complete. Count Doriano had specifically requested the safe return of his administrator. She knew that he would not simply be content with her word that all was well, especially not after she explained what happened.

Unfortunately, it seemed the administrator had taken full advantage of the villagers' guilt last night, and she found him difficult to rouse.

"Tell him they've sacrificed me!" the man moaned through his front door when Orsina made it clear that refusing to answer would only result in more insistent knocking. "Tell him they murdered me on an unholy altar, and a demon ate my heart!"

"Even if I were capable of lying to his lordship, I would never say such a thing," said Orsina. "You have one hour to ready yourself for the journey. This is your own doing, I hope you realize."

For some reason, the man did not seem interested in hearing a lecture on the merits of sobriety, so Orsina left him to dress. She did still have a few questions for the villagers. She wanted to know how they had come to learn Aelia's name.

When she went back into the tavern, the only ones inside were the tavern-keeper himself, and his young son. All the other Sorians were busy, making up for the weeks of work they had neglected. That was not to say that these two were not busy as well—in fact, the innkeeper appeared to be washing several weeks' worth of tankards while his son scrubbed at the floor with a brush.

When she approached them, they thanked her profusely for at least the third time that day. The boy, Benigo, declared that he would join the Order of the Sun once he was old enough, and save villages just as Orsina did. He was not the first child to say this to her, and so Orsina knew not to take it too seriously. Instead, she sat at the stool across from the washing-bucket and said to the tavern-keeper, "I wonder if I might ask you some questions?"

"Benigo, see if the priest needs help," the tavern-keeper ordered his son. Once the boy was gone, he looked up at Orsina. She could tell he was struggling with the words.

"Take as long as you need," she said.

"It was the children first. We thought nothing of it. *Aelia*, they would say. They spoke as though she was a playmate of theirs. We thought it was a game. You know how children are. When chores went unfinished, it was because Aelia distracted them. When the cow got out, it was Aelia who'd unlocked the gate." He shook his head. "I'm ashamed now, that I didn't see it for what it was."

"You could not have known," Orsina assured him.

"What if it'd been Issapa? Or Edan?" There was a glint of panic in the man's eyes. "We were lucky it was only her. She hardly meant any harm, compared to what some of the others might have done."

"That is true," Orsina acknowledged. Though Aelia was a chaos goddess, she was practically benign compared to what some of her siblings were capable of. Still, that was not to say she could be allowed to influence Inthya. The damage to Soria had been small because Orsina caught her quickly. Orsina shuddered to think of what the village would look like if Aelia's influence continued through the summer. The harvest would be ruined. All the livestock would die of neglect. There would be nothing stored away for winter.

"And then she started speaking to the adults, too. I can't remember what she said, but at the time it..." he put up his hands in defeat, "...it just made sense. When she told us to lock away our priest, none of us could remember why we had never done it before. She told us we were..."

"You were...?" Orsina prompted.

He shook his head. "She told us we were spending too much time worrying, and working. Our lives were so short, she'd say. Better to enjoy it while it lasts. As I said...it made sense at the time."

"I see," said Orsina quietly.

"It all sounds so foolish, now that I say it out loud," said the tavern-keeper. "You must think very little of us."

"Not at all," said Orsina. "It is the nature of men to trust the words of our gods, just as children trust their parents. Unfortunately, not all are deserving of that trust."

"I cannot disagree with that," he said. After a moment, he added, "I heard it was the reports that alerted the Count."

"Yes," said Orsina, who had seen several of the aforementioned letters during her initial meeting with Count Doriano. The reports themselves were unremarkable, containing the usual expenses and estimates and predictions. It was the personal notes at the end that had caused the Count to call upon Orsina. "I expect none of you had any way of knowing that his lordship does not have a cousin in Lonada, nor a great aunt in Sabaga. Nor is he courting a lady from Vazerta."

"Ah," said the tavern-keeper. "Yes. That might have been it."

Orsina looked down at her hands. "These things happen," she said. "Do not think less of yourself or your neighbors for it. If it had not been you, it would have been another village. It is in our nature to fail. Forgiveness would not be nearly so precious if we never required it."

You have done enough, said the memory of the goddess. *More than enough.*

Orsina raised her hand to her lips, remembering.

"Will you return home now?" asked the tavern-keeper.

"No," admitted Orsina quietly. "It seems Aelia was not the evil I was meant to defeat."

There was genuine sympathy in the man's eyes. "I'm sorry to hear that. Nevertheless, I'm glad you came to us."

"As am I," said Orsina. She forced herself to smile. "Well, if you are ever in need again, do call on me. I'm always looking for work."

Chapter Two

AELIA

Aelia watched the last of the villagers vanish into the darkness with a great deal of relief. At the paladin's orders, they had constructed a pyre to burn what they believed was Aelia's body, the remains of which were now little more than ash.

She was lucky, she supposed, that the dame had not noticed that the version of Aelia she killed was a fake. But then, for all their abilities to sense deception, paladins tended to believe whatever was put in front of their eyes.

Unfortunately, to make the ruse believable, Aelia had been forced to release her hold on the villagers' minds. Their support, unwilling as it had been, had given her power—power that she seldom felt. Gods were generally only as powerful as their worshippers, and Aelia had no worshippers at all.

Tens of thousands of years ago, Aelia had been classified as a chaos goddess by the organization that would later become the Temple of Iolar. All it really meant was that she represented something that Iolar disapproved of...and that his followers drove her out from wherever they found her.

Aelia slipped down from her hiding place in the trees. The wound in her stomach still ached, even as she pressed her magic into it. As long as she didn't expend herself, it would heal in a few days.

There was no moonlight to see by, but she at least had enough power left to sense her way out of the grove. She began moving in the direction opposite of Soria, determined not to be caught again.

Aelia had two options. The first was to simply kill herself and wait to regenerate. But regenerating from nothing was so painfully dull, and would take years, given how seldom anyone invoked her name. And then, once she was back in Aethitide, it would take ages for her to become strong enough to manifest on Inthya again. If she'd wanted to do all that, she would have just let the paladin kill her avatar.

Her other option was to perform the ritual to unbind her from her mortal body. This was far more desirable. The only problem was the ritual required the use of the Unbinding Stone. And Aelia had no idea where on Inthya it might be.

The Unbinding Stone was not, as it sounded, a simple stone. It was an ancient dagger, all carved from a single piece of violet crystal, forged in the early days of Inthya when the gods were not so powerful as they were now. If she used it to stab her own heart out, she would be free from her awful flesh prison, without the need to regenerate.

Aelia made it out of the olive grove and on to the main road. Weakened as she might be, she had no fear of bandits. In fact, a group of bandits might make satisfactory thralls. At least no paladins would come investigating when *they* started behaving strangely.

Aelia walked until the sky began to lighten to misty gray. Her body was horribly exhausted, and she wanted nothing more than to climb out of it. Several times she tried to free herself, but the binding magic held strong.

Iolar would regret teaching those rituals to Men someday. The Ten liked to believe themselves infallible, to pretend Men would venerate them until Inthya came to its end. But for all of Iolar's tedious laws, Men were wild, fickle, easily distracted. One day, they might all rise from their beds and decide to worship Aelia instead.

Aelia tried to imagine what it must be like to have thousands of worshippers scattered across the world. The thought warmed her. Then *she* would be the one sending her followers to chase her siblings out of miserable little villages she didn't even care about.

A glimmering light caught Aelia's eye, and she squinted into the woods that bordered the road. Deep in the trees, she could see water. A river, perhaps, or a pond. Aelia looked down at her bloodstained avatar. She should clean up before she tried to interact with any mortals.

Aelia gathered up her skirts and pushed through the underbrush. It was a pond, with one end completely coated in something green and fuzzy, but it was better than walking into a new town covered in blood.

Aelia knelt down by the water and took a moment to study her reflection. The paladin had said the binding words as Aelia had been between two forms: her usual avatar, and the Vesoldan noblewoman that she'd drawn from the paladin's memories. Now it seemed the two had mixed together to create someone new.

She supposed the paladin may have done her a favor, for she would have a difficult time passing as a Man in her old avatar. Her hair no longer had an iridescent sheen. Instead, it was the same dark brown color that was common in this region. Her skin was not quite olive-toned, but still dark enough to pass for a native Vesoldan if she claimed she was from the north, near the Ieflarian border.

Turning her head from side to side, Aelia examined her new face. Her cheekbones were more pronounced, as was her nose. Her eyes were brown—not the lovely golden color of the noblewoman's, just ordinary brown. She was a bit shorter than she preferred, though not nearly as short as the noblewoman. She was also a bit skinnier than she liked, but there was nothing she could do about that now. She could not alter an avatar once trapped in it.

Aelia peeled the bloodstained dress off. Her undergarments were equally stained, but nobody would ever see those. She soaked the dress in the water, but the blood had already dried and refused to come loose, no matter how Aelia scrubbed at it. At least the wound in her stomach was nearly healed. She wouldn't have any trouble convincing anyone that she had been attacked by bandits.

She needed a map. She needed help. And, apparently, judging by the buzzing in her head, she needed food. Aelia gave a little shudder at the thought. Her body might require sustenance, but that did not make the idea of consuming organic matter any less disgusting.

Aelia set her dress out in a patch of sunlight. It had started off existence as part of her form, but now it was a separate entity. It, too, had been midway between shapes when she had been locked into Inthya. The result was a dress sewn from dark red fabric.

At least the color matched the bloodstains.

But the dress was slow to dry, and Aelia quickly grew bored. She splashed some water on her face, trying to make herself look presentable. When there was no more she could do for herself, she entertained herself by catching frogs and letting them leap around in her hands. Could one eat a frog? Aelia could not recall. Men did not raise frogs, to her knowledge, so probably not. But then, Men did not raise deer, either. And she knew they ate deer.

A goddess ought to know more about Men and how they lived, but Aelia always struggled to pay attention to such mundane things, let alone remember which practices corresponded with which region. Besides, even when she did put in the effort, Men changed their ways so quickly. Entire continents could become unrecognizable after only a few hundred years.

Aelia poked the creature with a finger, feeling the blobby, pebbly skin. No, she decided. She would never be hungry enough to eat a frog. She allowed it to jump out of her hands and vanish into the long grass.

Why had Cyne put frogs on Inthya? Maybe she would ask him when this was all over. Cyne was the Eleventh in Ioshora, but he never acted as though he was too good to speak to Aelia. His plane, Ferra, was an endless expanse of rolling green hills and emerald forests, the eternal home to every animal that had died since the creation of Inthya. Sometimes his cats, with their strange ability to pierce the barrier between planes, came wandering into Aethitide.

She needed to find the Unbinding Stone. Everything else was secondary. Cyne would not help her, not once he learned she had been enthralling people. He did not understand what it was like to have his worship outlawed. He did not know what it was like to only have his name invoked as a curse. Men had loved him from the moment they'd first opened their eyes.

No, she would have to locate some of her fellow chaos gods and hope they were feeling charitable. There were hundreds of them, struggling to teach their names to every new generation of Men as to not be forgotten completely.

One of the most prominent among them was Edan, God of Wrath. Few worshipped him directly, but he was one of the lucky ones who did not really need worshippers to accumulate power. Instead, he gained his strength from the spiteful violence that Men inflicted upon one another. The souls that dwelled in his home plane, Aratha, were those rare few that had been deemed too vile for any of the other gods to take in after their deaths.

Edan had come to Aelia...how long ago? A month? A few years? A decade? She had no idea. He wanted her to join him for...something. Aelia had not really been paying attention as he'd explained it. She had no interest in working with Edan. She had no interest in working at all, but *especially* not with him.

Where had he asked her to meet him? Somewhere near the Xytan border, probably. Everything important seemed to be happening in Xytae this century, including Reygmadra's most recent fight with Dayluue over... whatever it had been.

Aelia never knew what was going on.

Well, she would seek out Edan. It was not as though she had anything else to do. And perhaps he would be able to point her to the Unbinding Stone if she agreed to ally with him for a while.

Her dress would be a long time in drying. Aelia moved away from the pond and found a patch of grass that didn't have any large stones or fallen branches. Her body was so exhausted that she barely noticed how uncomfortable it was.

Within only a few minutes, she was asleep.

A HAND ON her shoulder ripped her back to full awareness. Aelia screamed and threw a wild, directionless punch, only for her fist to meet with something that sent pain shooting down her arm.

"By the gods!" yelped a voice. Aelia scrambled backward, squinting in the darkness. The sun was already slipping below the horizon. How long had she slept for? A day? Longer?

"I was afraid you might be dead!" said the Man—a woman, probably. The armor made it even harder to tell than usual. "By Iolar, are you all right? You need a healer!"

Aelia stared up at the woman, disbelieving. She sometimes had trouble telling Men apart, but she was almost completely certain that this was the same paladin that chased her from Soria!

But...it seemed the paladin had not recognized her. Was her face really that changed?

"Here, we're not far from Antocoso," said the paladin with an encouraging smile. "I have a horse you can ride. Are there any others with you?"

Aelia shook her head, afraid to speak. Surely the paladin could sense what she was! Any moment now, she would draw her sword and finish the work she had begun.

But instead, the paladin went to retrieve the dress. It was halfway dry, stained with blood, and had a hole in the middle where her blade had pierced it.

Why was she not attacking? Was Aelia's flesh body shielding her from the paladin's magic? Or was it because Aelia was so low on magic of her own? Perhaps a combination of the two factors?

"I don't think there's any saving this," said the paladin, examining the dress. "I have extra clothes in my bag, though, and when we get to Antocoso—"

"No," interrupted Aelia, curling inward on herself. "No. Please. I don't want anything."

"Don't be silly," said the paladin. Her voice was gentle, as though she thought Aelia was a frightened child. "You need a healer. Was it a Man that attacked you, or an animal?"

"Please, I'm fine. I swear it."

"You are not," said the paladin. She unclasped the cloak from her shoulders and handed it to Aelia. The fabric was the garish yellow color that Iolar's followers were fond of. Aelia did not want to accept it—she did not want to accept *anything* from this woman—but she had to admit she was not looking forward to getting back into a cold, wet dress. She wrapped it around herself as best she could.

The paladin seemed to take Aelia's acceptance of the cloak as a victory.

"My horse is just back there," she said, gesturing in the direction of the road. "And I do have one dress in my bags. You're welcome to it, I hardly use it myself. And you must be hungry."

That caught Aelia's interest. She hadn't eaten once since manifesting on Inthya last night, and her stomach felt as though it was attempting to consume itself. "Yes," she said quickly.

"Follow me, then," said the paladin. She drew her sword, and Aelia flinched, but she only used it to slash through the underbrush so the sticks and briars would not tear at Aelia's bare limbs.

Aelia stepped out onto the road cautiously as the paladin began searching through her saddlebags. The horse was pale gray, and taller and wider than Aelia had been expecting. She had only really seen horses from a distance and thought they looked delicate and graceful, like overgrown deer. But up close her impression was quite different. This beast could kill her if it was so inclined.

"Star won't hurt you," said the paladin, noting the expression on Aelia's face. "I promise. She's the best horse I've ever owned." She withdrew a crumpled garment from the bottom of her bag. "Here, it might be a bit long, but you'll hardly notice when you're riding."

The dress was far too long and so tight across the bust and hips that she heard stitching tear when she put it on, but Aelia did not complain. Once she was dressed, the paladin handed her something that Aelia eventually identified as bread. Aelia tore into it, not even minding the sensation of it sliding down her throat in a moist lump and settling in her stomach. It was gone in moments, and so the paladin gave her another small loaf. This time, she ate more slowly.

"Antocoso is close," said the paladin. "Is that where you're from?"

Aelia shook her head around her mouthful of bread, afraid to lie outright. Some of Iolar's blessed, truthsayers, had the ability to detect lies. Fortunately, they were extremely rare, and logic decreed that if this paladin *was* one, she would be standing at the right hand of whoever was currently ruling Vesolda, not galloping around the countryside on the most dubious quest ever heard of.

"I'm traveling," explained Aelia. "One of my brothers... I believe he is living in Sabarra. I was hoping to reunite with him." Again, it was not an outright lie. Edan had asked her to meet him somewhere on the border that Vesolda shared with Xytae. Sabarra was the only area that fit that description that she knew the name of.

"That is quite far from here," said the paladin. "Surely you were not traveling alone?"

Aelia pretended to be too focused on her bread to respond. But instead of objecting, or demanding answers, the paladin helped her onto Star's back, knitting her fingers together so Aelia could use them as a step. Because of the skirt, Aelia was forced to sit sideways on the saddle, the way some nobles did, with her fingers gripping Star's mane.

"What is your name?" asked the paladin.

"Elyne," said Aelia, preparing for Orsina to declare her a liar. But instead, Orsina only took the reins and began leading Star down the road. Definitely not a truthsayer, then. Emboldened by her success, she added, "My family are vintners, in Ortradosa."

"I am Orsina of Melidrie," she said, turning back to look at Aelia. "My family has served as common guards for the Baron of Melidrie for generations."

"But not you?" asked Aelia, forgetting her fear for a moment.

"No," agreed Orsina. "I was called to the Order of the Sun."

Aelia remembered the things she had seen in Orsina's memories at the olive grove: an enormous stone manor house at the center of a sprawling estate, guards in gleaming armor, a noblewoman with yellow eyes that Aelia now bore a passing resemblance to.

She wondered if she could use that to her advantage.

"Will you tell me how you came to be in those woods?" asked Orsina after a long silence.

"Must I?" asked Aelia. "I do not wish to revisit my own foolishness."

"If it was a Man that attacked you, I would like to bring them to justice. And if it was an animal, it should be put down. But if you are not ready to speak of it, I will not press you."

Aelia did not respond. She was unwilling to make up an elaborate story, for fear of being caught in a lie later. For now, she would merely remain silent and let Orsina imagine whatever terrible things she desired.

From the gentle, pitying looks Orsina kept giving her, Aelia thought refusing to answer might even work to her advantage.

Orsina explained that she had already been to Antocoso once today, delivering Soria's administrator safely to Count Doriano. He had been imprisoned, she explained, by villagers in the thrall of a chaos goddess. The villagers forced him to write letters to the count, claiming all was well. But the man added personal notes at the end of each, the sort a sycophant seeking to impress a lord might, wishing good health to various friends and family members. None of the farmers knew enough about the Count's personal relationships to realize he was asking after people who did not exist.

Aelia listened to Orsina's side of the story with interest. She had to admit, she was impressed by the administrator's cunning, especially since her impression of him had been that he was a pompous old fool. But then, he had managed to fight off her influence when she'd first made herself known.

Perhaps she ought to have paid more attention to him. Still, what was done was done, and Aelia hated to dwell on the past.

They arrived at Antocoso as the sun was setting. It was a large town, or perhaps a small city. Aelia wasn't certain. Even though the day was over, the streets were still filled with people hurrying about, conducting last-minute business or just heading for home or the taverns.

Aelia wondered if they would go to the Temple of Adranus to find a healer, but instead, Orsina brought her to an inn. Unlike the tavern in Soria, this inn was clean and comfortable, with floorboards that gleamed and oil lamps casting the rooms in a golden glow.

Once they were through the doors, Orsina further surprised her by renting two rooms and asking for a hot meal to be brought to Aelia immediately.

"I did not realize that accepting your help meant that I'd become your ward," remarked Aelia.

"Did you think I'd leave you to sleep in an alleyway?"

"No. A temple."

"Would you be more comfortable with that?" Orsina looked concerned, even anxious. "I'm sorry. I should have asked. I just assumed..."

"It's all right!" said Aelia hastily. Too late, she realized that she probably should not have said anything. She already knew that Orsina could not sense what she was. A temple priest might be a different story. "I was only surprised. By...your generosity. I'm sure you have better things to do than look after me."

"It's nothing," Orsina assured her. "And besides, it's nice to have someone to talk to."

She really *was* lonely, Aelia realized. She'd seen it last night, in Soria, but hadn't thought much of it until now. Men were not meant to be alone for extended periods of time; even the most introverted of them required interaction with their own kind occasionally.

Despite everything, Aelia felt a little sorry for Orsina and her blind devotion to Iolar's ridiculous mandates.

When the meal arrived, Aelia identified more bread and some sort of meat on the plate. There was also a collection of small, bitter green fruits that each had a large, inedible seed inside. She almost broke a tooth on the first one. Was there a way to ask what they were called without arousing suspicion?

She ate everything on the plate, except for the meat. Consuming plant matter was one thing. Animal matter was quite another. Her own mortal body was made of meat, was it not? Meat consuming meat. It unsettled her. Luckily, the serving-maid brought her an entire bowl of figs, (announcing what they were called as she set the bowl down) and so Aelia could eat to her heart's content.

Orsina did not join her for the meal, though Aelia hardly noticed this. But just as Aelia was finishing the last fig, the paladin returned, accompanied by a healer from the Temple of Adranus.

Orsina heard no protests, and so Aelia was forced to show the healer the wound in her stomach. The healer tutted and poked, and Aelia worried that he might announce that her injury had already been touched by magic. But he set to work without saying anything, and by the time he was finished, Aelia's injury was little more than an ugly scar.

"You were lucky it wasn't too deep," the healer told her before he left, and Aelia did not contradict him. She counted herself lucky that her own healing had been enough to disguise the true nature of the wound. "Do not over-exert yourself for the next few days. And come to the temple if the wound re-opens or shows signs of infection."

The healer left to consult with Orsina, and Aelia went downstairs. This establishment was a nicer one, so there were no drunken brawls or patrons belting out bawdy lyrics, but Aelia found herself drawn to the musicians in the corner, where a woman plucked out notes on a lute while a neutroi sang wistful songs about years gone by.

Hours slipped past, but Aelia was not tired yet. She supposed it was because she'd already spent the entire day asleep. Aelia could not help but be concerned. Ordinary Men did not conduct their business at night and sleep during the day. It would arouse suspicion. How could she correct this? Aelia did not know enough about Men to be sure.

Finally, it seemed even the musicians were too exhausted to go on. They left the tavern with a good night to the owner, and Aelia was left with nothing to do but try to sleep.

As she passed the door to Orsina's room, she saw the door was open and the paladin was still awake. She was dressed in a long tunic and sitting at a desk, composing a letter. Orsina gave her a soft smile as she passed.

"How are you feeling?" she asked.

"I'm fine," Aelia assured her. "I'm hardly even tired. I only came up because the music was done."

"Let me know if your wound gets worse. I'll send for a healer again."

"I'm sure it will be fine. I don't feel it at all anymore."

They stayed like that for an awkward moment, Aelia in the doorway and Orsina staring back at her.

"Well, goodnight," said Aelia. Without waiting for a reply, she hurried to her own room.

Aelia had never slept in a bed before, but she had observed Men doing it. She removed the too-tight dress and settled herself beneath the blankets. It was much, much nicer than the forest floor. She'd hardly noticed that her back ached until now.

Despite the long sleep she already enjoyed today, Aelia was asleep before the candle even burned down.

"WE'LL GET YOU another dress today," reported Orsina over breakfast. "Maybe two."

"One is enough," said Aelia hastily, a little bit surprised that Orsina had even remembered her promise from yesterday. If their positions had been reversed, she knew she probably would have forgotten.

Except, according to Orsina, one was not enough. When they entered the seamstress's shop, Orsina told the women that Aelia needed two dresses and a new set of undergarments to replace the bloodstained ones she wore now.

This all required the seamstresses to measure, cut, sew, pin, and stitch while Aelia stood in the middle of the room like a living doll, a little dazed by the speed of it all. It felt like a strange, incomprehensible ritual and Aelia could not help but be impressed by the women's craftsmanship.

Orsina left the shop with a promise to return, which Aelia only half-believed. But the paladin returned a little after midday, carrying bread and cheese and some strange, pink thing that had been sliced into thin discs, and a wineskin to share.

"I thought paladins were not allowed to drink," Aelia said. They were sitting on the steps of the workshop, waiting for the second dress to be finished. As much as Aelia wanted to mock Orsina for her generosity, she was happy to be in a garment that fit.

"There is a difference between drinking and drunkenness," explained Orsina. "The former is allowed. The latter is not. I don't think Iolar could reasonably expect us to be able to find priests to purify water every time it's needed."

"What else is forbidden by the Order of the Sun?" Aelia asked, genuinely interested in what sort of absurd restrictions Iolar was forcing upon his children.

"Lying," said Orsina. "But you probably already knew that one, it's quite famous. We're discouraged from owning land or property, or accumulating too much money, though it isn't outright forbidden. Whenever I find myself with too much coin, I give it to the temple, or send it home to my parents."

"Did the Count give you a reward?" asked Aelia.

"Yes," said Orsina.

That explained the dresses, at least.

"And romance?" asked Aelia. "Is that forbidden as well?"

"Oh, of course not," said Orsina. "But...we are warned that it can be difficult to fully devote oneself to Iolar while pursuing a courtship. Because of that, many paladins choose to refrain from it entirely."

Aelia thought, yet again, of the golden-eyed noblewoman that lived in so many of Orsina's memories, but she said nothing.

"Do you think you will continue on to Sabarra, or return home to Ortradosa?" asked Orsina, changing the subject.

"Sabarra, I think," said Aelia. "I've made it this far. I'd hate to have to turn around."

"I will find passage for you," Orsina said. "I'm sure there's a traveling caravan of some sort going in that direction—"

"You don't have to do that," Aelia objected. The idea of spending weeks in the company of an entire troupe of strange Men was extremely unappealing. She knew she would not be able to behave as a mortal woman should for such a long time. Sooner or later, they would grow suspicious of her.

"Do you intend to walk to Sabarra, then?"

"Maybe I will!" Aelia retorted, suddenly feeling very contrary. Orsina rolled her eyes.

"Don't be ridiculous. You are lucky to be alive! You can't just go wandering around alone. Even with your magic, it is easy to be overwhelmed—"

"My magic?" repeated Aelia with a frown. As far as she knew, she had not used any magic in front of Orsina.

"Don't you have Talcia's magic?" asked Orsina. When Aelia's frown only deepened, Orsina added, "My ability to sense chaos magic also picks up Talcia's magic, since they're so similar. That's how I was able to sense you in the forest when we first met."

"Oh," said Aelia. "I—yes. You, you surprised me. I didn't realize..."

Orsina gave a soft laugh at that. "Most people don't."

"Does it bother you?" asked Aelia cautiously. "Being so near to someone with Talcia's magic?"

"No, not at all," Orsina reassured her. "When a chaos god is near, or a demon, I feel burning. Those with Talcia's magic are far more benign. My awareness is simply that—an awareness. If we traveled together for many weeks, I would eventually cease to notice it at all."

Aelia could hardly believe her luck. It seemed Orsina had an innocent explanation for everything Aelia said or did. Were all paladins this single-minded, or was Orsina just exceptionally trusting? Either way, it could be advantageous.

Perhaps it was time to reconsider her plan of getting away from Orsina as quickly as possible.

"If we traveled together?" repeated Aelia. "Would you do that?"

"What? Oh," Orsina gave an awkward shrug. "I'm sure you'd be more comfortable in a caravan. And you'd get to your destination more quickly, too. I'd be stopping nearly every day to help people...I'm sure you'd find it tiresome?"

"I don't think so," asserted Aelia. Perhaps, if she was lucky, Orsina would even be able to locate another chaos god who could help her. "I think I'd rather travel with you. Unless you were going in a different direction?"

"Well," Orsina scuffed her boot into the dirt, "I actually hadn't decided where I'm going next. I'm not exactly...I don't have a..." she seemed to be struggling to explain. "I'm on a quest, but I don't know what it is."

"How can that be?" asked Aelia, feigning ignorance.

"Iolar spoke to the Baron of Melidrie," Orsina explained. "He told him that there was a task waiting for me, a great evil that I must destroy. But he did not say where it was, or what form it might take. I have been searching for two years, but I have not found it yet."

"Are you certain that they were not just looking for an excuse to send you away?" asked Aelia with a mischievous smile. Orsina jostled her with her shoulder, nearly sending Aelia off the step and into the dirt.

Aelia screamed, but her fingers grabbed hold of Orsina in time to save herself from falling. It would not have been a terrible fall, no more than a few hand-spans, but Aelia was surprised nevertheless.

"So much for honor!" cried Aelia. "Did anyone else see that? This paladin just tried to throw me to my death!"

None of the passers-by paid her any mind.

Orsina laughed. "Very well, I apologize," she said. "But I do not think you'd enjoy traveling with me. It would be far more strenuous than what you're used to. And I cannot justify putting you in harm's way."

"I'd feel safer with you than without you," said Aelia.

Orsina seemed thoughtful but unconvinced. Aelia decided that it was time to play dirty. She pressed her lower lip out and pouted in the exact same way she'd seen Perlita do in Orsina's memories.

The result was instantaneous. Orsina swallowed visibly and pulled back a little, and for a moment Aelia was afraid she'd gone too far. But the moment passed as quickly as it had come.

"If...if you wish me to accompany you to Sabarra...I suppose I can do so," said Orsina slowly. Aelia's face lit up. "But I meant what I said about frequently stopping to aid others. I must pursue every trace of chaos magic that I detect, or else I might miss the quest that Iolar has intended for me."

"I do not mind," Aelia assured her, and it was the truth. The more chaos gods Orsina found, the better Aelia's chances of locating the Unbinding Stone. And if Aelia had to turn on Orsina and kill her when she outlived her usefulness, well, that was Orsina's own fault for being so absurdly terrible at detecting chaos.

"Stay here, then, and wait for the other dress," said Orsina. "I need to go and purchase the supplies we will need for the journey."

But Aelia was now thoroughly bored of the seamstresses. She had no intention of remaining at the shop any longer. Once Orsina was out of sight, she decided to go in search of something interesting to do.

The city was loud and colorful, completely unlike the village of Soria or the other small settlements that she generally restricted herself to in order to avoid detection. She had no money, which she understood was important, but there was still plenty to see. There were so many different types of Men in Antocoso. Some made shoes, or baked breads, or sold fish. Some, blessed with Inthi's fire, worked at hot forges shaping metal. Guards patrolled the streets, and the city walls, while children ran through the streets shouting to one another.

She spent some time watching the produce vendors at work. They yelled out the names of their wares, and over the course of a half hour, Aelia learned the names for artichokes, cabbage, garlic, peas, and carrots. She also learned that the pretty colorful fruits she ate last night were olives. It amused her to realize that she had known about olive trees, but never realized what their fruit was. A Masimi merchant in white robes introduced her to dates, which he swore were also a fruit, and were only small and shriveled because they had been sun-dried.

As she moved into the quieter, more expensive area of the marketplace, tables of glittering gemstones caught her eye. The merchants here were ebony-skinned and dressed in brightly colored clothing: diamond merchants, from the myriad nations of Nazaquai. This area was also filled with armed guards who glared at anyone whose hands strayed too near to the wares.

"This one cannot afford anything," said one of the merchants dismissively, as Aelia stopped to examine her table. She spoke in Benai to her guard, apparently confident that she would not be understood. Aelia raised her head and gave the merchant a withering look.

"I could be the Queen of Vesolda for all you know," she replied in the merchant's own language.

The woman's mouth fell open in shock, and she glanced over to her guard for verification that he had heard this too. The guard looked as though he had no idea how to react, until he finally burst out laughing.

"Ah, this is justice!" he said when he could finally speak. "Masedi, the gods have finally punished you for insulting your own customers."

"She isn't a customer, Lesego. I stand by my words," said Masedi, but Aelia could tell she was embarrassed. She got up and vanished into the tent behind her.

"Forgive my sister's rudeness," said Lesego. "It is extremely rare that Ioshorans choose to learn our languages."

"Well, she was right," Aelia granted. "I don't have any money at all."

"Ha!" yelled Masedi from inside the tent.

"Oh, good," said Lesego, sighing in relief. "I was afraid she'd be so shamed that she'd force us to leave the country. I am enjoying the climate here."

"We can spend the next six months in Cilva if you don't shut up," said Masedi, emerging once again. "Or maybe Domeysil."

"You trade in Domeysil?" asked Aelia, alarmed.

"No," admitted Masedi. "Other merchants do. But it seems a waste of time. Elves have little interest in diamonds. And besides, they make me uneasy."

Aelia was relieved to hear this. The Ten had been unable to keep the Elven Gods out of Inthya, but at least they were somewhat contained on their own lands. She knew that the entire race was not to be trusted, just like their creators.

"I have heard tales," said Lesego. "They say that if you sail too far past Thiyra, the Mer will warn you to turn around or offer to guide you back. But I cannot tell you if those stories are true. I, myself, have never met a Mer who was interested in anything but music or food or gold."

"Not so different than Men, then?" Aelia teased.

Lesego laughed, and Aelia decided that she liked him enough to try to give him a warning. "All mortal races have a common enemy in the elves. You are wise to stay out of Domeysil."

"I don't know if I believe that," said Lesego. "It seems impossible that an entire race could be evil. Some of them must be good. We only hear about the bad ones because it makes for more interesting gossip."

"I don't think they're evil. They just..." Aelia paused, realizing she was not certain how to describe it. Elves were not evil, in the same way earthquakes or plagues or poisonous snakes were not evil. They simply *were*, wild and untamable as the sea. "...you should keep away from them."

"We do not have any plans to go to Domeysil," Masedi assured her.

After a while, Aelia bid goodbye to the merchants and continued her aimless adventure through the city. She wished Orsina had given her a few coins to spend, even though she had been more than generous already. But Aelia was starting to get hungry again.

She eventually happened upon a group of children playing in an alley and, remembering the fun she'd had with the children in Soria, approached them. She'd been afraid they might all run away when they noticed her, but they didn't seem too bothered by the adult woman in their midst. In fact, they appeared to enjoy the novelty. They loaned her their skipping-rope and laughed hysterically as it got tangled in her skirt and caught on her boots, yelling advice from a safe distance.

When Aelia suggested that maybe they play something else, something that did not involve ropes, the children asked if she had any money for sweets. Aelia turned out her pockets to prove she did not. So instead, the children took stones and drew a strange, segmented path into the dirt. This, they said, was the court for a game of scotch-hops.

The game required Aelia to stand on one foot and leap through the squares without touching a line or falling out of bounds. It was simple enough to understand, but surprisingly difficult, especially when one was surrounded by children who yelled confusing advice in hopes they could cause her to make a mistake. Aelia was midway through her third turn, leaping over the square that contained her stone, when Orsina found her.

The children all gasped and drew back at the sight of the paladin in their midst, as though they thought Orsina had come specially to scold them for whatever crimes a child might commit. But Orsina barely seemed to notice them as she approached Aelia.

"What are you doing?" Orsina demanded, as though the answer to that was not obvious.

"Wait until my turn is finished," instructed Aelia, never slowing in her step. As she passed her stone, she swept it into her hand and tossed it to the next square in the sequence. But before she could begin again, Orsina caught her by the arm. Aelia lost her balance and set her other foot down to catch herself.

"Out!" cried all the children happily. Aelia stuck her tongue out at them, then stepped aside so the next child could take his turn.

"I was worried about you!" cried Orsina. "I thought you might have been kidnapped!"

"What?" Already, Aelia's irritation at having her turn ruined was melting away. "Why?"

"Because I couldn't *find* you! I was on the verge of asking the city guards to start a search! Why didn't you at least tell the seamstresses where you were going?"

"I didn't know where I was going," sulked Aelia.

"Elyne, that's dangerous!" Orsina gave her a searching look, and for some reason, Aelia could not stand to meet her gaze. "Why—I don't understand—why would you—?"

"Does it matter?" asked Aelia. "You found me. I'm not kidnapped, or dead. Everything was all right."

"This time!" said Orsina. "You must promise me, if we are to travel together, you must promise me you won't wander off without telling someone where you've gone."

Aelia paused, considering. She supposed Orsina's request really couldn't be called unreasonable, even if it was against her nature. In the past, when Aelia allied with fellow chaos gods, she found them to be unreliable. But she could not complain, because she was equally unreliable. It was part of the reason why they had never been able to band together and fight the Ten.

"Very well," agreed Aelia. "It will not happen again." Probably. Aelia knew herself too well to claim complete certainty.

Orsina sighed, but there was a smile on her face when she shook her head. She seemed to have forgotten her anger already. "And who are these children?" she asked.

Aelia turned and saw that instead of continuing with their game, the children were now watching the conversation with interest.

"These dirty cheaters?" asked Aelia, raising her voice so they would know that she was teasing. "Children of Antocoso, I am afraid. Do not play dice with them."

"Dice?" repeated Orsina dryly.

"It wasn't for money, Dame!" cried one of the braver children. "Only for pebbles! We swear it!"

Aelia wondered if Orsina was going to lecture them about gambling, but she merely shook her head again.

"We should return to the inn," said Orsina. "It will be dark soon, and you must not stay up so late tonight. We'll be leaving early tomorrow morning."

"For Sabarra?" asked Aelia eagerly.

"Yes, though the journey will take two weeks, at minimum, if we are not waylaid," warned Orsina. "I have mapped a route that will take us through several cities, so we will have chances to replenish our supplies."

As Aelia followed Orsina back in the direction of the inn, she considered the fact that Orsina had gone to the trouble to locate her after she'd wandered away from the shop. Aelia knew she would not have done the same for Orsina if their positions had been reversed. It was rather touching. It almost felt as though Orsina cared about her.

Of course, that was because Orsina believed her to be a woman, not a chaos goddess with barely enough magic left in her to light a candle. The moment Orsina learned the truth, she would be drawing her sword and chanting prayers again.

Aelia could not allow herself to become too comfortable around Orsina, no matter how thoughtful or generous the paladin was. Their alliance, if one could call it that, was based on lies. It could not last.

But Aelia was determined to enjoy it while it did.

Chapter Three

ORSINA

Orsina's irritation with Elyne was already beginning to fade away when they arrived back at the inn. The idea that something terrible had befallen the young woman made her sick with worry. Elyne had just survived something terrible. What would it do to her mind, to endure it twice?

Stabbed, I'd wager, the healer had said to Orsina privately, after treating Elyne's wound. *By a sword, or maybe a dagger. She's lucky indeed. And in very good spirits, considering.*

Orsina felt rage building up inside of her chest whenever she remembered. Elyne was a light-hearted young woman who liked music and played street games with children and was frightened by horses. Whoever attacked her needed to be brought to justice immediately.

But Orsina was aware that such matters could be complicated. In her training, they emphasized the importance of being respectful toward victims who were unwilling to testify against the ones who wronged them. Paladins, with their strict sense of justice, often struggled to understand why anyone did not wish to see a criminal punished, even if that criminal was a family member, or lover, or friend.

Orsina did not believe that Elyne had simply fallen afoul of a highwayman. If that had been the case, there would be no reason for secrecy. No, whoever attacked

Elyne was someone she knew. And Elyne was refusing to name them, either out of sentiment or fear of reprisal.

Maybe, on the journey, Elyne might come to trust her enough to tell her the truth.

Orsina found that she was looking forward to the journey with Elyne. Apart from the manticore adventure, she had traveled alone for the last two years. It would be good to have someone to talk to on the road, aside from Iolar and Star.

And Perlita. As always, Orsina had started a new letter to her once the old one was complete, but she had not managed to write much last night. The initial pain of being kissed by a chaos goddess wearing her face had faded, but the feelings of abandonment had not.

Perhaps Perlita's silence was an answer of its own.

Orsina wondered if she should stop writing letters. What if she was only an irritant to Perlita? The thought was mortifying.

But if Perlita no longer cared for her, why did she not simply say so?

She watched Elyne pick at her meal, testing each vegetable individually, as though they might be poisonous, and avoiding the meat outright. Elyne left the meat last night as well, Orsina noticed. There were a few religious sects that refused to eat meat, mostly tied to the temples of Cyne or Eyvindr. But Elyne had mentioned no such affiliation. And besides, she had eaten a few slices of dried sausage when Orsina offered it to her earlier that day.

"I purchased another horse," said Orsina. Her reward from Count Doriano had been enough to cover the price. "I know you don't ride, but it's not terribly difficult to learn. It will save us many days of traveling."

"Oh," said Elyne. She seemed to be at a loss for words. "Oh."

"Don't worry. I'll show you everything you need to know."

Elyne nodded and looked toward the musicians. This was a different group than the ones in the tavern yesterday.

"Do you play?" asked Orsina.

"Play what?" replied Elyne.

"An instrument. You seem to enjoy—"

"Oh! No. Not at all." She paused. "Do you?"

"I was forced to learn the harp during my training, but I was never very good. Perlita was excellent at it, though, and sometimes—" The words caught in her throat.

"Perlita?" asked Elyne.

"The daughter of my Baron," explained Orsina, picking her words carefully. "We were friends in childhood. She was furious when I left to join the Order of the Sun." Orsina smiled fondly at the memory, though at the time it had not been so amusing. Perlita had screamed and screamed until she was red in the face, swearing she would never forgive Orsina for leaving. It had almost been enough to make Orsina forget her calling. "But she forgave me quickly enough. When I returned home, I was assigned to guard her."

Elyne appeared to be considering this. "And you have not seen her since you left on your quest?"

"Yes," said Orsina. Then, surprising even herself, she added, "Sometimes I feel as though she must have forgotten me by now."

Elyne's eyebrows shot up. "That cannot be, if you were friends since childhood."

Orsina shrugged, unwilling to say more. But it seemed that Elyne's interest was piqued.

"You said earlier that most paladins don't bother with romance."

Orsina stood abruptly. “I’m going to bed.”

“Oh, come back here!” cried Elyne, grabbing her by the wrist. “You can’t run away from me! I’m staying in the same room as you!”

“You won’t tell me what happened to you yesterday, but I’m expected to tell you my entire history?” retorted Orsina. Perhaps she wasn’t being fair, but she suddenly felt ill. The mentions of Perlita were making her chest ache.

“What happened to me isn’t important!” Elyne proclaimed brashly. “And it’s not interesting, either.”

Orsina gave her a skeptical look.

“Alright,” said Elyne, perhaps sensing that this line of questioning was fruitless. “Sit down, sit down. I’ll stop asking about it.”

Orsina sat slowly.

“Why does a paladin need to know how to play the harp, then?” asked Elyne.

“We don’t, exactly,” said Orsina. “But the Justices don’t want us to be dumb soldiers who don’t know how to do anything more than take orders and stab monsters. A paladin ought to be well rounded, or at least skilled enough to not be an embarrassment to the Order of the Sun. In training, we spent half the day learning combat, or riding, or survival. The other half was in the classroom. Some of the initiates came from farming families and didn’t know how to read or write anything more than their own names, but those of us who did not require extra assistance after class were told to select an instrument to learn. I chose the harp because Perlita always made it look so easy.”

“I do not care much for learning,” said Elyne. “But I think if I were to learn something, it would be an instrument. The musicians here play so beautifully.”

"Well, it is never too late to learn. The Temple of Merla has a strong presence in the south, if you want to learn from the best. Or were you planning to stay in Sabarra?"

"I do not know," admitted Elyne. "I suppose it depends upon what we find there."

"Is your brother expecting you?" asked Orsina.

"No. It is...the situation is complicated."

Orsina waited to see if Elyne would say anything more on the subject, but she didn't.

THE MOUNT THAT Orsina purchased for Elyne to ride was a pony, a docile ten-year-old blue dun named Lavender. Orsina had ignored the graceful, hot-blooded Masimi mares and flashy Vesoldan stallions in favor of something a novice like Elyne would actually be able to ride.

One of the dresses that Orsina bought for Elyne featured riding skirts, so Elyne could ride astride. Riding skirts, despite their name, were actually not skirts at all. They were wide-legged trousers, fashioned to look like skirts when one was standing still. The nobility tended to reject them, but they were popular with ordinary citizens of Vesolda. The most expensive designs had an additional flap of fabric that buttoned across the waistline to complete the illusion.

Elyne still needed help getting up onto the pony's back, but she seemed more comfortable around Lavender than Star. After a few false starts and a bit of hysterical screaming from Elyne, they left Antocoso by the east gate and set off in the direction of Sabarra.

Orsina alternated their pace between a trot and walking, as to not tire Star. Galloping, she explained to

Elyne, was really only for emergencies, or if they were losing daylight. Elyne was quiet at first, watching their surroundings with wide eyes. Orsina wondered if she was anticipating a second attack, and could not help but hope that the assailant would be foolish enough to strike while Elyne was still in Orsina's presence.

But either the assailant was no longer following Elyne, or he knew that he was no match for a paladin and kept his distance. After a few hours, Elyne was comfortable enough to begin complaining that she was bored.

"How did you entertain yourself on the trip from Ortradosa?" asked Orsina.

"I don't know," sulked Elyne.

"What do you mean you don't know?" Orsina laughed. "You've forgotten?"

"When will we arrive at a town?" demanded Elyne, ignoring the question.

"At this rate, midday. But we're not staying the night."

Elyne groaned.

"I did say you might prefer a caravan," added Orsina. "It's not too late to join one. You can sit in a wagon and work on your embroidery."

"That sounds even *worse*," declared Elyne.

"Well," said Orsina, "why don't you tell me about your family? You said they were vintners?"

"Oh." Elyne shifted uncomfortably in her saddle. "Yes."

"And you mentioned several brothers?"

"Sisters, and brothers, and neutroi siblings. My family is quite large. I expect they've hardly noticed my absence."

"I'm sure that's not true," Orsina reassured her. But Elyne merely shrugged. "Do you intend to take up your family's business?"

"I suppose I must," said Elyne. Then, after a moment, she added, "I've never felt as though I had any other prospects."

Orsina looked at Elyne, who was now staring down at Lavender's bridle, fiddling with the leather straps.

"Well," said Orsina. "If you could do anything in the world, what do you suppose it would be?"

Elyne seemed surprised by the question. "I don't think I ever really considered that."

"Perhaps you should," encouraged Orsina.

"I don't know," Elyne mused. "It's probably too late for me. I'm too old and set in my ways to start anew."

"Too old?" repeated Orsina. "What madness! How old are you? Twenty-five?"

"Fourteen billion," said Elyne.

Orsina could not help but laugh at the absurdity of the number. "Fourteen billion years, and you have not found the time to learn the harp?" she teased.

"That's not fair. The harp was only invented a few thousand years ago."

"Oh, how foolish of me to have forgotten. In that case, I retract my statement. A thousand years is hardly enough time to accomplish anything at all."

"Shame on you for speaking so disrespectfully to a frail old woman!" Elyne cried. "I will write to your commander."

"My sincerest apologies, grandmother," said Orsina, who had completely given up on trying to hide her amusement. She decided if Elyne did not want to reveal her age, she would not pry. "It will not happen again."

True to Orsina's prediction, they arrived at the first town a few hours after midday. It was a bit larger than Soria, but not nearly so large as Antocoso. Orsina had not been planning on stopping for any longer than it took to water the horses and check their hooves, but when they rode into town, she saw there was a small crowd gathered outside the temple.

From atop Star's back, Orsina could see two women at the heart of the crowd, arguing passionately. One was young, and the other was middle-aged. From their similar faces, Orsina thought they must be mother and daughter.

When the daughter spotted Orsina, her face lit up with hope. She pointed at her and said, "Here! She'll tell you! She'll tell you I'm right!"

Orsina was used to being waylaid like this, so she pulled Star to a halt and dismounted. "What is the problem?" she asked.

"I'm supposed to be married today!" cried the young woman. She was dressed in a blue gown, beautifully embroidered with a colorful floral pattern, and fresh flowers had been woven through her braids. "But she says our sacrifice to the temple is not enough, and that it is a sign we are not ready to be married."

Orsina looked at the mother for confirmation.

"Well, it's true," said the older woman. "If you can't even afford to pay the priestess, you can't afford to live a good, comfortable life together. Why not wait a few years?"

"We can afford to pay the priestess!" cried the girl. "She has already said that what we plan to give is sufficient. It's just not enough for your pride!"

"Where is the priestess now?" asked Orsina.

"Inside," said the girl, gesturing toward the temple. The building was a Temple of Eyvindr, but small towns like this were usually visited by traveling priestesses of Pemele, who performed weddings when they were in the area. Lacking a physical temple of their own, they borrowed the temple of whatever god had one in town—usually, given that most of the towns were farming communities, temples of Eyvindr.

"If the priestess is pleased with your offering, I see no issue," said Orsina. "What is your trade?"

"I am a seamstress," said the girl. "And Alexius is apprenticed to the apothecary. We may not be as wealthy as some, but we will not starve."

Orsina looked at the girl's mother. "But you disagree?" she asked.

"My daughter has no idea how harsh the world can be," said the woman. "This will only end badly."

"And what is your reasoning?" Orsina asked patiently.

"We have always taken care of her," said the woman. "She is supported by my husband, and myself. She cannot live on her own, her income would not be enough to sustain her."

"That's not true!" cried the girl. "I have shown you my figures! You're only embarrassed because I won't be living in luxury. But I do not need such things to be happy, and neither did you when you were married! You expect Alexius to have the sort of wealth that takes decades to build!"

Orsina raised her hands slowly, and the girl fell silent.

"I do not know if your daughter will be able to sustain herself," she said to the girl's mother. "But even if she cannot, Pemele does not forbid the impoverished from being married."

"She is not *ready*," insisted the woman.

"That's for me to decide, not you!" cried the girl.

"We have supported her for her entire life!" cried the woman, as though her daughter had not spoken. "We raised her, and fed her, and educated her—"

"Yes. You did all that you agreed to do when you asked Dayluue for a child." Orsina did her best to quash her own impatience, but she was afraid it was showing through in her tone. "I have given my answer. There is no legal or moral reason why your daughter should not be married."

"Oh, what do you know?" cried the woman. "You're just a girl yourself, and I'm certain you have no children of your own!"

Orsina turned to the daughter and gestured to the temple. "Go. Be married." Then she addressed the crowd. "Attend the wedding, or don't. I am finished here."

The daughter gave a laugh of triumph, for apparently this small bit of validation from a stranger in armor was all she really needed. She turned on her heel and vanished into the temple.

Orsina went back to Star as the other villagers looked at each other, apparently trying to decide on a course of action. It seemed they were not sure whether they wanted to support the mother or the daughter.

"Come on," said Orsina to Elyne. "We're leaving."

But to Orsina's surprise, Elyne was now struggling to get down from Lavender's back. "We can't leave!" she cried, one leg flailing madly in midair. "I've never seen a wedding before!"

"What?" asked Orsina.

"I want to *see*," Elyne insisted. She landed in the dust but leaped back to her feet. "There's no harm in it. We're not in any hurry, are we?"

"Nobody invited us!" protested Orsina, but Elyne was already moving toward the temple, looking over the architecture appraisingly. "Elyne!"

It was impossible to grab Elyne and pull her back, with the crowd of townspeople as large as it was. Orsina sighed in defeat and went to tie the horses. Meanwhile, the crowd of villagers seemed to have decided in favor of the bride and were moving toward the entrance as well.

She caught up to Elyne in the anteroom that led to the main area of the temple, where she'd been distracted by a selection of climbing vines that trailed up along the walls. When Orsina took her by the arm, she turned around and smiled.

"Oh good, you're here," said Elyne. "Come on. Let's sit in the back. I don't know how this is supposed to go. Is there something we're supposed to do?"

"It's not too different from an ordinary service," Orsina advised as Elyne pulled her along. "Just follow what everyone else does."

The interior of the temple was also filled with live plants, mostly colorful flowers in ornately decorated pots. But the most striking feature of the temple was the small stained-glass window just behind the altar, which depicted a scene of emerald fruit trees and golden fields.

Standing before the altar was a priestess wearing soft lavender robes. Just beside her was a neutroi youth, whose clothes seemed to have been cut from the same blue fabric and embroidered with the exact same colorful floral design as the bride's. Orsina realized the girl probably made each garment herself, patiently sewing and embroidering by candlelight in anticipation for this day.

Orsina and Elyne took seats in the very last row and therefore were the first to see the arrival of the bride. Smiling radiantly, she all but ran down the center aisle to take her position by her partner and the priestess. Traditionally, she should have been waiting at the altar with her spouse-to-be before the arrival of all the guests, but the priestess did not seem to mind very much.

The hymn to call Pemele's attention to the couple was beautiful, floating and ethereal. Orsina did not know any of the verses, only the chorus, for she attended weddings so infrequently. Fortunately, the villagers were not so ignorant, and so the priestess did not have to sing alone.

Orsina looked down at Elyne. Her mouth was open, but she was not singing. She seemed to be dumbstruck, and Orsina was not certain what to make of it. She did not know what to make of most of the things Elyne did.

Orsina was beginning to suspect that Elyne had been isolated from the outside world for much of her life. She might even be a runaway, fleeing a restrictive family. What if the one who attacked her was a relative, seeking to bring her back home?

That might explain why she was so reluctant to name her attacker.

A merchant's daughter ought to be well socialized and business-savvy so that she could make an advantageous marriage or become a respectable business partner. But Elyne reminded Orsina of a foreigner, still learning the ways of a new land.

The wedding ceremony began with the priestess addressing the congregation. Orsina supposed she must have been familiar with the couple, because she spoke about their occupations and their lives. The girl was named Evi and was well known for her skills with a needle. The neutroi was named Alexius, and though their blessing from Adranus was weak, too weak for them to ever become a full healer, they made up for their lack of magic with an impressive work ethic.

Evi seemed to have completely recovered from her argument with her mother and was smiling radiantly as the priestess spoke. Orsina admitted to herself that she was glad she'd been able to help the two get married, even though she really had no place making such decisions. But she'd long since become accustomed to people seeing her insignia and assuming she could help them, no matter how far removed their problem was from Iolar's domain.

Orsina knew that the length of a wedding ceremony could vary wildly. Back when she had been Perlita's guard, she had once been forced to attend a wedding ceremony that had taken up the better part of a day, and then the celebration afterward continued well into the night. The entire thing had been an opulent display of materialism, with both noble families attempting to prove they had the most money to waste. Orsina found the entire affair offensive.

But it was not always so. Orsina's fathers told her that their own wedding ceremony had not even lasted half an hour, and been little more than a particularly joyful worship service. Fortunately, it looked as though this one would be similar.

Orsina wondered if she would ever be married. Probably not, she decided. She could not see herself falling in love with anyone besides Perlita, but the daughter of two common soldiers had a better chance of walking to the moon than marrying into Vesoldan nobility. If she had to choose, she supposed she might consider a fellow paladin. They would understand one another, at the very least. Most paladins were men, but Orsina didn't think she had a preference regarding that.

Well, it was a moot point until her quest was finished.

The ceremony came to an end and Orsina and Elyne followed the laughing, singing villagers back outside. It seemed the earlier conflict had been completely forgotten already. Orsina had been hoping to slip away quickly, but Elyne was clearly in no great hurry.

"They're saying there's another celebration at Alexius' parents' home," Elyne informed Orsina eagerly. "Can we go?"

"No," said Orsina. "Watching a public ceremony is one thing. Turning up at a party uninvited is quite another. Surely even you can understand that. We should leave immediately."

"What?" cried a voice from behind them. Orsina turned, and saw Evi standing there, her hands still entwined with Alexius'. "Of course you should stay! None of this would have happened, if not for you. You are welcome to join in the celebration."

"But—" Orsina protested.

"Come on!" Elyne wheedled, smiling brightly. "You can't say no to the bride on her wedding day. Besides, I've never been to a party before."

"Alright," Orsina reluctantly said. "But we can't stay longer than an hour. We've already lost far too much daylight."

It was only a short walk to the home of Alexius' parents, which had been decorated with flower garlands and tables filled with all sorts of traditional Vesoldan foods. The celebration was nothing compared to what Orsina had seen when accompanying Perlita, but Orsina appreciated that it was a demonstration of joy, rather than wealth.

Elyne immediately gravitated toward the musicians, while Orsina found a seat near the back of the crowd and kept an eye out for Evi's mother, in case the woman planned to return and make trouble. But there was no sign of her, and soon Orsina forgot about her entirely.

Some of the villagers had apparently taken up the task of teaching Elyne one of their local dances. Elyne's steps were uncertain, but she seemed to be having fun, her long dark hair flying behind her as she spun with her partner.

Elyne claimed she'd never been to a wedding, despite having at least six siblings. It seemed unlikely, but still within the realm of possibility. But her claim that she'd never been to a party was...worrying. Either she was lying, or she was exaggerating.

Or she had spent the first twenty years of her life locked in a cellar. Orsina did not want to believe such a thing, but it explained too much. *Far* too much.

Once she delivered Elyne to Sabarra, perhaps she would pay a visit to Ortradosa and investigate any vintners living there.

Orsina looked at the sky and sighed, realizing there was no way they'd be back on the road today. She might as well find them somewhere to stay for the night. She remembered passing an inn when they'd first come into town. Slipping away from the party, she began walking back in the direction they'd come from, following the road. The distance between the too-loud music and her ringing ears was a relief.

Fortunately, the innkeeper still had a room available and was happy to rent it to Orsina. She took her time in bringing up the bags, for she was in no hurry to return to the celebration. Somehow, celebrations left her exhausted.

A time such as this was ideal for working on a letter to Perlita, so Orsina unpacked her writing instruments and laid them out on the room's small writing-desk, reviewing the letter she'd started composing yesterday. Staring at the words, she found that she lacked the will to write any further.

Orsina's last letter left off just before she defeated the chaos goddess in Soria. She wondered what Perlita might think if there was no follow-up. Would she worry? Would she think Orsina had been killed?

Would she even notice?

In a sudden, impulsive move that shocked her for days afterward, Orsina swept the page into her hand, crumpled it into a ball, and threw it on the fire. The edges glowed for a moment before it was consumed.

She would trouble Perlita no longer.

THE WEDDING CELEBRATION seemed to have only grown in Orsina's absence, spreading to the street outside Alexius' parents' house. After a few minutes of searching, she found a very red-faced Elyne laughing with a few of the villagers.

"Are we leaving? Already?" Elyne yelled as Orsina approached.

"No," said Orsina. "I rented us a room at the inn. We will leave tomorrow instead."

Elyne smiled brightly. "Good! I'm having fun!"

"I can see that," said Orsina, stifling a laugh. "But we really should be going. We must leave early tomorrow, to minimize the loss of time."

Elyne threw her arm over her eyes and groaned dramatically. "Must we? Why don't we just stay here forever?"

Another laugh escaped Orsina, and she reflected upon how she had done more laughing in the last two days than in the past year. "Come on. Or you'll regret it in the morning when I wake you at dawn."

Elyne, unsurprisingly, was more than a little unsteady on her feet. She leaned heavily on Orsina's arm the entire way back to the inn, explaining in a too-loud voice about the different foods and drinks she had tried. When Orsina shushed her, explaining that the residents of the village were surely trying to sleep, Elyne nodded and fell silent for a few moments before picking up again at full volume.

By the time they finally arrived at the inn, Orsina had given up on silencing Elyne and was instead offering prayers to Iolar that none of the village guards would come over to reprimand them.

Once they were safely inside, Orsina helped Elyne up the stairs. This was the most difficult part of the evening so far, and took at least a quarter of an hour, by Orsina's measuring. When they finally made it to their room, Orsina gave silent thanks to Iolar and began searching for her nightclothes.

Something light and soft touched the back of her head. Orsina straightened and began to turn—

"Wait," Elyne murmured into her hair.

Orsina froze as Elyne's hands swept down her body.

"I never thanked you for saving me, did I?" Elyne's breath was warm and sweet. "Let's fix that."

"You're drunk," said Orsina.

Elyne laughed. "No! I can't be!"

"You most certainly are," Orsina said, prying Elyne's hand off her. "And don't think that will stop me from waking you at sunrise tomorrow morning."

"Do you know—" Elyne swayed a little, "—what your problem is? Do you?"

"I know that it is *not* drunkenness," retorted Orsina, walking Elyne over to her own bed.

Elyne laughed again. "I always thought paladins were humorless. But you're not. You're just very...very...dry." She looked around at Orsina. "Did you, did you notice what I did there? That was a pun. Did you catch it? I can do it again."

Instead of responding, Orsina pushed Elyne onto the straw mattress. Elyne apparently was not in the mood to fight and collapsed on top of the blankets without another word. In fact, she was silent for so long that Orsina thought she had fallen asleep.

"She's an idiot," proclaimed Elyne at last.

Orsina turned her head partway, "Pardon?"

"She's an idiot," said Elyne. "For letting you go."

There was no sense in arguing with a drunk, but she was compelled to defend Perlita. "Iolar's orders outrank any of those of any Man. Even if she tried to keep me at Melidrie, I would have refused."

"I don't understand anyone less than I understand you," murmured Elyne, closing her eyes again.

"Go to sleep," commanded Orsina sternly.

Elyne spoke, but Orsina did not understand any of the words. It was not the Vesoldan language, nor did it sound anything like Xytan or Ieflarian or Masimi.

"Pardon?" said Orsina, frowning slightly. But Elyne chose that moment to succumb to sleep, and Orsina decided that it was not worth the trouble to wake her.

Chapter Four

AELIA

Aelia awoke the next morning with an indescribable pain pounding through her skull. When she opened her eyes, the sun cut through her vision, and she covered her face with her arm, groaning.

"I would like to leave within the hour, if at all possible," came Orsina's voice from somewhere nearby. In response, Aelia flailed her other arm in Orsina's general direction, hoping that she might be lucky and manage to hit her.

"Stop that," said Orsina. "You did this to yourself."

Aelia removed her arm from her eyes and squinted at Orsina. Then she flicked her fingers in Orsina's direction, sending a few tiny sparks of violet light at her. Orsina yelped in surprise.

"I could have woken you up at dawn, you know!" Orsina reprimanded. "You might at least show a little gratitude!"

"I'm never drinking again," moaned Aelia.

"The Order of the Sun supports your resolution," said Orsina. "There's tea on the windowsill."

"Everyone always made it look like so much fun. Nobody ever told me about this part. This is terrible. I'm going to die." Rage flared in her chest, and it was enough to give her the fortitude to sit upright in bed. "Why did *nobody* warn me?"

"I refuse to believe nobody ever told you—" began Orsina, but Aelia wasn't in the mood to listen. The events of last night were starting to come back to her, starting with dancing with the villagers and ending with her lips against Orsina's hair.

Oh.

Mortified, Aelia got out of bed and shuffled over to the windowsill, where a heavy earthenware mug rested. She picked it up and took a few sips of the lukewarm liquid. The tea was bitter, unsweetened, but Aelia could not bring herself to complain.

It wasn't forbidden, exactly, but gods always had to be careful when pursuing mortals. The Ten kept well away from such entanglements, believing the power imbalance between themselves and mortals to be irreconcilable. For one as insignificant as Aelia, it could hardly be called a concern. Orsina had already proved that she was Aelia's equal in a fight. And it was not as though Orsina venerated her. She would not see refusing Aelia's advances as sinful or arrogant.

But did Aelia even *want* to pursue her? It had all the hallmarks of a terrible idea. But it also sounded like it might be fun. Orsina was pretty, and she apparently had money, and she seemed like she'd be easy to manipulate. And besides, if Orsina became infatuated with her, she would be even more inclined to turn a blind eye to anything questionable Aelia might do...

Until Iolar found out.

That was a sobering thought. No, it was a better idea to keep the relationship professional. She didn't want to spend the next thousand years confined to her plane.

Aelia combed her hair with her fingers and tried not to think of how terrible she must look. Within half an hour, they were on the road again, alone save for the singing of birds in distant trees.

Orsina must have noticed how quiet Aelia was being, and so today it was she who filled the silence. They would pass through a few more villages, and then, in a day or two, reach a large lakeside town called Catorisci. Catorisci was known to be prosperous despite its remote location, and Orsina promised Aelia would be able to have a bath in warm water when they arrived, as the town was home to one of Inthi's temples.

Orsina did not mention what had happened last night, and Aelia eventually began to relax enough to ask her more questions about herself and her quest.

"Have you left Vesolda in your travels?" asked Aelia.

"No. Last year, I was considering going to Ieflaria, to help with their defense against the dragons. But it seems that situation has been handled now. And of course, I could not go to Xytae even if I wanted to."

"Why is that?" asked Aelia.

Orsina gave her a strange look. "Are you joking?" she asked.

Aelia shook her head, and Orsina drew Star to a halt. Aelia's heart sank as she realized that she had given herself away already, missed some crucial element of Orsina's culture—

"The Order of the Sun has withdrawn from the Xytan Empire," said Orsina. "Had you truly not heard?"

"No!" cried Aelia. "When did this happen?"

"Several years ago," said Orsina. "You are certain you did not hear of it?"

Aelia felt sick. Xytae was undefended? She could have taken over *six* towns if she'd gone there instead of Vesolda! Why had nobody told her? Why hadn't she taken the time to study Inthya, instead of manifesting in the first town that caught her interest? Why did she always have to be so—

"Let me think. It would have been...two autumns ago." Orsina nodded. "I was still at Melidrie at the time."

"What happened?" asked Aelia.

"What do you know of Emperor Ionnes?"

Aelia shrugged. "Just...little things," she lied. "I've never really..."

"His mother is Irianthe of Xytae, but she was only Empress for a very short time. As soon as Ionnes came of age, she gave the throne to him, though she is still extremely influential at the Xytan court."

"Why did she give up her throne?" wondered Aelia.

"I do not know. Perhaps she was not suited for it. Ionnes married a noblewoman named Enessa, and they have three daughters. His eldest, and heir, is named Ioanna, but I understand that she is seldom seen in public. I suppose they are afraid of assassins."

"Oh," said Aelia.

"Even before his ascension, Ionnes frequently spoke of returning the Xytan Empire to its former glory. It was not long before the paladins grew displeased with him. They believed that his veneration of Reygmadra was...excessive. And his wars of conquest did not sit well with them. But the Order of the Sun was not powerful enough to stand against him without destabilizing the empire and potentially plunging the entire country into chaos."

Reygmadra, Goddess of Warfare and Eighth of the Ten, was extremely influential in Xytae. Even though Xytae's glorious, uncountable legions were a thing of the distant past, Reygmadra was still at least equal to Iolar in power within the empire's borders.

The Ten always tried to present a united front, but even Aelia knew that Iolar and Reygmadra frequently had difficulty coexisting.

"Then one day, Emperor Ionnes called the Knight-Commander to him. He said that the Order of the Sun had done well protecting his lands, but now they needed to fight alongside his armies in Masim."

"You're making that up!"

Orsina shook her head. "As a result, the Order of the Sun withdrew from Xytae. At that time, dragons were terrorizing the Ieflarian countryside, so most of the paladins went there. But Ionnes would not apologize for his actions, or even retract his decree. That is why the Order of the Sun has been absent from Xytae for so many years."

"But what about protecting people? From chaos gods?" asked Aelia. "You just left them all to fend for themselves?"

"The situation is undesirable, but the Temple of Iolar is still there. It is not as though there is nobody there who can sense the presence of chaos magic and drive out demons. We can only hope that the priests are enough to keep the Xytan people safe."

Aelia fell silent, pensive. Iolar had enough power stockpiled to ensure his status for the next millennium, but he was not at all generous with it. Most of the gods' magic came from their worshippers, with faithful and willing ones generating the most power.

Some gods, like Eyvindr, gave back as much as they were given. Others, like Iolar, only made grandiose demonstrations very rarely. She wondered how far Xytae would be allowed to fall into chaos before Iolar stepped in.

She wondered if Edan's plans had something to do with it.

"It is unfortunate, but sometimes I think all paladins must eventually choose between the laws of Iolar and the laws of Men," said Orsina. "I came upon a similar problem when I was a girl."

"What happened?" asked Aelia.

Orsina paused for a moment to collect her thoughts. Then she said, "I have mentioned before that my parents were two of Melidrie's guards. I was expected to follow in their footsteps. My training began at a very young age, with a wooden sword and shield. But there were always a few paladins from the Order of the Sun stationed at Melidrie, serving as personal guards to the Baron and his family.

"The paladins looked intimidating, but they were actually very friendly. Looking back, I think they could tell that I had Iolar's magic, even at my age. They told me legends of paladins long past, of ancient adventures into cursed ruins and battles with incredible monsters. Perlita always dismissed the stories as boring or false, but I could not hear enough of them. While I sat in the Temple of Iolar for the Sunrise service, I wondered if someday I might become a paladin as well.

"But I did not wish to leave Melidrie, or Perlita, or my parents. Initiating into the Order of the Sun required me to travel to the Great Temple of Iolar, in Bergavenna. So I decided I would serve Iolar quietly, in my own way, rather than leave everything behind."

"But obviously that didn't happen," said Aelia.

"No," agreed Orsina. "But it might have been so, if not for the irritable phase Perlita went through when we were about ten years old. One day she woke up and decided that the weekly Sunrise services were a waste of her time and she would no longer be attending. I might have turned a blind eye to it, but Perlita ordered me to join her in her delinquency."

Aelia considered this. She always swore that she would never force her followers to conduct tedious rituals in her name, not that she'd ever had a chance to do so. But the wedding ceremony yesterday had been beautiful.

"I protested, of course," Orsina went on. "I enjoyed the Sunrise services. And even if I had not, attending them was mandatory. I would not disobey my parents."

If Aelia focused, she could see Orsina's memories: the ethereal sound of the hymns drifting up to the high ceilings, the warmth as the rising sun poured light through the east window onto the congregation, the feeling of Iolar's nearness. And she could also see skinny ten-year-old Perlita, declaring that the old-fashioned hymns were droning, that being forced to stand facing the rising sun hurt her eyes, and that she had never once felt Iolar's presence in the temple. *And furthermore*, Perlita argued, *it was every soldier's responsibility to follow her lady's orders, and right now her lady was ordering that they skip the services to climb trees together*.

"I didn't know what to do," said Orsina, pulling Aelia's attentions back to the present. "How could I choose between Iolar and Perlita? So I went to the paladins for help. I asked them what they would do, hypothetically, if the Baron asked them to do something they knew Iolar would not like. I did not mean for them to catch on to my problem, but I knew from their faces that they had. I was afraid they might instantly demand to know what Perlita was up to, but instead, they invited me to sit with them while they talked."

The memories sharpened as Orsina focused on them, and for a moment Aelia could see the events as they had played out that day.

"The Baron rules Melidrie," Sir Biagio said. He was about the same age as Orsina's fathers, and patient despite his powerful, calloused hands and scarred face. "But he cannot make a law for Melidrie that contradicts the laws of King Marcius, can he?"

Orsina had never considered that question before, but she shook her head.

"Why not?" the paladin prompted.

"Because..." Orsina chewed her lip, "...because the King is a higher station than the Baron."

"Yes," said Sir Biagio. "And Iolar holds a higher station than even his majesty. That means that the laws of Inthya come even before the laws of Vesolda, does it not?"

That was about what Orsina had been expecting to hear, but for some reason, she was not comforted. She struggled to explain. "It's just...the Baron is right here. And Iolar is all the way in Solarium. And if we don't do what the Baron says, he could lock us up, or worse."

"Perhaps so," said Sir Biagio. "But how long can the Baron imprison us for?"

"The rest of our lives. If he really wants to."

"Would you be willing to endure fifty years imprisonment if it meant an eternity in Solarium afterward?"

"I don't know," Orsina whispered. To her young mind, fifty years and an eternity were practically synonymous.

"I would not expect you to. These are questions for adults, not children."

"But you can't do any good if you're locked up," Orsina said. "Maybe it's better to stay free. And help more people. Even if you have to break some rules."

"How would you decide which rules are worth breaking?"

Orsina shook her head. "I don't know."

"Shortly after that, the paladins recommended to the Baron that I be sent to Bergavenna to be formally assessed," concluded Orsina. "I was invited to become an initiate only a few months later."

"But you said that wasn't what you wanted," Aelia said.

"I think there was a difference between asking and being offered," Orsina admitted. "I think I'd managed to convince myself that wanting to be a paladin was a silly fantasy, and I'd only embarrass myself if I asked. But knowing that adults that I admired thought I was capable of it changed things. My parents were proud of me, but Perlita was furious. She swore she would never forgive me if I went to Bergavenna."

Aelia looked down at Lavender's mane. She wouldn't claim to approve of little girls devoting their lives to concepts they couldn't possibly understand, but she also couldn't help but wonder why Perlita would be so deliberately cruel.

Aelia was very quickly beginning to dislike Perlita, and Orsina's veneration of her only made her irritation burn brighter. From what she could glean from Orsina's memories, Perlita was nothing more than a spoiled young noblewoman who had never been denied anything.

Not that she cared very much about what Orsina did in her personal life. Aelia would probably end up killing Orsina in the end and it would all be a moot point—

Well. Maybe she wouldn't have to kill Orsina. Orsina might be a paladin, but Aelia could not seem to muster up very much hatred for her. If Aelia could think of a way to get her hands on the Unbinding Stone and destroy her mortal body without letting Orsina know the truth, she might try it.

Orsina fell silent, now lost in her own memories, and Aelia did not ask any more questions.

RIDING A HORSE, even a docile pony like Lavender, was far more difficult than Aelia would have ever guessed. After two days in the saddle, her legs were numb and sore, whether she was on horseback or not.

As they approached Catorisci, the sun was slowly beginning to set over the lake, dying the water beautiful shades of orange and pink. Aelia thought it looked pretty, but Orsina pulled Star to an abrupt halt, her eyes narrowing.

"There is something evil in that lake," she announced.

"What?" asked Aelia. The water was still and tranquil, and she had not sensed anything within. She brought Lavender around, reaching out with her mind, but Orsina grabbed the reins from her.

"Don't go *closer!*" she cried. "I'll have to investigate in the morning."

"What do you think it is?" asked Aelia, squinting as she focused her thoughts in the direction of the lake.

"With any luck, it's just an ancient relic that fell to the bottom centuries ago," said Orsina. "Or perhaps there's an old shrine to a chaos god on one of those little islands."

Aelia's magic was still weak enough that she would need to get nearer to sense whatever Orsina was sensing. Frustrating, but not very surprising.

Catorisci was medium in size and clearly prosperous, just as Orsina had said. The inn was even nicer than the inn back in Antocoso. In fact, even in the dim light, Aelia could see that Catorisci was a beautiful, well-kept town. Several of the houses had glass in their windows, and even the stones in the streets seemed to have been scrubbed clean by someone with too much time on their hands. It was all so orderly and calm that Aelia wondered if Orsina might be mistaken about the presence in the lake.

But it seemed Orsina was not at all comforted by their absurdly pristine surroundings. While Aelia tried to enjoy the evening meal and listen to the musicians, Orsina did nothing but press the tavern's employees for information.

"I expect most of your wealth comes from your lake?" asked Orsina.

"Not at all, actually," said the barmaid who had come to refill their drinks. Her name was Claretta, and Aelia supposed she was probably around twenty years old. "There's not a single fish in that lake. It's been empty for generations."

For a moment, Orsina seemed to have been stunned into silence. "Are you certain? A lake of that size—"

"No, it's true. Ask anyone," said Claretta cheerfully. "There's a legend that some lord or another, ages back, tried to stock it with fish. But the fish all died within the month."

"Surely you find that alarming?" asked Orsina.

Claretta laughed. "You know, I'm so used to it, I forgot how strange it must sound to outsiders! But in truth, we hardly even need the lake. We've been so lucky with trading and commerce, most days I forget it's even there unless I feel like sketching it."

"Sketching it?" Aelia spoke up for the first time.

"Oh, it's nothing," said Claretta hastily. "Just little drawings. I don't fancy myself a lady or anything, I've never had proper lessons."

"I'd like to see."

But Claretta just waved her hand, as if embarrassed.

"Have you noticed anything else unusual about the lake?" Orsina pressed. "Maybe an excess of drownings?"

"There is the occasional accident, but no more than you might expect. There are some superstitions, I suppose, but when I was a girl my friends and I built rafts and went sailing or swimming, and nothing ever befell us. Why? Has the Order of the Sun received complaints?"

"Not to my knowledge," said Orsina. Aelia wondered if she would tell the barmaid about sensing evil in the waters, but she did not.

"Well," said the young woman, moving away from the table. "Let me know if you need anything more."

"I want to swim," announced Aelia to nobody in particular. Last night's activities, followed by the long day on the road, had left her feeling heavy with grime. How did anyone tolerate living in a flesh body for decades and decades? It was enough to drive one mad!

"You are absolutely not going in that lake," said Orsina. When Aelia pouted at her, she added, "If you want a bath, ask one of the maids to draw you one."

"You're no fun," grumbled Aelia.

"Do you even know how to swim?"

Aelia lapsed into baffled silence, turning the words over in her mind. Know how to swim? Was there something to know about swimming? Surely swimming just happened, like walking, or breathing. Men made it look easy, and the Mer made it look even easier. The idea that it might be an acquired skill was something she had never considered before.

"Tomorrow I'll begin a true investigation," said Orsina, more to herself than Aelia. She got to her feet. "I'm going to turn in early. Stay out of trouble, won't you?"

"I'm tired as well," Aelia assured her. "I'll be along as soon as the musicians are done for the night."

Orsina nodded. "Very well. I will see you in the morning."

Aelia did as she'd promised for a while, listening to the soft, drifting music. She really did want to learn an instrument, she decided. She watched the mortal with the lyre as his fingers moved over the strings with impossible speed and grace. Could she really learn to play like that? It seemed utterly impossible.

Once she was certain that Orsina was in bed and not coming back down again, Aelia got up and left the inn. She had to admit, she was curious. What had Orsina sensed in the lake? And could it be of any use to Aelia?

Dense woodlands separated the lake from the town, and Aelia quickly realized that she had no idea how to reach it. She didn't really want to go wandering through the forest in the dark, but it seemed she had few options. Then she noticed a few small children playing in the fading light.

"Hey!" she called to them. They both looked up at her, squinting a little in the darkness, but did not run away as she approached. "How do I get to the lake from here?"

The children exchanged looks.

"There's a path through the trees," said the elder one, indicating what, to Aelia's eyes, was an impenetrable forest. "Only you're not supposed to go down at night. Everyone knows. 'S bad luck."

"I'm not afraid," said Aelia. "Come on, show me where the path starts. Just the start. You don't have to walk it."

The older child pressed his lips together, but the younger raised her hand and pointed. Aelia went over in the direction indicated and saw that there was indeed a very faint path through the trees, so faint that she could not be sure if it was just her imagination. She pointed at it questioningly, and the child nodded.

The path was long and winding, and Aelia stumbled more than once over an exposed root or fallen branch. By the time she reached the pebbled shores of the lake, only a silver moon lit the night.

But, she realized, Orsina had been correct. There was something in the lake, something active and malicious. She could sense it just as she could sense the mosquitos biting into her arms.

Aelia closed her eyes and focused on the presence. It was familiar; someone she knew. One of her siblings. A brother. Sleepy and lethargic and greedy and hungry, hungry, eternally hungry.

"Iius?" called Aelia in Asterial. She picked up her skirts and took a few cautious steps into the lake. "Iius, is that you?"

The surface of the water rippled. Then...

Aelia? asked a lazy, leviathan voice.

"Yes, it's me!" cried Aelia. "What are you doing in there?"

Waiting for my next meal. Are you sure you're Aelia? You smell like a Man.

"A paladin trapped me in this avatar. Only a few days ago."

She could sense her brother's slow, lazy amusement in her mind. *Would you like me to free you of it? It will only take a moment.*

"No thank you," said Aelia, taking a few rapid steps backward. "Do you know where I might find the Unbinding Stone?"

I have no need for such trinkets. But you might ask Edan. He always seems to be plotting something. Perhaps he would know.

"Did he come to you looking for an ally?"

Yes.

"Do you remember where he asked you to meet him?"

No. I was hardly listening. But you might try the Xytan Empire. Many of our siblings are settling there since their emperor managed to chase away the Order of the Sun.

"I heard about that," said Aelia. She found a dry patch of stones and sat down to gossip properly. "Was it Reygmadra's doing?"

She claims the emperor acted of his own accord. There is no proof that she is lying. And it is unlike the Ten to betray one another. But she has always envied Iolar, hasn't she? The emperor might have come up with the idea on his own, but she certainly did not dissuade him.

That sounded likely to Aelia. "In that case, why are you here instead of Xytae?"

With so many of our siblings converging upon Xytae, it will not be long before Iolar is forced to intervene. I'd rather not be there when that happens. Besides, why should I leave when everything I require is right here? My priestesses bring me meat, and in return, I have made their pathetic village prosperous.

"Your priestesses?" Aelia repeated in shock. "Are you serious?"

If you get them when they're young, they're less likely to turn on you, advised Iius. *Years ago...don't ask me how many, they all run together...I made myself known to two children as they played. They brought me frogs and worms to eat. Then fruit. Then a chicken. A stray dog. A child who displeased them. And so on.*

"That's disgusting." Aelia wrinkled her nose. "Meat is revolting."

To each his own, said Iius. *Are you sure you don't want me to help you out of that body?*

"You might want to return to your plane in Asterium for a few days," said Aelia, deciding to ignore the question. "There's a paladin here, and she's already sensed you."

Is that so? She could sense his amusement, his eager anticipation. *In that case, point her my way. It's been weeks since I last ate a Man.*

"I find that difficult to believe," said Aelia.

It is the truth. Men love to tell themselves that nothing is amiss, that they are safe, that there is no monster lurking near. So long as I restrict myself to outsiders, or what my followers bring me, they turn a blind eye to my presence.

"Maybe so, but you can't eat my paladin," said Aelia. "I need her alive for a while longer. Just go, so she forgets about it and we can be on our way."

Playing games, are we, Aelia?

"That *is* my domain," she retorted. "I'm going to bed now. Thank you for your help."

She could feel his derision in her mind all the way back to the inn.

THE MUSICIANS WERE gone and the tavern employees were wiping down the tables when Aelia arrived back. It seemed the citizens of Catorisci were not inclined to stay out late, for there were only a few lingering now.

Aelia was about to go upstairs and join Orsina in their room, but Claretta caught her eye and waved her over. When Aelia came nearer, the woman withdrew a few folded papers from the large pocket of her apron.

"I was afraid I'd missed you for the night," she said. "If you meant it, I have some drawings. They're not very good, especially compared to some others I know, but..." She lowered the pages so that Aelia could see the lead and charcoal sketches. As mentioned, two of them featured Catorisci's lake. Others were clearly taken from things Claretta saw around town: a bird resting on a blossoming tree, a dog sleeping in the sun, a clump of wildflowers. Aelia found the subjects a little dull, but even she could appreciate the skill that had gone into the act of creation.

"I don't think they're bad at all," said Aelia. "I can tell what they're meant to be. That's a good thing, isn't it? And they're probably better than anything I can do."

"Don't you have any pieces of your own?" asked Claretta.

Aelia shook her head. "I've never even tried."

Claretta seemed very surprised. "I took you for an artist. I don't know why, though. I apologize for troubling you."

"I asked to see, didn't I?" pointed out Aelia.

"Come to the Temple of Inthi tomorrow," said Claretta. "There's a group that meets there, and they're all more talented than I. You don't have to have Inthi's fire to join, the priests just let us use the space. You might like it."

"I'll be there," said Aelia. She was glad for something to do while Orsina ran around the lake getting mud on her boots. Hopefully, Iius would be sensible and just return to Asterium. Orsina would give up the chase by noon, and they could be on their way.

But there was no telling what foolishness Iius's mindless hunger might drive him to.

As Aelia lay in bed that night, she resolved that she would not get between Orsina and Iius if it came down to a fight. If they wanted to be violent fools, that was their choice. She would have no part in it.

Her thoughts drifted for a while until they landed on the memory of the wedding yesterday. Aelia had a rather loose understanding of how marriage worked or why it was so important to Men, but she could not pretend that she had not been impressed by the ceremony or the beautiful songs that the attendants sang for Pemele.

Nobody had ever sung for Aelia before.

The realization hit her surprisingly hard. Nobody sang for chaos goddesses, that was simply the way it was. Nobody wanted the attention of the embodiment of sloth, or greed, or uselessness.

For that was really what she was, wasn't it? Uselessness. Fickle and shallow, with not enough of an attention span to accomplish anything. Hardly anyone ever came to her willingly, and her followers always eventually died of starvation if they weren't rescued first. Aethitide was empty, save for the cats that sometimes wandered through from Ferra. No Men loved her enough to call her plane home after their deaths.

If she had to be a chaos goddess, why couldn't she at least be like Edan or Iius, utterly without remorse or compassion? She was too erratic and irreverent to ever hope to have her worship legalized but also had no desire to perform an act of great evil that might gain her some much-needed prestige.

At least her magic was starting to return. She would never be at full power, not while she inhabited a mortal body, but being able to sense the presence of her siblings and catch on to Men's thoughts gave her some measure of security. She raised her hand to her face and called her magic forward, the purple light that could pass for Talcia's blessing if she was careful.

By the colored light, she could see Orsina, sleeping peacefully on the other side of the room, dreaming nonsense dreams. Most Men believed that Eran, God of Dreams and Ninth of the Ten, constructed dreams especially for mortals, and brought them to Ivoria every night to show them whatever they wanted.

The truth was not quite so romantic. Men's brains naturally generated dreams as they slept for reasons Aelia was unclear about. Eran did sometimes bring Men into Ivoria to give them visions of the future, or show them something meaningful, or pass along messages to their followers. But the majority of Men's dreams were just that: dreams.

Aelia might have been a little bitter that Eran got so much more credit than they really deserved, but she did not have much animosity toward them. Eran might have been one of the Ten, but they tended to stay out of disputes and power struggles, and their followers never gave Aelia any trouble.

Aelia sighed to herself and pulled the blankets closer. Within a few minutes, she was asleep as well.

ORSINA WAS GONE by the time Aelia woke the next morning, already off on her quest to restore order to Lake Catorisci. It was extremely pleasant to get to stay in as late as she wanted, with the morning sun slowly warming the room. Only her promise to Claretta got her out of bed.

The Temple of Inthi was Catorisci's only religious organization unless one counted Iius' little cult. Aelia had to admit that she was impressed. She would never have expected someone like Iius to manage to secure worshippers loyal enough to call themselves his priestesses.

The temple was not difficult to find, located near the center of town. Inthi was the neutroi God of Creation and had been the one who first forged Inthya into being. Their status as First of the Ten reflected their place in the creation story.

Of course, the creation of Inthya had been *far* more complicated than the temples could ever hope to explain. But the stories that Men told each other had the order of events more or less correct. First had been Inthi, then Merla had covered the world in oceans, and then Eyvindr had brought forth the land.

Aelia had existed back then, too. She'd been little more than a stray thought, drifting in and out of awareness as the more powerful gods, still filled with magic left over from their last failed enterprise, continued to construct their new world.

The Temple of Inthi was built in strange red stone, or perhaps ordinary gray stone painted a rusty red color to reflect Inthi's fire. When she opened the door and stepped inside, she was immediately blasted with hot air. Judging by the temperature, this temple contained at least two forges.

At the center of the room was a strange fixture. Aelia approached it, unsure of what she was looking at. It seemed to be twisted sheets of copper and other colorful metals, all forged in such a way that they gave the impression of a blazing fire.

Aelia took a moment to appreciate the piece. She did not understand the principles behind most of what Inthi did, but it was nice to see one of their followers create something that did not serve an immediate practical function.

Most of the people inside were dressed in protective leather garments so that Aelia could not tell the priests from the acolytes or the apprentices or the master craftsmen. Instead of flowing robes, which would flutter into open coals and ignite, the common garb was thick gloves and heavy aprons. There was nothing ethereal or otherworldly about this temple, even in the entrance hall. It smelled of iron and sweat and steam.

"Elyne!" That was Claretta, waving at her from the other end of the room. She was dressed normally, not like a smith. She held a folio close to her chest. "You're here! I'm so glad."

Aelia brushed a few beads of sweat from her forehead as Claretta drew nearer.

"How do you get any work done in here?" asked Aelia. "It's so hot!"

"It's cooler in the upstairs rooms, where we meet," said Claretta. "The warm air rises, but the worst of it is over the furnaces, and those are outdoors. Still, I wouldn't try to paint in here."

"Who made that statue?" Aelia waved her arm toward the abstract depiction of the fire that she'd been admiring.

"Lucil did that," said Claretta. "They're an acolyte here, and a sculptor. One of their pieces is in the Great Temple of Inthi in Bergavenna. I wouldn't be surprised if they get a patron and never have to take a smith's job."

Claretta led Aelia upstairs, where it was indeed more comfortable in temperature. The temple had several large windows built into the stone. Today, all the heavy shutters were open, allowing fresh outside air to mingle with the smoke and steam.

Carved chairs formed a circle at the center of the room, where a group of people were gathered. All of them held rolls of canvas or leather folios.

"Everyone, this is Elyne," announced Claretta. "She arrived with the paladin yesterday."

Aelia was suddenly the center of attention, all curious eyes upon her.

"This is Riana. She does painting, mostly," Claretta went on with her introductions. "And Sabela, she weaves. And this is Lucil, the one who did the sculpture downstairs."

As Claretta went on naming her fellow artists, Elyne looked at Lucil. She could sense Inthi's fiery blessing radiating from their heart, invisible to the eyes of Men but obvious to her and any other gods that might be looking.

Riana was unrolling her canvas, laying it out on the floor so that everyone could gather around to look. It was a portrait, done in what Aelia supposed was a traditional Vesoldan style, all dark, heavy oil paints and soft lighting. The subject was a pair of children, dressed in clothes that were doubtless expensive, but it was otherwise unremarkable. Aelia found herself disappointed.

"If it is a bad likeness, I will not be blamed. Those dreadful children refused to hold still while I worked. The younger was all but climbing the curtains." Riana wiped her hands on her skirt and looked at Aelia. "This one was a commission from Giuliano, one of the richer merchants in our town. He heard King Marcius recently commissioned a painting of his daughter in this style, and so he wished to do the same."

"Will King Marcius be visiting his home?" asked Aelia.

"Only in Giuliano's fantasies!" Riana laughed. "I can't imagine what our king would say if he came to Catorisci."

"'Help me, I am terribly lost,'" suggested one of the other artists, prompting laughter from the group.

"Do you often take commission work?" asked Aelia.

"It is the only way to pay my landlord," said Riana. "Perhaps I could have a proper studio if I was in

Bergavenna or one of the other cities. But at least with a commission, I do not have to worry about dreaming up my own subject."

"I'd expect that to be the easy part," said Aelia.

"Maybe if I lived in Bergavenna, there would be more to inspire me," said Riana, looking down at the canvas. Aelia could sense the longing in her heart, the vague but colorful fantasies that Riana had difficulty pinning down. "And even when I do get an idea, I struggle to finish a piece. With a commission, I cannot afford to delay. If not for that, I doubt I would get anything done."

After that, each of the artists took a turn to show their most recent work. Claretta had more charcoal sketches, similar to the ones she'd shown Aelia last night. The others encouraged her to practice drawing from life, for her figures were often not-quite-right.

Sabela's work was beautiful, an intricately woven tapestry that showed olive trees in bloom over a rocky cliff that led down to bright, blue water. Sabela even let Aelia touch the fabric with her hands.

"I cannot take all the credit for this," Sabela explained in a somber voice. "It was Gina's. Her mother asked me to finish it."

"Gina?" asked Aelia.

"She died about four months ago," explained Claretta. "She was a member of our group."

"Oh." Aelia was not sure how to respond. She looked down at the tapestry again. "I'm sorry. What happened?"

"Drowned, we think," said Sabela. "But then, they never found her body. Just bits of her dress washed up on the shore."

"At the lake, you mean?" Aelia frowned. That did not fit with what Iius told her—that he left the townspeople in peace. Had he lied? Certainly, he was capable of it, but why bother? There was nothing to gain from lying to Aelia, at least, not about this.

"I don't understand it. She knew better than to swim alone. It's so easy to get pulled under." Sabela shook her head, frowning. "Sometimes I get so angry, remembering...I know I shouldn't, but I can't help it."

Aelia had no idea what to say. Luckily, it didn't seem like anyone was expecting her to say anything, and the subject quickly turned back to the artist's latest projects.

Lucil did not have any new sculptures, but they did bring a handful of sketches for a new piece they were hoping to forge soon. The design was difficult to make out, for it had been made with a light hand, but Aelia could identify the shape of a woman, more or less, with wildly curly hair and a pair of enormous feathered wings emerging from her back.

"Zeneen," said Aelia in surprise.

"Yes! You're the first one who hasn't said Nara," Lucil laughed.

"Nara doesn't have hair like that."

"I met a Masimi trader who kept a statuette of her, and I was inspired. She's not just the goddess of the desert there, you know. She's also associated with fire and the sun. I was going to cast her in copper, but I don't want her turning green someday. I'm going to try bronze instead."

"I think she would like that," said Aelia.

The mood in the room was still pleasant when the meeting ended. There seemed to be a little bit of a competitive edge between a few of the artists, but they were honest with one another when they made suggestions. At the end of it, Aelia and Claretta walked back to the inn together.

"You could build a little temple to Ridon," said Aelia, naming the God of Art. "There's certainly enough of you." And the protection of another one of their siblings might stop Iius from eating any more of her new friends.

"I don't think Ridon cares much for small towns in rural Vesolda," said Claretta.

"You might be right," Aelia nodded. "He does think highly of himself, doesn't he?"

Claretta gave her a strange look. "If anyone had cause to think highly of himself, it would be one of the gods, wouldn't it?"

"Oh, you know what I mean! I can't stand gods who only give their best blessings to nobles, or the children of heroes, or the same family line for generations. A handful of mortals get to go through life with an advantage, while all the ordinary ones have to work twice as hard—"

"Do not stand so near. I do not wish for the lightning to strike us both," said Claretta, edging away.

"You know what I mean!" Aelia threw up her hands. "Ridon keeps his gifts within a few families. Meanwhile, people like you and Riana had to work for your skills, showing genuine devotion to his domain, but he never acknowledges you, does he?"

"I am sure he is very busy," said Claretta. "And besides, I do not begrudge those who are born with his gifts. Having talent is not the same as having discipline. He might grant a blessing onto one of his followers, only to see it go to waste if the person is without passion."

Aelia had never thought of it that way. "You think someone would really do that? Waste a blessing?"

"Why not?" said Claretta. "We squander money and love and time. Why not gifts from the gods as well? It is in our nature, I think. I would rather be blessed with inspiration than talent."

Aelia contemplated this new perspective as she walked along. She'd never had enough magic to give a mortal a blessing, nor had she ever encountered a mortal that might be worth the effort.

"Well, never mind. I'm glad you decided to come today. It's so nice to have someone new around."

"I'm sorry I can't stay longer," said Aelia, and she meant it. "Maybe I'll find my way back someday."

As they came back to the center of town, Aelia spotted Orsina. She was on the other side of the road and speaking to two women. But that was not what made Aelia stare. Just as Lucil glowed with Inthi's fire, these women had blessings as well—but it was not any of the blessings that were common on Inthya. They were twisted and hateful, shimmering greenish-black, and wrapped around both women's hearts like the roots of a terrible weed.

My priestesses bring me meat, Iius had said.

"No," muttered Aelia.

"What's wrong?" Claretta asked. Aelia only shook her head and hurried over to Orsina.

"Oh, Elyne!" said Orsina, breaking away from the conversation. "There you are. I was just—"

"Are you ready to leave?" Aelia interrupted, ignoring the dirty looks that both the women were giving her. "I'd like to go, soon."

"Be patient," said Orsina. Her smile was so relaxed that Aelia realized she had not sensed what the two women were. Perhaps because they had not used their magic yet? "I warned you that if you traveled with me, I'd be stopping frequently..."

"But there's nothing here to stop for!"

"Maybe," said Orsina. "But maybe not."

Aelia pouted, this time more out of instinct than any real desire to manipulate. "I'm hungry," she complained. "Do you want me to starve?"

Orsina rolled her eyes. "I was just about to go down to the lake."

"You haven't been yet?" Aelia was surprised. She'd have thought that would be Orsina's first stop.

"I got sidetracked," Orsina said. Aelia glanced at the women again, briefly. She was not afraid of them, exactly, but she did not know how much Iius told them about her, or what his orders to them had been. The two gave her identical looks of cold disdain.

"Let's eat something first," Aelia suggested. "So if you drown yourself, at least I won't die of starvation today."

If the two women appreciated Aelia distracting Orsina, they did nothing to show it. As Orsina and Aelia began to walk away, Aelia gave one last glance over her shoulder and saw they were still watching her.

"What was that about?" Claretta asked, once Aelia and Orsina were near enough.

"I'm still not completely sure," said Orsina with a frown. Aelia waited to see if Orsina planned to elaborate, but she didn't.

"Oh, don't pay any mind to them," said Claretta. "Miserable old hags. Let me guess, they were complaining about everyone else in town?"

Orsina looked surprised.

"I don't think they cared much for me, either," Aelia admitted.

"It's not you, it's everyone outside their families." Claretta shook her head. "Don't pay them any mind, Dame."

“Have they given you any trouble before?” asked Aelia.

“Oh, not really. Sousana’s been cross with me for a month, but she’s so sour all the time I’ve hardly noticed the difference.”

“Whatever for?” asked Orsina.

“Her son, Vissente, was hired on at the inn three months ago, but he thought he was too good for the work. Wouldn’t sweep a floor or wash a dish. Kept trying to get better jobs, even though he hadn’t earned them yet. I had to tell him to leave, and not come back. She seems to blame me, as though it’s my fault she raised a layabout.”

“Are you worried?” asked Aelia.

“What, about Vissente? I don’t think he could do anything to me even if he wanted to. It would be too much like work.” Claretta shook her head. “Before you think I’m some slave driver, he had that job two months longer than anyone else in town would have, since we all felt so sorry for him.”

“Sorry for him?” repeated Aelia. But now they’d arrived at the inn, and Claretta’s shift was about to begin. Her questions would have to wait.

As they ate lunch, Orsina reported on her findings for the morning.

“There have been no disappearances, or murders, or anything that suggests an active cult,” Orsina said.

“So, nothing to worry about, then?” asked Aelia.

“I’m not so sure,” said Orsina, frowning down at her plate. “There have been drownings, and I forced the watchmen to admit the bodies are almost never recovered. Besides, haven’t you noticed? This town has no beggars, or pickpockets, or petty criminals.”

“I thought you’d approve of that?”

"That's not the point," said Orsina. "It is unnatural. I know something is going on, but nobody is interested in uncovering the truth. It is as though they would rather people go on dying than have something uncovered that might disgrace the town."

"Well, if that's what the people want, let's give it to them. We should probably be moving on anyway, shouldn't we?"

"I know what I sensed last night. I'm going down to the lake right after this. Maybe I'll find some evidence that they won't be able to ignore."

"Well, be careful," said Aelia. "I'll be greatly inconvenienced if you don't return."

Orsina laughed. "I will try my best."

"What did those old ladies want? The ones you were talking to when Claretta and I came up?"

"Oh." Orsina shook her head. "Sousana and Vasia? They were just curious about me, and if I'd learned anything significant. I think they're just town gossips. They didn't seem too bad, really. I think Claretta was a little harsh. Sousana lost her daughter-in-law only a few months ago."

"Really?"

Orsina nodded. "I understand she drowned. Or at least, that's what they want us to believe..."

"Wait." Aelia frowned. "Was her name Gina?"

"Yes. You heard of her?"

"She was married to Sousana's son? The one Claretta fired?" *We all felt so sorry for him...*

"They were engaged. Set to be married when the priestess came by. I think Claretta could stand to be a little more compassionate. It's only—"

Orsina went on talking, but Aelia wasn't listening anymore. Why would Sousana kill Gina? Had she disapproved of the relationship? Or had Gina learned about Iius from Vissente, and threatened to turn them all in?

"Where is Vissente now?" interrupted Aelia.

"What?" Orsina looked confused. "Who?"

"Sousana's son. Where is he?"

"I don't know, I haven't met him. Why? Do you think he knows something?"

"I'm not sure." Aelia sat back in her chair and folded her arms, replaying her conversation with Iius over in her head.

So long as I restrict myself to outsiders, or what my followers bring me, they turn a blind eye to my presence.

Realization struck her like a runaway carriage. Iius had never claimed he only ate outsiders! Aelia just assumed it. He would eat anything Sousana and Vasia brought him. Including their neighbors...

And if Gina hadn't been safe, neither was Claretta.

Aelia's stomach clenched with anxiety. No, she told herself. Claretta was smart. She would never put herself in a position where she might be attacked.

But fear, it seemed, could not be reasoned with.

I do not care. She is just another Man. Why should I care?

And it was not just Claretta who was in danger. All the inhabitants of Catorisci had the potential to become Iius' victims. Riana, Sabela, and Lucil and everyone else she met today at the temple...

Aelia leaped to her feet, and Orsina gave her a curious look.

"Excuse me," said Aelia. "I'll—I'll be right back."

She all but ran for the lake, tripping over roots and stones the entire way. It seemed to take an eternity to reach the water, but she did not slow her pace even when it finally came into sight. She ran into the lake, splashing in up to her knees.

"Iius!" she yelled.

Silence. Had he gone back to Asterium after all? As the last echoes of her shout died away, she was aware of the cold water seeping into her stockings, and her skirt. What was she doing? What was she *doing*?

The surface of the water rippled.

Aelia? her brother sounded as though he'd just been woken from a nap. *What do you want now?*

"Listen, Iius," said Aelia. "I don't care what you do, but there's a group of Men in this town that I like. I want to make a deal with you, for their protection."

We both know you have nothing to offer me, said Iius. *And besides. How am I meant to tell your Men from all the others?*

Aelia paused, realizing he had a point.

This town is mine, Aelia, said Iius. *You have no rights to anything within its borders.*

"I do have things to offer," Aelia lied. "Once I get free of this body—"

No. I am not interested.

Something brushed up against her leg. It was probably just some rotted plant matter, but it made her jump nevertheless. Aelia looked down at the murky lake water, which barely reached her knees. Whatever form Iius had taken, it probably was too large to come into the shallows.

Still, Aelia edged backward toward the safety of the muddy banks.

Why have you come here? asked Iius. *Your pet has been upsetting my priestesses and irritating the authorities. I do not understand what you hope to accomplish.*

"I have no control over what she does. We'll be gone as soon as I manage to convince her there's nothing to investigate here. Which I'm not going to be able to do unless you can guarantee the safety of my friends."

What makes you think I intend to allow her to leave?

"Iius!" Aelia cried. "I told you, I still need her!"

Iius did not reply, and Aelia pouted and kicked the water. "Fine," said Aelia. "But if she kills you, it's not my f—"

Something struck her over the head, and for a moment Aelia thought she had been freed of her mortal body. She collapsed forward into the lake, unable to control her own limbs anymore. She was aware that she needed to push herself upward, to get her face out of the water, but it was as though she had lost her arms.

She could feel hands on her back, but they were not helping her up. Instead, they seemed to be dragging her further out into the water. Aelia tried to shake free, the only movement she could manage, but it did little good.

Aelia twisted her body around and saw an old woman staring down at her. It wasn't Sousana, it was the other one. His other priestess. Vasia.

"Iius!" Aelia shrieked as her face broke the surface. "Tell her to stop!"

You may thank me after you have regenerated, said Iius. *Be honest. You probably weren't going to find the Unbinding Stone in any case.*

But Aelia was beginning to regain control of her body. She grabbed the priestess by the arms and dragged her down into the water with her. Aelia should have been stronger than her—the woman's body was old and frail. But somehow, it seemed she was being overpowered. The old priestess's hands wrapped around her throat and forced her beneath the surface of the water.

In a blind panic, Aelia called her magic to her hands and began striking wildly, aimlessly. Even as she attacked, she knew she was outmatched. How many had this woman killed in this exact same way? Aelia was about to be just one more victim. It was actually rather embarrassing.

Next time around, she would pick a body with muscles.

But then the pressure around her throat lifted, and Vasia was yanked up and away, into the open air. Aelia scrambled upward, choking and sputtering as she broke through the surface once more.

When her vision cleared, Aelia realized Orsina was knee-deep in the lake and holding the priestess by the collar. Her sword was unsheathed and glowing with the golden light of Iolar's blessing. Aelia kept her distance, though her mortal body protected her from the brunt of it.

The priestess pulled her fist back and punched Orsina directly in the chest. Aelia would have laughed, but she caught sight of the shocked expression on Orsina's face, as well as the freshly broken links in her chainmail. Orsina took a few staggering steps backward, her grip on the priestess loosening enough for the old woman to break free.

"I am giving you this opportunity to turn yourself in," called Orsina. "If you renounce your—"

Vasia leaped forward, her face twisted with hatred. But instead of tackling Orsina into the water, she collided with a spectral shield made of golden light that blossomed from Orsina's palm. It vanished as quickly as it had come.

"I recommend you surrender," said Orsina, seizing the woman by the neck. "If you agree to name your fellow cultists, I may be able to—"

The woman raised her face, opened her mouth, and lunged for Orsina's throat with her teeth. Aelia had just enough time to wonder if Orsina would still spare the priestess since she was a woman and not a chaos deity or demon. But that question was answered a moment later, when Orsina sliced through the woman's stomach, cutting her in two.

"Elyne!" yelled Orsina as the water around her changed from green to crimson. She stumbled nearer, clumsy and unsteady in the water until she caught Aelia by the arms. "Are you all right?"

Aelia nodded, unable to speak just yet.

"Gods," said Orsina. "What on Inthya is going on here?"

"Priestess," Aelia stuttered out. "They—the lake. They've been feeding him."

"Feeding *who*?" Orsina's fingers dug into Aelia's arms as she looked at her intensely. Aelia looked back out to the water, which was now beginning to stir.

"Iius," Aelia stammered. "God of Gluttony. He's going to eat both of us!"

Orsina released Aelia's arms and drew her sword again. "Go," she said, turning to face the deeper part of the lake. "I'll take care of this."

Iius was laughing, the eerie sound echoing across the water. Orsina only raised her blade, waiting. Aelia staggered back toward the shore, then turned around just in time to see Iius surface.

Iius' form was a massive gray fish, larger than any animal Aelia had ever seen before. He had rows of pointed teeth like a Mer, and beady black eyes. Orsina took a single step backward at the sight, and Aelia thought she saw the paladin's hand tremble a little.

Aelia summoned her magic again, intent on helping Orsina. Her magic was weak, and she doubted she'd be able to do any real damage, but she could at least cause a distraction.

Iius propelled himself into the shallows, his massive head thrashing around and teeth slamming open and shut, biting at the empty air around Orsina. Orsina was forced to keep in constant motion to avoid his mouth. A single bite would bring the fight to a rapid end.

Aelia could see how limited Orsina's range of movement was in the water. It was only a matter of time.

Aelia flung her arms outward, sending purple sparks in Iius' direction. They danced around his beady eyes, limiting his vision enough that his movements slowed and became more careful. Orsina struck forward with her sword, and crimson blood spilled forth from Iius' gray hide.

But a single, shallow cut would not be nearly enough to stop her brother. Aelia looked around for something, anything, that might be useful. Her eyes fell on the severed lower half of the dead priestess's body, and she seized the legs. They were far heavier than she'd anticipated, but she was able to drag them through the water.

Orsina and Iius were keeping one another busy enough that neither of them noticed Aelia moving nearer and nearer, pulling the dismembered legs after her. When she was a mere handful of steps away from Iius's flailing body, she steadied herself and waited.

Iius opened his mouth again to bite at Orsina, and that was when Aelia lifted the dead hunk of flesh out of the water and flung it at Iius's face with all her strength. In Aelia's imaginings, it landed squarely in his massive mouth. But instead, it fell just short of her target, landing at a midway point between Iius' nose and Orsina's blade.

But Iius could not ignore a meal any more than Aelia could ignore a sudden distraction. He lunged forward again, his jaws closing around the remains of his own follower. Orsina took advantage of the distraction and rushed forward. Aelia closed her eyes, knowing that it would only take Iius a moment to swallow and resume fighting—

There was a terrible squelching sound, followed by a shout. Aelia opened her eyes to see Orsina leaning her entire body's weight on her sword, which thrust vertically downward into Iius' brain.

But Iius' body was not dead. Not yet. It flailed with supernatural strength, sending Orsina's sword flying off into the depths of the lake. Orsina herself was struck in the torso by that immense, powerful tail, and went flying backward into the rocky shallows. Aelia turned and ran for the banks, knowing there was nothing more she could do now.

But Iius' flailing was beginning to slow as the water around him turned a deeper and deeper shade of crimson. Aelia stumbled and landed on the banks, her palms sinking into the mud. When she twisted around to look back at her brother, he gave a hateful snarl.

Aelia! Iius bellowed into her mind. *I won't forget this! You will regret ever coming here! Once I have regenerated, I will have my revenge!*

"This wasn't my fault," Aelia whimpered, but there was no way he could hear her in his death throes.

It seemed to take an eternity for Iius' body to grow still and cold. When it was finally done, Orsina got to her feet and staggered toward Aelia.

"Are you—?" Aelia began. Orsina's face was covered in cuts, and her chainmail was missing more than a few links. Aelia couldn't see any serious injuries, but Orsina had landed quite hard on the stones. Even Aelia knew that head injuries could be fatal, from the inside.

"What were you *thinking*?" cried Orsina, once she staggered near enough to reach out and catch Aelia by the arms. She leaned forward, breathing heavily, apparently unable to stand upright on her own. "Elyne, what—what—I don't even know where to begin!"

"I'm sorry," said Aelia. "I thought I could reason with him."

"You *what*? Elyne, how could you be so...?" Orsina's voice trailed off and she shook her head. "Are you injured?"

"I don't think so," said Aelia. Every inch of her body ached, but she didn't think anything was broken or bleeding out. She looked down at herself and saw she was caked in mud and blood. If she did have any injuries, she could not see them.

Orsina crumpled against her, as though the strength had gone out of her body. Aelia wrapped her arms around Orsina's torso as they both went crashing to the soft, muddy ground.

"I'm sorry," said Orsina faintly. But she gave no indication that she planned to stand up again.

Aelia had always thought of Men as bags of water and meat, but now she found herself noticing how finely all the pieces fit together. Orsina's body was made up of a million tiny parts that spoke to one another in a language of lightning and chemicals. Her heart pulsed, her veins surged, her mind was aglow as it worked to interpret all the information it was receiving.

But parts of Orsina's brain were dark and eerily quiet. The lightning seemed to take too long to move through it. Aelia moved so that she was sitting up and rested Orsina's head in her lap. Resting her fingers across either side of Orsina's head, Aelia set to work.

Aelia knew nothing about healing, or biology, but the brain remembered what it wanted to look like, and to feel like. She followed the natural pathways, fixing the damaged connections and dead tissue as she went. After a few minutes of work, Orsina opened her eyes again.

"What happened?" she mumbled.

"You killed the shark and then you fainted," said Aelia. "Also. You lost your sword. I'm sorry."

"It's still got a blessing on it. We'll be able to see it when it gets dark," Orsina murmured. "I'll retrieve it tonight."

Aelia looked down at Orsina's bloodstained face. Her body was already rallying against her wounds, coating each injury with a protective mix of clotted blood and sticky organic glue.

"Also," said Aelia, "Sousana killed Gina. Her son's fiancée."

Orsina sat upright, pulling away from Aelia's lap. *"What?"*

"What, you think you're the only one around here who knows how to ask questions?"

Orsina shook her head incredulously. "Alright, well, that's one more thing to deal with before we go. Though if she had a mental link with Iius, she's probably already fled."

Aelia expected Orsina to stand up and start walking back to Catorisci, but she did not. Instead, the paladin closed her eyes and her breathing became slow and measured. For a moment, Aelia was afraid that she was about to collapse again. But then she realized that Orsina was reaching out with her thoughts, reaching upward—reaching for Iolar's approval.

No response came.

Orsina got to her feet without a word, but there was no missing the disappointment in her face. Aelia looked down at her own dirty hands and said nothing, unable to even bring herself to tease Orsina for her devotion. It seemed like there was no kind way to make light of the situation.

"I really thought this one might be it," said Orsina with a loud sniff, wiping at her face. "I'm sorry. You must think—"

"No," said Aelia. "Whatever you're thinking I'm thinking, you're wrong."

Orsina laughed weakly, and that was when Aelia pressed her lips to Orsina's cheek.

The kiss was soft and fleeting, but Aelia would not have been surprised or offended if Orsina screamed or shoved her away. But Orsina's brown eyes seemed to be regarding her thoughtfully.

"Alright," said Orsina.

Aelia kissed her again, on the lips this time. She brought her hands up to cradle Orsina's face, half-expecting Iolar to reduce her mortal body to cinders on the spot. But Iolar's attentions must have been elsewhere, for nothing happened.

Orsina's powerful arms encircled her, pulling her close. Aelia melted into the embrace, suddenly understanding why Men were so obsessed with romantic love. Perhaps Orsina would never need to find out the truth about Aelia. Perhaps Aelia could live alongside her as a mortal until she died of old age.

I'm being ridiculous, Aelia told herself. There was no way she could pass herself off as a mortal woman for fifty years. Orsina would catch on eventually—assuming she even had any interest in keeping Aelia around for decades and decades.

"What's the matter?" asked Orsina.

"Just thinking," Aelia murmured into her chest, closing her eyes and savoring Orsina's warmth. It felt like the light of Solarium, but gentle and forgiving rather than harsh and punishing. Aloud, she said, "I don't know what I'm doing anymore."

"We're going to Sabarra," Orsina reminded her. "We're going to find your brother."

Yes. Edan. Would Orsina destroy him, just as she destroyed Iius? Just as she'd tried to destroy Aelia?

The memory of running through the olive grove struck her like a blow. This was foolish. This was *dangerous*.

But Orsina's hand was rubbing soothing patterns across Aelia's back, and Aelia's mortal body was beginning to respond. She suddenly wanted to feel those strong hands on her hips but did not know how to ask.

After a moment, Orsina released her.

"We should go," she said. "We have a lot of explaining to do."

Chapter Five

ORSINA

Catorisci's municipal council was not convinced or impressed when a bloody, battered paladin staggered into the center of town and announced she killed a chaos god that had been living in their lake for generations. So, despite her exhaustion, Orsina led them all back down to the lake, where Iius' corpse was still trickling blood into the water.

They had to burn it, Orsina explained, or else something new might crawl inside, heal the worst of the injuries, and start menacing the town once more. After a rapid discussion of how they could possibly hope to haul a monster the size of a small hut out of the shallows, the town butchers sent their apprentices off to fetch their knives.

Convincing the council that Iius also had devoted priestesses—one of whom was now in two separate pieces—was not so easy, however. Orsina was fully prepared for someone to tell her she was under arrest.

Orsina wasn't terribly worried for herself, for she knew the Order of the Sun would send their best magistrates to defend her if it came to a trial. But she was unwilling to leave Elyne unprotected.

Especially now.

Catorisci's officials wanted a formal written statement from her, so she set to work composing a detailed report of her morning investigation. Claretta directed her to a private dining-room in the tavern where Orsina could write in peace.

Orsina was careful to leave out any implication that the townspeople had been complicit in the disappearances due to their fear of scandal. Then, she wrote, she paused around noon, and returned to the tavern with Elyne...

And then Elyne had rushed out. Orsina had to pause in her writing and pace angrily around the room at the memory. What had she been thinking?

"I thought I could reason with him."

Orsina groaned and rubbed at her eyes. She knew Elyne was naive, but there was a difference between naiveite and outright stupidity.

And just what had Elyne been doing all morning? Somehow, while Orsina had been struggling to get the townspeople to even acknowledge there *might* be something amiss, Elyne managed to uncover the name and domain of the chaos god in the lake and draw out one of his priestesses.

Sousana's house had been empty when Catorisci's guards went to check in on her. Her son, Vissente, was in the middle of being questioned when Orsina left to write her statement.

There was a soft knock at the door, and Orsina turned around. Elyne was standing in the doorway, still in her bloody and mud-covered dress and wringing her hands awkwardly.

"I was wondering if you needed a healer," said Elyne. "Just. Just in case."

"I'm fine," said Orsina, and it was true. Somehow, miraculously, it seemed she had come out of the fight with only some cuts and bruises.

Elyne laced her fingers together. "I didn't mean for any of this to happen."

"You could have been killed," said Orsina. "Elyne, what were you thinking?"

"I told you. I wanted to try talking, instead of stabbing. I won't do it again." That, at least, sounded earnest.

"Did you speak to him?" asked Orsina. Elyne nodded. "That's very odd, that he responded to you. I'd have thought he'd want to stay hidden."

"I think he was looking forward to eating both of us," said Elyne. "From what he said to me, it seemed like he couldn't eat just anyone who came into the lake, or else the townspeople wouldn't have been able to ignore him. But outsiders, like us, nobody would notice or mind if we went missing."

"You said Sousana might have drowned her son's wife?" Orsina asked.

"I don't have proof," said Elyne. "But Claretta told me she drowned, and they never found her body. And Iius told me that Sousana and the other woman did sometimes sacrifice other townspeople. If Sousana didn't like Gina, or thought she was stealing her son from her..."

"How terrible," said Orsina. "To think ordinary women would be so cruel to their neighbors."

"Men are not wicked because of chaos gods," said Elyne. "It is Men's wickedness that brings them into existence."

Orsina raised an eyebrow. "How philosophical of you."

Elyne's cheeks flushed red. "Well, it's the truth, isn't it? I think the world could be improved if people stopped blaming the gods for their faults and started improving their own character instead."

"I do not disagree," said Orsina. "But surely you realize Iius needed to be stopped?"

“He did.” Elyne wrapped her arms around herself and hugged her sides. “I was foolish for thinking it might turn out differently.”

Orsina sighed, torn between delivering a lecture and letting the issue go. “Just...if we are to travel together, you must understand. I encounter evil regularly. I hate to be cynical, but I have never encountered a chaos god that is open to the idea of changing their ways.”

“Do you frequently suggest it?” asked Elyne.

“I cannot say that I have ever had the opportunity,” admitted Orsina. “They tend to attack on sight. Besides, gods are not easily persuaded to behave against their own natures—and even if they were inclined to, it is more difficult for them than it is for us. To alter the domain of even a minor deity would be an unbelievable feat.”

Elyne said nothing more, and Orsina looked down at her half-complete report on the desk. She sat down again and picked up her quill.

“I’ve asked for a warm bath,” said Elyne. “I’ve got blood and mud everywhere.”

“Good,” said Orsina absently, chewing on the end of her quill. How much of Elyne’s side of the story should she add to her report? Elyne’s knowledge did provide important information, but the magistrates might dismiss it as hearsay if it was coming from Orsina, rather than Elyne herself.

“You’ve got mud and blood everywhere too,” Elyne added.

“Mm,” said Orsina.

Elyne simply stood there for a few moments longer, silent.

“Right,” she said at last. “Well. Then. You do that, then.”

Orsina turned back around to look at Elyne, whose lips were now pressed together in irritation.

"Elyne, I just killed a woman," Orsina said. "I know you want to talk. I want to talk too. But complying with the authorities in this town is the only way we'll be able to get out of here within the next few days."

"Do you regret it?" asked Elyne.

"What? Killing her? I had to, she was—"

"No!" Elyne's face was red, and she waved her fists in the air. "By Asterium! Do you regret letting me kiss you?"

"What?" Orsina rose so quickly that she nearly knocked her chair over. "Is that what you think?"

"What else am I meant to think?" retorted Elyne. "I know...I know you hit your head. If. If you were still confused when I—"

"No," said Orsina firmly. "My head is fine. I knew what I was doing. I just..."

Sometimes, occasionally, Elyne reminded her so much of Perlita that it hurt to look at her. Orsina wasn't totally sure why. There seemed to be some faint similarities in their facial structures, but that very well could have been wishful thinking.

But whether the physical resemblance was real or just a product of Orsina's imagination, there was no denying that Elyne's impulsive, inquisitive nature, her delight in the world around her, and her infuriating stubbornness were all traits that Perlita also possessed.

Guilt clenched at Orsina's stomach. She would not turn Elyne into a substitute for Perlita.

"I'm sorry," said Orsina. "I've been alone for such a long time, I..."

"You don't deserve to be alone."

"Maybe, but..." Orsina floundered. "I...I just..."

It had seemed so simple when she'd thrown the letter onto the fire. It had seemed simple when Elyne kissed her, and Orsina kissed her back, heart still pounding from the battle and blood trickling into her eyes and righteous fury surging through her veins.

But now, with Elyne staring up at her, expecting answers and promises and reassurances, she knew that it would never be simple.

"Just what?" asked Elyne. "You just what?"

"I just don't want to hurt you," said Orsina.

Elyne actually laughed at that, like Orsina had told a good joke. "You! Hurt me!"

"I'm serious, Elyne!"

Elyne sobered quickly. "What's wrong, then? You don't like me after all? Is that it? You're just too polite to turn me down directly and this is your way of trying to get rid of me?"

"Elyne!"

"What? It wouldn't surprise me!"

"You know I cannot lie, Elyne," Orsina reminded her.

"You can't lie, but you can refuse to give a straight answer and hope I hear what you want me to hear! Everyone knows that!"

"I would not do that to you." Orsina met Elyne's eyes. "You deserve honesty. Genuine honesty. And you deserve someone who could devote themselves to you fully. I'm afraid I cannot do that right now."

Elyne's lips quirked again. "I never took Iolar for a jealous husband."

"Elyne!" Orsina cried, scandalized by this blasphemy. "That's—that's not what I meant."

"It's Perlita, then?"

"Yes," admitted Orsina, lowering her gaze. "I know there is nothing romantic about chasing after one who has made her feelings clear. But it hurts, knowing I meant so little to her."

"What would you do if she wrote to you right now, then?" asked Elyne. "If she asked you to come home?"

"I cannot return home until Iolar tells me so," Orsina reminded her.

"That's not the point! What would you do if she wrote to you now?"

"She will not," said Orsina.

"But if she did!" Elyne insisted. Realizing she was serious, Orsina paused to fully consider this scenario.

"I suppose," Orsina began slowly, "it would all depend upon the contents of the letter. I would require an explanation for her silence, first and foremost. Unless Melidrie was swallowed by an earthquake, which I would have heard of, there is no reason that she could not have written to me even once. I. I can forgive a lot, especially from Perlita, but I don't deserve to be ignored for two years."

It almost felt like sacrilege, to say such a thing—to say anything that implied Perlita was imperfect. But it was all true. Orsina deserved better. Expecting basic decency from those she loved wasn't selfish or unreasonable.

"If nothing else, I am glad you realize that," said Elyne. She tilted her head to the side, an odd smile on her face. "I should let you finish your report, shouldn't I?"

"I won't be too much longer," promised Orsina. "Go, before your bathwater gets cold. We can talk more later."

ELYNE WAS STILL in the bath when Orsina finished her report, so Orsina went to the stables to clean her armor. She was nearly done with that when a group of older children arrived, soaking wet and bearing her still-glowing sword. They had apparently been set to the task by parents who wanted them out of the way while they gossiped and speculated and waited for official statements to be made.

To Orsina's relief, none of them had injured themselves on the blade or managed to drown themselves in the process. As she ended the blessing and set the sword aside for cleaning, the children told her eagerly of their adventure, and then began asking her questions of their own.

"Did Vasia really try to feed your lady to the shark?" asked one of the younger children of the group.

"That is what I saw," confirmed Orsina. She examined the broken links in her chainmail and decided it needed to be fixed before they left. With a temple of Inthi in town, the work would be good, and probably fast, but not cheap.

"They went to her house," said another child. "And they found something! But they won't tell us what. We think it's a body."

"I doubt that," said Orsina. "She would have little use for a body, and there would be no missing the smell. It was probably an altar."

This got some impressed murmuring.

"How did a shark get in the lake?" asked an older boy. "The merchants say sharks can only live in the sea."

"Gods can live wherever they like," said Orsina. "In this case, I believe Iius materialized in the lake from his plane in Asterium a very long time ago." She picked up her sword and a cloth. The blade was undamaged, save for a few new scratches, and only needed to be cleaned and re-oiled.

"Old Sousana disappeared," reported another child. "Do you think she'll come back for revenge?"

"I don't know," said Orsina. "If she did, she would probably come after me. I'm the one who ruined her plans. I don't think she would return to Catorisci. Too many people know her. She would be caught quickly."

One by one, the children were called away. When they were all gone, Orsina decided to go see if Elyne was finally done with her bath. She had not been when Orsina finished her report.

Orsina found Elyne in her bed, under a pile of blankets. Her hair was still wet, though the rest of her seemed to be dry.

"You should lay your hair out by the fire so it will dry more quickly," suggested Orsina. "It's not so crowded downstairs yet."

"No," said Elyne. "I'm never getting up again. It's too cold out there."

"You're only cold because you're wet," said Orsina. "And if you don't comb your hair, it will dry in knots."

Elyne sat up reluctantly, keeping the blankets wrapped around herself like heavy cloaks. Orsina picked up a carved wooden comb from the bedside table and sat down behind Elyne.

"Are we under arrest or not?" asked Elyne.

"Not, I think," said Orsina as she began to work on Elyne's tangles. "The dead monster in the lake does lend a great deal of credibility to my claims. But if they detain us longer than a few days, I will send for a magistrate. From what I have seen of the people of Catorisci, they may let us go simply to avoid the embarrassment of a public trial."

"A magistrate?" asked Elyne.

"The Order of the Sun is more than just paladins and justices. Magistrates are responsible for hearing internal disputes. They are also qualified to serve as advocates when a case involving one of us goes before the Temple of Iolar, as it might in this instance."

"I hope it does not come to that," said Elyne.

"I do not believe it will." Orsina paused. "I only wonder how many followers Sousana and Vasia had."

"Maybe Vissente could tell you."

"They're questioning him. I'm interested to hear the outcome. Though, perhaps he didn't know anything, if his mother drowned his fiancée and he said nothing."

"Or maybe he was too scared to say anything," Elyne suggested. "Maybe he was afraid he'd be next."

Orsina bit her lower lip, thinking.

"What are your parents like?" she asked Elyne, after a considerable pause.

Elyne did not respond immediately. She seemed paralyzed.

"Mothers? Fathers? One of each?" Orsina prompted.

"Parents. Both neutroi. They...they retired a long time ago and left the family business to us. We try not to trouble them too much."

"Who runs the business now?"

"One of my brothers controls most of it," said Elyne. "My other siblings usually defer to his judgment. They've been successful, but it's still a bit of a mess. I'd rather not be involved."

Orsina continued to pull the comb through Elyne's dark hair. "Have you considered the Temple of Talcia? If you have her blessing, they'll accept you."

"Perhaps," said Elyne. "But I don't think I'd make a very good priestess."

"You don't have to be a priestess. You could just stay an acolyte or another low rank. If nothing else, you'd be safe."

"I suppose it depends on what happens when we reach Sabarra," said Elyne. She was quiet again, and then added, "If we cannot find my brother..."

"We will think of something else," Orsina assured her. "I won't just abandon you in a strange city."

Elyne leaned her head forward a little. "I know I was careless today. But it won't happen again."

"I believe you. If nearly being drowned wasn't a learning experience, nothing would be."

Elyne's hair was finished, laying smooth and flat on her back. But Orsina continued to run the comb through it, mostly to give her hands something to do.

"I think you might be the kindest person I've ever met in my entire life," whispered Elyne, so softly that Orsina would have missed it if they had not been in a silent room.

"Most people are kind," Orsina said. "I...I know your family hasn't treated you well. But the rest of the world isn't like that. You can have a good life, away from them."

Elyne leaned back, and Orsina wrapped her arms around her instinctively. Too late, she realized this was probably a bad idea. But Elyne was already beginning to relax, and Orsina could not bear to ruin the moment.

"If you want to talk about it..." Orsina ventured.

"I do," said Elyne. "But I just...I can't find the words."

"Tell me who attacked you?"

"Someone sent by my brother," Elyne said. "A mercenary, I suppose you could say."

"Would you like to press charges?"

Elyne laughed as though she had said something absurd.

"I'm serious! That was attempted murder. He shouldn't be allowed to get away with it."

"Even if we had proof, which we do not, my brother would never go to trial," said Elyne flatly. "My family is far too powerful. And besides, I'd rather not alert him to the fact that I'm still alive. At least now he will leave me in peace."

Orsina struggled to balance her innate desire for justice with her knowledge that Elyne was right: being presumed dead by her awful family was the surest way to her freedom. Still, she *would* be investigating Ortradosa once Elyne was somewhere safe. Even if Orsina could not have the brother tried for attempted murder, surely the family had committed other crimes that only needed to be uncovered.

"It's all right, Orsina," said Elyne, as though sensing her discontent. "I hardly think about them. It all feels so far away now."

Orsina unwrapped one of the blankets from Elyne's shoulders and squeezed the moisture from her hair. "You should get dressed," she advised. "The day's not over yet. And I need to get cleaned up myself."

Warm baths were a luxury that Orsina seldom indulged in, but she supposed today could be an exception—though she did not spend nearly as long in the water as Elyne had. Checking herself over for injuries, Orsina realized she had been fortunate indeed. Nothing was broken, or deeply cut, and she did not feel light-headed or confused.

The water turned an unappealing shade of reddish-brown within only a few minutes of Orsina sitting down in it, but Orsina reclined in the bath and let her thoughts wander.

She had never encountered a chaos god in such a terrible body before, though her teachers had warned her of the possibility. Orsina hoped it would not be the start to a new trend. Chaos gods were dangerous enough when they looked like Men. The last thing they needed was one deciding it would be a good idea to manifest as a dragon.

She also could not help be a little bit hurt that slaying Iius had not warranted personal recognition—not that she felt entitled to a moment of Iolar's attention! It was only that Iius had been an impressive foe, and even if he was not the great evil she was destined to destroy, it was still a feat to take pride in.

If Iius wasn't evil enough to end her quest, what would be? Orsina had no illusions about the fact that she would have lost the fight without Elyne's aid, minor as it had been. Was her destiny against a foe even worse? How could she be expected to defeat something like that alone?

Or maybe she wouldn't do it alone. Maybe this battle was a sign that she needed to start working with other paladins, rather than believing herself capable of beating any foe she happened upon. That was hubris, wasn't it? Maybe she would never be strong enough to face her destiny alone.

Orsina was happy to admit her own weakness and ask for help, though she found herself worrying about how Elyne might react to a few more paladins joining them on the road, or how they might react to Elyne. She was an unusual young woman, anyone could see that, and paladins were not known to keep their opinions of anyone hidden.

Perhaps that could wait until Elyne was somewhere safe before recruiting more help. Elyne had just escaped a terrible situation. Orsina did not want to put her through any more unnecessary stress.

The walk to the Temple of Inthi was not long. It was very nearly evening, but the days were growing longer, so there was still plenty of light to see by.

"I don't think it looks so bad," said Elyne as Orsina showed her the damaged links in her chainmail. "But I suppose if we're going to be stuck here, now's the time to get it fixed."

"Even small holes will grow larger if they are not mended immediately. I just hope they don't overcharge us too badly."

"They should be giving it to you for free!" huffed Elyne. "You saved them all from being eaten."

"All of Vesolda benefits when I pay for my goods. Besides, paladins do not serve in hope of favors. We serve because it is right." At the unconvinced expression on Elyne's face, she added, "And I do not think Iius was foolish enough to attempt to eat someone blessed with Inthi's fire."

Elyne did not reply, and they walked along in silence for a while, moving at an unhurried pace in the direction of the temple. Something struck the back of her hand, and Orsina looked down. Elyne's own hand was very near to her own. Orsina took it, carefully. Elyne's fingers curled to meet hers.

"You're not hoping to repay a debt, are you?" asked Orsina.

"What?" Elyne stopped walking and looked up at her in confusion. "What are you talking about?"

"You think Catorisci owes me something for saving it. Do you think that you owe me something for saving you?"

"No, I—" Elyne shook her head. "That's not why—no."

"Are you sure?"

"Yes!"

Orsina did not want to disbelieve Elyne, nor did she think Elyne was lying outright. But she was not entirely convinced yet.

"On the night of the wedding, you said..."

"I was drunk! For the first time in my entire life!" Elyne's face was turning red. "And, if you *must* know, repaying you was just an excuse. I just...I thought you were pretty."

"You what?" An incredulous laugh escaped Orsina's mouth. "You—*what?*"

"What?" Elyne looked a little offended. "Nobody's ever told you that before?"

"Well..." Perlita had always been the sort to receive compliments, not give them, and nobody from the Order of the Sun had any reason to comment on anyone's physical appearance. Orsina lived in a very practical world of cold iron and carefully drawn runes. Beyond making sure her hair wasn't too tangled, she had no real reason to worry about her looks.

Her fathers thought she was pretty, but they were her parents so that hardly counted. Companions from the Temple of Dayluue called her all sorts of nice things as she walked past, but that didn't mean anything, either. They were just hoping for customers.

Orsina released Elyne's hand at last. "I suppose I've never thought about it. Is *that* why you're so persistent?"

"No. I meant what I said before. You've been kind to me. That's all. Can't that be enough?"

"Plenty of people will be kind to you," said Orsina.

"And plenty won't. Why shouldn't I want to hold on to the ones who will? Besides, you were the first. I'm allowed to be sentimental about it."

"I don't want to take advantage of you."

“Don’t treat me like a child,” said Elyne. “I might be silly sometimes, but I’m not stupid.”

“I...” Orsina began to object, but then she realized that perhaps Elyne was correct. “...I’m sorry.”

From the expression on Elyne’s face, she had been expecting a very different answer.

“Be patient with me,” said Orsina. “Please. I’ve been alone for...such a long time.”

Elyne took her hand again. “I know,” she said. “I have too.”

CLARETTA RARELY LEFT their table that night, except to occasionally refill someone’s drink. The discovery of Iius was clearly the most exciting thing to happen to the town in living memory.

Several of Elyne’s new friends from the Temple of Inthi had come, too. Orsina listened in calm silence as they traded stories of the lake or strange sightings that they’d thought nothing of until today. It was a little frustrating to see just how much had been brushed aside, but Orsina kept that to herself.

The group that Elyne had befriended were an interesting and colorful group, and Orsina could not help but smile at the knowledge that Elyne managed to make friends on her own. One of them even brought Elyne a sketchbook. So she could learn to draw, they said. Elyne rubbed her palms against the smooth paper and declared she would never ruin it by attempting to use it.

But Orsina was exhausted, and it seemed Elyne was as well. They returned to their room early that evening. Orsina had nothing on her mind but sleeping well into the next morning, but Elyne went to the window and stared out into the darkness, obviously unsettled.

"What's wrong?" asked Orsina.

"Good things never seem to last very long, do they?"

Orsina tilted her head to the side, surprised by this line of conversation. "That's not always true. And besides, new good things always come to replace the old."

"Not always," said Elyne.

"Did something happen tonight? You seemed happy before."

Elyne turned and looked up at her, a smile brightening her features. "No. I'm fine. Just thinking too hard, probably." She reached up to touch Orsina's face, her smile turning mischievous. "Why don't you distract me?"

"Elyne."

"All right, I'm just teasing. I'll stop, I promise."

"Thank you," said Orsina, but she could not deny that she felt a little twinge of disappointment at the words. It was so nice to feel wanted. "I...I am glad you're here with me."

"And I'm glad you found me." Elyne's face was suddenly very close to hers.

"I hate to think what would have happened if I hadn't."

"Oh, I'd have found a way through. I always do."

Orsina could not help but be skeptical—Elyne had appeared to be *very* close to death when she'd found her—but there was no point in arguing now. Elyne seemed to sense her dissent and leaned in to very, very rapidly press a soft kiss to Orsina's cheek.

"I'm sorry." Elyne did not sound very sorry at all. "I broke my promise already, didn't I?"

"I think I'll manage to forgive you," said Orsina.

Elyne pulled away, but Orsina could still feel the echoes of her fingertips on her face.

ORSINA WOKE EARLY the next morning to check on the status of Catorisci's investigation, only to be told that her presence was no longer required, and she could leave whenever she pleased.

Orsina did not find this terribly reassuring, given Catorisci's history of covering up unpleasant truths. Eventually the council admitted to her that they had identified all of Iius's worshippers with the help of Sousana's son Vissente. There were nine of them in total, and all but Sousana herself had been arrested.

There would be a trial, and representatives from the Temple of Iolar were expected to arrive in Catorisci by the end of the day. A few of the council members seemed optimistic that perhaps the entire thing could be handled quickly and quietly, with minimal embarrassment to the town.

Orsina decided not to tell them that a cult that fed innocents to a chaos god was unquestionably the single most dreadful thing she had encountered in the last two years, and they could expect the Temple's investigation to take at least six months. They would find out for themselves soon enough.

Instead, she asked after Vissente. They were reluctant to bring her to him, at first. They seemed afraid that Orsina might attempt to execute him on the spot. Even after Orsina swore she only wanted information for her own report to the Order, she could sense their discomfort.

Vissente was being held in his mother's home, under guard. Apparently there had been a fear that his fellow cultists would kill him before the trial if he was imprisoned with them. Orsina realized that had probably been a wise decision.

When Orsina entered the home, she found the young man sitting at the kitchen table, staring down at his own hands. A look of horror came over his face as he looked up at her, and his entire body tensed as though he wanted to leap out of his chair and run.

"It's all right," said Orsina, raising her hands in a gesture of peace. "I'm not an executioner. I just want to talk to you."

Vissente did not look at all reassured by this. Orsina sat down in the chair across from him, hoping that he would relax more if she did not tower over him.

"Can you tell me about Gina?" she asked.

Vissente blanched. "Whatever you're thinking—"

"Your mother fed her to Iius," Orsina pressed. "You stood by and let it happen?"

Vissente shook his head vigorously. "No! It wasn't like that!"

"What was it like, then?"

Sweat trickled down Vissente's forehead. "I, I tried to tell Gina. To convince her to join us. I didn't think she'd take it as badly as she did."

"You didn't think she'd object to learning you were murdering people and feeding them to a monster?"

"You don't understand." Vissente looked desperate. "I was born into it. I never knew anything different. I thought...I never questioned...I thought it was normal. It wasn't until I saw how horrified she was that I realized what we were doing was wrong."

"You must have known it was wrong, else you wouldn't have kept it a secret your whole life."

"I..." Vissente struggled with his words. "I don't know."

Orsina gave a small sigh. "And what happened after you told Gina the truth?"

"She wanted to run away. Just the two of us. Get away from the lake, and my family."

Orsina frowned. "She wasn't going to turn you all in?"

"I don't. I don't know. Perhaps, eventually. But in that moment, all she wanted was to run." Vissente shook his head. "I was careless, in those next few days. Of course, my mother learned what we were planning. We should have left that night. If we had, Gina might still be alive."

"Why didn't you report your mother after Gina died?"

"She is still my mother," said Vissente helplessly. "And...I think she managed to convince me the whole thing was my own fault. If I'd just listened...if I hadn't courted a girl outside the cult...if I'd kept it a secret. I forced her hand, in a way. She was only doing what Iius commanded."

"She was not in thrall, so that is no defense."

"You do not understand." Vissente shook his head. "You were lucky enough to be chosen by a god who loves you. Do not mistake your good fortune for moral superiority."

Orsina stood up, and Vissente flinched like he was expecting her to draw her sword. But instead, she just walked to the door.

"I was hoping I'd find you penitent," she said, resting one hand on the doorknob. "But all I've heard are excuses. I've nothing more to say to you."

"Wait!" There was true panic in his voice. "Wait! I am penitent! I will prove it! The girl you travel with—she is not what you think she is!"

"What?" It took a moment for Orsina to comprehend the meaning of Vissente's words. "What are you talking about?"

"He told us, he warned us!" Vissente looked around, like he thought someone would leap out of the shadows and attack him. "She is using you for protection. She's tricked you into trusting her!"

Orsina had enough experience with cultists to know that they would claim just about anything when truly desperate. Apparently Vissente had finally reached that threshold. She rolled her eyes and opened the door. "I'm done here. I suggest you rethink your approach, sir. The magistrates will not be nearly as patient as I."

She could still hear Vissente shouting at her as she closed the front door and walked away from the house.

ORSINA'S CHAINMAIL WAS repaired and ready for her by midday, just as the first Temple representatives were arriving in a flurry of bright yellow robes and paperwork. Reassured that justice would be done whether Catorisci's council liked it or not, she went to retrieve Elyne, who was in the middle of saying long goodbyes to all her new friends.

They left Catorisci from the west gate, moving closer and closer to Sabarra and the border that Vesolda shared with Xytae. They passed green barley fields and then verdant woods as they continued down the dusty road. The sun beat down on Orsina's back, and she shifted as the chainmail began to grow uncomfortably warm. She directed Star closer to the edge of the road, where they might catch some shade from the trees.

Elyne was talkative today, sharing every thought that came into her head. But Orsina did not mind. It was nice to see Elyne happy and confident.

Still, she could not shake Vissente's words from her mind. She knew that they were nothing more than the desperate rantings of a doomed man. But for some reason, they remained with her.

Could Elyne have been affiliated with a chaos cult? Loathe as Orsina was to admit it, such a thing was possible. Was that the reason she'd fled her home and family? It did make a horrible amount of sense.

Orsina knew better than to ask outright. She would have to either wait for the right moment to raise the subject or hope that Elyne soon came to trust her enough to tell her the whole story.

They would not make it to another town before sunset, so Orsina kept an eye out for a good place to set up camp for the night. Perhaps they would be lucky and find a roadside campsite meant for merchants or soldiers, though she doubted that since they were in such a rural area.

"We're stopping already?" asked Elyne, when Orsina pulled aside to examine a flat clearing just off the road, sheltered by a copse of trees. She sounded disappointed. "I don't want to sleep on the ground."

"You have a bedroll," said Orsina. "Besides, it's not so bad. It's warm out."

"The ground hurts my back," Elyne sulked. "I'm sure we'll pass a village soon enough."

"According to the map, we should reach the next town tomorrow afternoon. If we try to make it tonight, we'll just end up riding in the dark, and you won't enjoy that."

"You might be wrong," said Elyne. "Maybe they've built a second village between the time your map was drawn and now."

Orsina dismounted and surveyed the area. She had not heard any tales of bandits, but she would draw a protective circle around their campsite tonight just to be safe. Not far away, a small stream sparkled in the light.

"Will you eat fish?" asked Orsina, eyeing the stream thoughtfully. Some people who would not eat meat still made an exception for fish, she knew.

"I..." Elyne looked uncertain.

"You do not have to, if you don't want to."

"No. I'll try it." Elyne's uncertainty was replaced by a bright smile. "As long as you don't burn it."

Orsina began pacing the perimeter of the campsite, looking for good places to anchor a protective circle.

Elyne had dismounted and was now sitting in the grass looking blank. Orsina wanted to ask her to set up a fire, but she had a feeling that was outside of Elyne's realm of knowledge. So instead she said, "Why don't you lay out the bedrolls, or collect firewood?"

Elyne looked doubtful. "Do I need an ax?"

"No, just pick up what you find on the ground." Orsina found a stone that she could use to carve the protective sigils in the dirt. "Make sure it's not wet."

Elyne disappeared into the woods and returned a little later, her arms full of sticks of all shapes and sizes. When she saw what Orsina was doing, a strange look came over her face.

"What's all that?" she asked, and some of the sticks on top of her bundle fell out of her arms.

"It's just a protective circle. See?" Orsina stepped back so she could examine the runes. "Once I bless it, it will alert me if anything crosses. It doesn't catch animals, but it will stop bandits from taking us by surprise."

Elyne frowned but didn't say anything. Orsina retrieved her hook and line from her bags and went to the stream to see if there were any fish. From a distance, she watched as Elyne dropped all the gathered wood into an awkward pile and then put her hands in her pockets.

Elyne came back to Orsina and sat beside her, staring into the water. "How long do you think it will be?"

"I think I saw a bream. Don't worry, we have supplies if I don't catch anything. You will not starve."

"I could try to blast it out of the water," suggested Elyne, her fingertips glowing violet.

"That...strikes me as excessively cruel," said Orsina. "I don't think Cyne would approve."

Elyne looked contemplative, then she nodded. "You're right." The violet light vanished.

"Did your family worship Cyne? You seem to have great respect for him."

"Cyne is...nice," said Elyne. "There are many stories about him that I like."

"Well, we have some time," said Orsina. "Why don't you tell me one?"

Elyne thought for a moment. Then she said, "Do you know the one about Spring Frog and the Orb of Rain?"

Orsina shook her head.

"It happened among the Orogai people."

Orsina gave Elyne an odd look. "Where?"

"Their lands are around the middle part of Hedoqua," said Elyne casually. Orsina frowned. She liked to think that she had been well educated by the Order of the Sun, but she could not recall ever having heard of the Orogai.

"There are many nations of people in Hedoqua, all with different customs. The Orogai are primarily farmers. Their lands are fertile and green, and they grow corn and squash—"

"You are making words up," interrupted Orsina, but Elyne ignored this and went on with the story.

Spring Frog was not, in fact, a frog. She was an adventurous mortal girl who apparently featured in many Orogai legends. Orsina was skeptical at first, but Elyne spoke with complete authority, weaving the story as though she had been there to witness it firsthand. She explained the Orogai people called Iolar 'Father-of-the-Sun' and believed that his wife was not Talcia, but Nara, who was called 'Song-of-the-Wind.'

At the beginning of time, Song-of-the-Wind had given the orb of rain to the Orogai people, so that their crops always grew. The orb was kept by Spring Frog's grandmother, a wise woman and healer of the tribe who Orsina supposed was a sort of priestess, even though Aelia said the Orogai did not keep temples. But one night, the Orb was stolen, and rain no longer fell on Orogai lands.

Thus began Spring Frog's adventure to recover the Orb, aided by Cyne (or, All-Wild-Things) in the form of a blackbird, though of course she did not know it was him at the time. As Orsina caught, cleaned, and cooked a silver fish from the stream, Elyne described Spring Frog's encounters with river spirits and fire demons and even a few chaos gods that had no names in Vesoldan.

As they sat in front of the firelight, Orsina was pleased to observe that Elyne seemed to be enjoying the fish she had caught—though Elyne was so busy telling her tale that Orsina wasn't sure if she really tasted it.

The story ended with Spring Frog outsmarting Whispers-in-the-Dark, the chaos god that had stolen the Orb, and returning home in triumph. Orsina had to admit that she'd liked it, even though it had been very odd and she wasn't sure if it really was a story from Hedoqua and not something Elyne invented herself.

As the sun set, Elyne wrapped herself in blankets and Orsina went to activate the protective circle she'd drawn around them. The runes glowed gold as she completed her prayer, then dimmed to amber.

In her bedroll, Elyne made a pained sound and curled inward.

"Elyne? What's the matter?"

"Nothing," mumbled Elyne. "Just tired."

Orsina wasn't certain if she believed that, but Elyne didn't seem to be in the mood to discuss it. "Well, tomorrow night we'll sleep in an inn. I promise."

Elyne nodded, and Orsina got into her own bedroll.

A few hours later, Orsina awoke with a start to the sound of Elyne choking. She lurched to her feet and found Elyne vomiting into the stream, tears leaking down her face. Orsina went to her side, pulling Elyne's hair back and rubbing a soothing hand across her back.

"Well, now we know you don't like fish," said Orsina, as Elyne went still.

The next morning, one of the anchor runes had been rubbed out, but Orsina blamed it on an animal.

Chapter Six

AELIA

They arrived in the small village of Sacisa at midday and, for once, nobody stopped to ask Orsina for help with anything. Orsina said that they would spend the night, then be off the next morning. Aelia, disoriented and tired from last night's protective circle, went to bed at three in the afternoon, much to Orsina's concern.

It transpired that there was one benefit to being sick, though, and that was getting to see just how attentive Orsina could be. She sent for Sacisa's only healer, an apothecary affiliated only loosely with the Temple of Adranus who had more experience with farming injuries than illnesses. He gave Aelia some terrible tea, told a story about a man who had been gored by a bull (as though he expected Aelia to be grateful that her situation was not much worse) and then announced that she would probably be fine by morning.

Orsina was openly dissatisfied with this prognosis and spent the remainder of the day at Aelia's bedside, offering her everything from fresh soup to soft bread to peeled oranges. When the room became too warm at the high heat of midday, Orsina folded a sheet of paper into an accordion and fanned her with it.

Aelia didn't understand why Adranus was always worrying about plagues. In her estimation, being sick was rather nice.

Still, she could not help but feel a little guilty that she was keeping Orsina from her work. She encouraged Orsina to go out and try to find something to defeat, but Orsina only laughed and said the town was showing no signs of evil influence.

As the day went on, Aelia drifted in and out of sleep, slowly regaining the energy that Orsina's protective circle sapped from her. She awoke sometime after sundown to see Orsina had fallen asleep as well, her head resting in Aelia's lap despite still being seated in the chair she'd pulled up.

Aelia reached down and stroked Orsina's hair, pushing it back behind her ear. Orsina did not even stir, and her breathing remained steady and even.

Aelia sat up, carefully, trying her best to not disturb Orsina. But as her legs shifted, Orsina's eyes fluttered open, and she pushed herself up from the bed.

"Elyne..."

"That doesn't look very comfortable," said Aelia with a smile.

"Mmm, you're right." Orsina stretched, and Aelia heard something in her bones make an odd noise. She rubbed the back of her neck. "How are you feeling?"

"A little better, actually. Maybe the healer was right after all. I think I'll be able to travel by tomorrow."

"I'm glad to hear it," said Orsina. "I've been worried about you."

Aelia shrugged, suddenly embarrassed. "I'm sorry to have delayed us."

"That wasn't your fault. You didn't get sick on purpose."

Aelia did not reply. If she'd been an ordinary woman, the protective circle would have had no effect on her. There was no sense in feeling guilty, for she had not asked to be a goddess any more than Orsina had asked to be a Man, but Aelia found that she could not help herself.

"You shouldn't sleep like that," said Aelia. "You'll injure your back."

"You're right. I'll—" Orsina got to her feet. But before she could take a step toward her own bed, Aelia caught her hand.

"There's room enough here," said Aelia.

The moment stretched on in the silence. She could feel the blood pulsing in Orsina's fingertips, could see it rising in her cheeks.

"Elyne," said Orsina, but there was no complaint or protest in her voice. It was as though she'd spoken her name for the sake of tasting it in her mouth.

"Only if you want to." Aelia loosened her hold on Orsina, only for Orsina to reach forward with her other hand and clasp Aelia's.

The bed really wasn't meant for two, but they both fit. Orsina's body was warm, and when she lay on her side, her shirt fell in such a way that Aelia could see a tattoo of the sun on her shoulder, just beside her collarbone.

Aelia pressed her forehead to Orsina's, and Orsina draped one arm over her side.

"Are we going to sleep?" Aelia whispered.

"Yes," said Orsina firmly.

That was probably for the best, Aelia told herself. But she was a little disappointed anyway.

AELIA WOKE TO Orsina holding her in a protective embrace, the paladin still fast asleep and the sun still below the horizon. The last traces of dizziness had left her, and she felt as good as ever.

Aelia wanted to go and explore Sacisa before they left, but that would mean waking Orsina. Orsina's mind was still dreaming, and if Aelia focused, she could catch pieces of it. But she was far more interested in studying Orsina's face, her messy dark hair and soft lips and tanned olive skin.

Aelia brought Orsina's hand to her lips for a soft kiss. Her skin was scarred and coarse from years of training and fighting and Iolar knew what else. In contrast, Aelia's hands were soft and delicate like a noblewoman's, or, more fittingly, a newborn child's.

She did not want to think about that, though. She wanted to pretend she was a mortal, no different from Orsina or any other Man on Inthya. She would live for another fifty or so years and die of old age and then whichever god she had served best would bring her spirit into their plane.

She wanted to tell Orsina the truth.

But she couldn't. Orsina would turn on her in a moment, this time making sure Aelia's body was well and truly destroyed.

Aelia gave Orsina's hands one last kiss and then carefully slipped free of her grasp. She was restless and needed to move.

Downstairs, the staff of the inn was preparing for the morning, yelling to each other as they baked bread and boiled water. Aelia sat at a table and picked at some figs discontentedly. Someone brought her a mug of tea, but it was too hot to drink and too bitter.

"She's pretty, isn't she?" said a new voice.

Aelia looked up, expecting to see Orsina. But the woman who had come up to her table was a stranger, one

Aelia was certain she had never seen before, for there was no way she could have forgotten a mortal so beautiful. A single dark ringlet had escaped from her elaborately pinned hair to cradle the side of her face so perfectly that Aelia refused to believe it was an accident.

Without waiting for an invitation, the woman sat down across from Aelia. She had softly tanned olive skin, and high cheekbones, and a strong Vesoldan nose. Her lips were painted bright cherry red, and her eyes were...

Were...

...red, like a rabbit...

Desire, crushing and burning and maddening. Desire beyond logic, beyond reason. Desire imperative as air or water. Fingers and lips and legs entwining. Love like sunlight, lust like firelight. And beneath that, something deeper. Calculations and charts, a twisting ladder made of chemicals—

Aelia broke free, gasping and coughing as though someone had been holding her underwater.

Dayluue, Goddess of Love and Seventh of the Ten, stared back at her impassively.

"Perhaps you'd like to tell me what you think you're doing?" she asked.

Aelia tried to respond, but all that came out was an incoherent mixture of excuses and apologies. Dayluue folded her hands in her lap and Aelia fell silent.

"You are not in trouble," said Dayluue. "Yet. Though I cannot say I approve of your actions, your goal of reaching the Unbinding Stone lies outside of my domain, and so I shall not interfere. I am concerned solely with the girl."

"I don't want to hurt her! I don't even want to kill her anymore."

"That, too, is outside my domain," said Dayluue, stealing one of Aelia's figs with her perfectly tapered fingers. "Though I am pleased to hear it nonetheless. She has been good for you, hasn't she?"

Aelia stared down at her hands.

"One way or another, you will become a goddess again," said Dayluue. "And on that day, you will no longer be her equal. I expect you understand my meaning."

"I'd never—" protested Aelia.

"You would never knowingly force her to be yours," said Dayluue. "But unknowingly? It is a possibility for all of us, and we must never forget that."

Aelia shook her head. "I wouldn't. I swear! I don't want a thrall. Especially not from her."

"And if that is the case, I will leave you both in peace," Dayluue's voice was calm, even friendly. "But if I find you are compelling her, it is not Iolar's wrath you need fear."

"Does Iolar...know?" asked Aelia.

"No," said Dayluue. "Our brother's attentions are elsewhere at the moment. There have been great changes in the north, and more still to come. Unless you do something terrifically stupid, you need not worry about catching his eye."

Aelia ought to be relieved to hear that, but she could not help but be annoyed on Orsina's behalf. She knew that Iolar had thousands of paladins and thousands of priests, but surely he could spare a thought for Orsina?

"If that is all, I will leave you to your quest."

"Wait!" said Aelia. She had no idea when her next chance would be to talk to one of her siblings. "I, I want to tell her the truth."

"A noble sentiment," said Dayluue, a strange smile coming over her face. "How very unlike you."

"I know," mumbled Aelia bitterly. "But I'm not a complete fool. I know that if I tell her, she'll destroy me without a second thought."

"Perhaps. But then, perhaps not." Dayluue got to her feet. "Good luck to you. I will be watching."

Dayluue walked out of the inn, and Aelia did not chase after her. She knew that if she went outside, the goddess already would be gone.

Aelia slumped forward and rested her head in her arms, wondering how she had managed to completely lose control of her own life in such a short period of time.

"Elyne?" That was Orsina, coming down the stairs. "There you are. Are you feeling better?"

"Yes," said Aelia, unconvincingly and a little muffled. She lifted her head. "I'm fine. Just...tired."

"I'd imagine. I don't think I've ever seen you rise so early of your own free will." Orsina smiled. "Let me eat something, and we'll head out. I don't think anyone here needs my aid."

Aelia was feeling restless, so she went outside to get some fresh air. This village was tiny, comparable to Soria, and completely unlike the bustling town of Catorisci. The sun was just barely beginning to rise, and she could see people shuffling to their work.

Aelia went to the inn's stables for lack of anything better to do. Lavender was in a stall, and her ears pricked forward when she saw Aelia. If the horses suspected that Aelia was not an ordinary mortal woman, they never did anything to show it.

Aelia petted Lavender's ears while the pony sniffed her hands, clearly hoping for a treat.

"I don't have anything," she informed Lavender. "They couldn't even be troubled to put sugar in my tea. I don't think they'd spare any for you."

"I need help."

Aelia jumped, startling Lavender enough that the pony shied away from her hand. She glanced around the stable and found it empty. But she was certain she had heard a woman speak...

"I don't know what to do!" moaned the voice that seemed to come from everywhere and nowhere. Aelia looked around frantically. *"I'm such a waste! Everyone's going to laugh at me. Or worse."*

"Riana?" asked Aelia, suddenly recognizing the voice of the painter from Catorisci. But Riana was miles away! Was she going mad?

"They're going to pretend they like it and then mock me once I'm gone."

But she could hear the girl as clearly as though she was standing before her.

Was this...

Was this a *prayer?*

Aelia closed her eyes and focused on the voice. *Riana?* she asked, cautiously.

Riana's mind lit with joy and delight. *"Ridon?"* she asked.

...no, said Aelia, and the realization that she had not been Riana's intended target crushed her.

"I'm sorry! I'm sorry!" cried Riana. *"Please don't go, it was just a guess! Nobody's ever answered me before!"*

Aelia swallowed. *What do you need?* she asked.

"Inspiration," said Riana. *"Or maybe just skill. The others are so talented. I think they only let me stay because I make them look better in comparison."*

You mean Claretta and Lucil and the rest?

"Yes!"

I don't think that's true, said Aelia. *But never mind. Tell me what you're working on now.*

Aelia's mind was filled with the image of a painting, or at least the beginnings of one. It was the lake, as seen from the banks. Not bad, but not remarkable, either.

Let me show you something, said Aelia. She thought of Aethitide, her plane. There was a lake there, too, but there was no mistaking it for a lake of Inthya. The water reflected the myriad colors of the sky, all greens and blues and purples. Along the banks grew flowers of Aelia's own invention, absurd creations that could never survive on Inthya, with all its rigid and unforgiving rules about energy and physics. They grew in messy clumps and clusters, choking one another and weaving together. Enormous, rugged trees lined the water, their black crystal trunks glittering in the dim light. At the center of the lake, a few stony islands hovered above the surface of the water, suspended in midair.

"*Oh!*" cried Riana. "*Oh, oh, thank you! I could cry!*" And from the sound of her voice, she was telling the truth.

Let me know when you are finished, said Aelia. *I'd like to see it.*

"I will! I promise! And—what is your name? So I can tell the others?"

Aelia's throat suddenly felt very strange. She swallowed and rubbed at her nose, which was stinging.

I am called Aelia, she said.

LESS THAN AN hour later, they left the village and continued westward. Aelia kept replaying the conversation with Riana in her mind, not entirely convinced that it had been real. It seemed more likely that being stuck in a meat body was driving her mad.

Orsina said that tonight, they would stop and make camp again, for the nearest town was too far to reach in one day. Aelia wouldn't be able to tolerate another night inside one of Orsina's circles. But how could she convince the paladin to forego this protective measure?

Aelia was in the middle of plotting an elaborate hoax to distract Orsina from remembering to put up a circle when two soldiers on horseback approached from the opposite direction. At first, Aelia paid them no mind, but they slowed down as they came nearer. Orsina pulled Star to a halt and watched as they did the same.

The soldiers were dressed in the uniforms of what was probably a local town, distinctive but not very impressive. By the way they looked from Aelia to Orsina, it was clear that they had come specifically for the two women.

Orsina raised one hand in greeting. "Can I help you?" she asked.

"We have come from the town of Aola," said one of the soldiers. "We heard that a lady paladin saved Catorisci from a chaos god, and hoped she might help us as well."

"That is I," confirmed Orsina. "What trouble is in Aola?"

"Some manner of monster," said the soldier. "Every night, it emerges from our forest. Every night, we slay it. But it returns the next evening no worse for it."

"A vengeful spirit, perhaps?" asked Orsina.

"That is what the priest we sent for thought," said the soldier. "He performed his exorcism, but there was no effect."

"How far is Aola from here?" Orsina asked.

"Two days' ride to the north. We are happy to escort you."

Orsina looked at Aelia. "I'm sorry," she said. "But I must see to this. I can pay for your passage to Sabarra from the first town we reach—"

"What?" asked Aelia. "No! I don't mind. You said yourself that this might happen. A day or two doesn't make a difference to me. Besides, I want to see what's happening in Aola."

Aelia could sense the relief that radiated from Orsina's heart at the words. She could not help but be a little offended that Orsina thought Aelia would abandon her so easily. But she did not say anything. She did not want to start a fight in front of strangers.

The two had weak blessings from Reygmadra, the sort the goddess commonly gave warriors. Aelia could see the magic for enhanced strength and prolonged energy coursing through their veins and permeating every part of their bodies. Aelia did not see any of Reygmadra's more dangerous gifts, like the blood rage or heightened animalistic senses, but that was to be expected since these men were only common soldiers.

Still, she was not pleased to have them around.

Aelia forced herself to be rational, for once. Why didn't she want the soldiers there? Was she afraid they would somehow determine what she really was? Or was she merely annoyed that they were cutting into her time with Orsina?

Perhaps a little bit of both.

Orsina conversed comfortably with the soldiers all day long, speaking of road conditions and healer's fees and other matters that concerned warriors. It took all of Aelia's meager self-control to keep silent. The soldiers would not be as understanding as Orsina when she inadvertently said something unusual.

Aelia could not be completely irritated with the soldiers, however, since their new northward route meant that they arrived in another small village just as dusk fell. They rented rooms in the inn and Aelia finally forgot the matter of Orsina's magic circles.

"You were quiet today," observed Orsina as they got ready for bed. "Was it the soldiers?"

"There's nothing wrong with them," said Aelia truthfully. "It's just that they're strangers."

"You've nothing to fear from them. I am certain that they would not be allowed to serve if their conduct was unbecoming," said Orsina. Aelia shrugged, unwilling to say more. Hopefully the two had not noticed anything strange about Aelia.

From behind, Orsina wrapped her arms around Aelia and pressed a kiss to the back of her neck. Aelia's body warmed in response.

"I'm so glad you stayed with me," said Orsina. "I know that sooner or later, we'll have to part, but—"

"Do we?" asked Aelia.

"Your brother is waiting for you."

Edan. Aelia nearly flinched as she remembered what waited for her at the end of the road. What would he demand in return for aid? Would it even be worth the price? Suddenly, she was not so certain. Edan never went halfway on his plans; it was against his nature. Would he expect Aelia to kill for him?

And would his victims only be evil Men who he hoped to drag, screaming, into Aratha? Or would they be innocents, like Gina?

Aelia suspected she already knew the answer to that.

"And besides, you're not meant for a life on the road," Orsina added, as though realizing Aelia had not been convinced by her first point.

“I could be,” Aelia said. “Don’t you ever think about the future? I want to stay with you.”

“It’s too dangerous. At least until I finish this quest. We’ll find a safe place for you to stay in the meantime, whether it’s with your brother or a temple or even with my parents at Melidrie. Then, when I’m done, we’ll...” Orsina’s voice trailed off. “We’ll think of something.”

“I can help you,” Aelia objected.

“Elyne, it’s dangerous out here. We were very lucky with Iius. I can’t justify taking risks with your safety.”

Aelia pressed her lips together, struggling with the words. “I. I’m not completely helpless,” she began.

“I know that. Still, it’s better this way. If something happened to you, I’d never stop blaming myself.”

“If something happens to me, it will certainly be my own doing!”

Orsina laughed. “Don’t speak about yourself that way!”

“I thought you were opposed to lying?” Aelia retorted, but it was hard not to laugh when Orsina was laughing too. She turned to face Orsina, and Orsina kissed her lips.

Aelia melted into Orsina’s arms, their argument already forgotten. What did it matter what happened tomorrow, or in the days after that? She didn’t want to think about that. She didn’t want to think about anything except the woman in front of her.

AOLA WAS A handsome town, quiet and well kept, with a sparkling river cutting through the heart of its valley. At first glance, it was difficult to believe that there was anything sinister happening within its borders.

Of course, Aelia knew that appearances were frequently deceiving. And if she focused, she could just make out *something* twisting across the town, seeping slowly through the air like spilled oil. She wanted to go off wandering in search of its source, but Orsina was already asking one of the soldiers for directions to the inn.

"You have been invited to stay in the home of our mayor," said the soldier in response. "He is very eager to meet you."

The mayor's home was a clean two-story building made from wood and stone. Carefully tended hedges surrounded the exterior, and a garden filled with fruit trees was in full bloom. Up in the branches, gray doves called softly to one another.

But despite all this, Aelia felt a strange dread rising up in her bones as they stood on the stone walkway.

The mayor himself was there to greet them, his servants hurrying to see to the horses and unpack their things. His name was Adamo, and he was a middle-aged man with curly dark hair. There were dark circles under his eyes, but his clothes were neatly pressed and there was nothing about his manner that suggested he was on the verge of panic. He confirmed the story that the soldiers relayed and told Orsina that she would be granted anything she required to conduct her work.

"Where is the apparition happening?" asked Orsina.

"Just inside the nearby forest," said Adamo. "You can see we have guards stationed there even now. The manifestation only happens after dark, but I don't want to take any chances."

"I'd like to take a closer look," said Orsina. "Elyne, stay here. Hopefully I can get to the root of this quickly."

"But—" Aelia protested.

"I won't be long," Orsina reassured her.

"My husband, Dion, is just inside. He will make sure you have all that you require. And..." Adamo's voice trailed off awkwardly. "...I think the company might do him some good."

Aelia did not want to be indoors, but she remembered her promise to Orsina and followed the servants inside. The interior of the house was even lovelier than the outside, with gleaming marble floors and expensive, hand-carved furniture.

And there was an undercurrent of sorrow here, muffled but unmistakable. She pressed one hand to the nearest wall to orient herself. It was almost like standing in a river, the pressure building slowly against her body, threatening to knock her over if she did not dig in her heels.

Mourning. This felt like a house in mourning.

But she could see no signs of it. No shrouds had been hung or laid over the ornamentation, the curtains had been pulled away from the large windows to let in sunlight and the scent of orange blossoms, and the servants scurried about their business as though this day was no different from any others.

Aelia weighed her desire to explore against her promise to Orsina that she wouldn't take any more risks. But surely there was nothing dangerous lurking in the mayor's home? The real danger was in the forest.

"Hello," said a new voice. Aelia looked up in surprise to see a man standing in the doorway. He was about the same age as Adamo, but his hair was longer and his face was remarkably handsome. He was also thinner, weary-looking, with rumpled clothes and sunken eyes. Such a corona of grief and exhaustion radiated from his heart that Aelia had to make an effort not to stare.

"You are the paladin's lady?" he asked.

"Elyne," she said. "You are Dion?"

The man nodded. "Come with me," he said. "I will show you the room the servants are preparing for you."

Aelia followed after him, trying to think of something to say that wasn't too intrusive or awkward. Finally, she managed, "It's so quiet in here."

Dion came to an abrupt halt, his shoulders tensing, but he did not turn around.

"Yes," he agreed in a hoarse voice that made Aelia's heart seize. "It is."

Aelia interlaced her fingers awkwardly. "Has it always been so?"

"No," said Dion. But then he began to walk again and said no more until they arrived at the door to the room that had been prepared. It had a large double bed, with soft blankets that Aelia immediately needed to rush to and run her hands all over.

"If you need a bath, the servants will draw you one," said Dion, but his gaze was far away. Aelia pretended to fluff the pillows as she pressed into his mind, only to recoil almost immediately at the maelstrom of anger and bitterness that was contained within.

She turned back to look at him, but Dion was already wandering away. She decided to follow.

"This is a lovely town. It seems strange that you're being visited by some manner of monster."

"Tragedy is everywhere," said Dion. "It is inescapable. I expect that when I reach Asterium, it will be more of the same."

Aelia frowned. Not because she disapproved of the sentiment, but because the words struck her as familiar. It was the philosophy of one of her siblings...

"Xara," said Aelia aloud.

"What?" Dion looked at her in confusion.

"Nothing!" Aelia shook her head. "Just...thinking."

Another man might have been suspicious, but Dion said nothing. He did not seem to have it in him to care.

Despite the despair that tore at Dion's spirit, Aelia could clearly see that he was not in thrall. Nevertheless, everything that she had sensed today—that slow, listless dread—told her that Xara could not be far away.

Aelia struggled to think of some way to continue the conversation. Finally, she asked, "Do you have any children?"

Dion stiffened again, and the grief that stabbed through his heart made Aelia flinch. "No," he said.

Aelia ran through the possibilities in her mind. Had Dion attempted the Change for the sake of carrying a child and found himself unable to hold the required shape for long enough? Was there no one in their town willing to serve as a surrogate? No family with more mouths than they could afford to feed? No orphans in need of a home?

Dion led her to an airy, open sitting room with soft couches and a low table between them. They sat across from one another while the servants brought them tea on trays with lemons and cream and a sugar bowl made from cut crystal.

As Aelia poured half the contents of the sugar bowl into her teacup, Dion stared blankly out the window, as though transfixed by the orange trees just outside. He did not touch the tea poured out for him.

"I expect the husband of the mayor has many responsibilities?" In fact, Aelia had no idea what the responsibilities of the husband of a mayor might be, but she had recently started to realize that people liked to speak about their work.

But Dion only nodded and continued to gaze out the window. Aelia drew the sugar bowl closer to herself.

"Have you seen the demon yourself?"

"Yes," said Dion. "One night, it came up to our window. The guards dealt with it. If it is allowed to leave the forest, it wanders through the town until it spots someone. Then it attacks. If we lock ourselves indoors, it destroys whatever it can get its hands on."

"That sounds frightening," Aelia commented as she squeezed some lemon onto her sugar mixture. "I can see now why you sent for Orsina."

Dion shrugged. "Perhaps if she fails, we will all be forced to move elsewhere."

"Would you like that?" Aelia asked.

"It hardly matters," said Dion.

The lemon and the sugar went well together, but the taste of the tea threw it off. Aelia squeezed in another few slices of lemon experimentally. Lemon and sugar together made a pleasant taste, in her opinion. Perhaps all it needed was some water to weaken the lemon juice?

She eyed the cream thoughtfully.

When Orsina and Adamo returned shortly afterward, they found Dion staring out the window and Aelia crouched in front of the table, which was now strewn with sugar, lemon rinds, and soggy handkerchiefs.

Aelia ignored the extremely judgmental and uncalled-for expression on Adamo's face and rushed to Orsina. "Did you find anything interesting? I've invented a new drink. Did you see the demon?"

Orsina took Aelia's hands gently. "I didn't see any overt signs of cult activity or any chaos gods that I'm familiar with," she said. "Tonight I will stand guard and see if I can identify the creature. If I'm unable to vanquish it, I will have to send for more aid."

"We have several hours until sundown," said Adamo. "You will dine with us tonight, and then you will be escorted to the site of the apparition."

"Very well," said Orsina. "In the meantime, I have some books that I would like to consult. I will admit that I've never encountered a creature like the one you've described before, and I wish to prepare as best I can."

"They put everything in a room for us," said Aelia. "I think I remember the way."

"Then lead me there," said Orsina with a smile in her voice. "And tell me what you've concocted."

"Oh! Lemon and sugar and water. All mixed together into a drink. I only need to get the portions right."

"Very good, my dear," laughed Orsina, pushing Aelia from the room. "You have invented lemonade."

WHILE ORSINA SPREAD her books out across the floor and began experimenting with various banishing diagrams, Aelia collapsed onto the excessively comfortable bed and burrowed under the covers.

"I wouldn't mind living here," announced Aelia. "Demon or not."

"I don't think Adamo and Dion would be pleased if we tried to remain here forever," Orsina commented.

"I know that! But if you save the town, they can't complain, can they?"

Orsina gave a small laugh and turned back to her books. Aelia closed her eyes and savored the soft, silk pillows and whatever cloud-like organic matter they had been stuffed with.

"Are you there? I think I've finished."

Aelia's eyes snapped open. *Riana?* she asked silently.

"Yes, it's me! I think I've finished the painting. Will you tell me what you think?"

Aelia glanced over at Orsina to see if she had sensed anything of this conversation, but the paladin was still pouring over her books, as peaceful as ever.

Show it to me, said Aelia.

At once, her mind was filled with a colorful canvas. Apparently Riana had been adequately inspired because the painting bore only a faint resemblance to the original sketch. Instead, Riana perfectly captured the image that Aelia sent her, so much so that for a moment Aelia was struck by a pang of homesickness.

It's perfect, said Aelia, as all other words failed her. *Thank you for showing me.*

"I'll do another!" said Riana. *"I want to focus on the trees this time. Maybe I'll even do a whole series. Oh, I can't wait to show everyone, they'll be so jealous! Just promise you won't give them better ideas than you gave me!"*

Aelia bit back a laugh. *I'll try to remember that you were the first to speak to me.*

"Yes! Exactly! I'll even be your priestess, if you like."

Aelia considered this. *I don't know. I've never had a priestess before. I'll have to give it more thought.*

"I have a spare room that I can turn into a temple!" Riana exclaimed eagerly.

Aelia turned her face to the pillow so that Orsina would not see her laughing. *Very well. But no mandatory services. And don't make the prayers go on too long, I'll get bored.*

"What sort of plants do you like?"

Aelia paused. *I don't know,* she said. *Figs are nice. Lemons are good, but only with sugar. I've been promised I'll like chocolate, but I haven't had a chance to taste it yet. Chocolate is a plant, isn't it?*

She could tell that Riana had seized a sheet of paper and was now taking down everything she said.

I also like the round pink salty things that you sometimes eat, Aelia added. *But I don't know what they are called.*

"I don't know..."

You cut it into thin discs and serve it with bread and olives, or cheese. I will show you. Aelia focused on her memory of the food that Orsina had given her several times on the trip.

"Oh, that? That's dried salami! It's not a plant at all, it's made from pigs."

Aelia felt herself frown. She had been tricked by meat-matter. *Really? I would not have guessed.*

Miles away, Riana giggled.

I won't lie, said Aelia, *there's so much I don't know about mortal life. I'm at a disadvantage. You are free to find a more competent goddess to serve.*

"Oh no, I wouldn't want to do that! Besides, it's silly to expect you to know about food when you don't need to eat."

Yes, well, said Aelia awkwardly. *Don't worry about offerings or decorations too much. Though... I wouldn't mind a song once in a while. If you're feeling up to it.*

She left Riana to her eager preparations and went to Orsina's side. Orsina was still kneeling over her books, studying texts and diagrams that Iolar should have never given to mankind.

"Do you know what those words mean?" she asked Orsina, gesturing to the sigils inside one of the banishment circles.

"This is for getting rid of demons," said Orsina. "But I don't know if the markings have any true meaning behind them. I just know it doesn't work if you draw them incorrectly."

So Iolar had not taught Men to read Asterial after all. She supposed that made sense. If they could compose their own banishing or summoning rituals, the Ten might be in trouble.

She rested her chin on Orsina's shoulder and watched her work. "Do you think it's a demon?"

"That seems likely," said Orsina. "Though I could not guess which deity it spawned from."

Xara, thought Aelia. But she said nothing.

Demons were interesting creatures, a side effect of the discrepancies in the flow of time between Inthya and Asterium. They could be created consciously by gods seeking minions, but this was rare. Creating a demon powerful enough to be of use generally cost more energy than it generated. If a god was powerful enough to create a demon intentionally, he was generally powerful enough that he had no use for one.

Most demons were created by accident. They were like shadows of the gods, embodying aspects of their domains but acting without true purpose or understanding. They could be extremely dangerous and were frequently impossible to reason with.

Luckily, they weren't particularly clever. Aelia supposed that demons were to the gods as animals were to Men. They could hardly even be held responsible for their own actions.

She just had no idea what would cause one to regenerate night after night.

A few hours later, a servant came to escort them to dinner and found Aelia and Orsina curled up on the bed together, half-asleep.

Adamo did most of the talking at the meal, while Dion stared at his plate. Orsina asked questions about Aola and its history while Aelia examined the food and tried to decide if any of it looked like it might be meat-matter masquerading as plant-matter. Fortunately, nobody but Orsina noticed when Aelia bit into a pomegranate like it was an apple.

After the meal, Orsina donned her armor once more and gave Aelia a soft kiss on the lips before departing with three other town guards, leaving her alone with Adamo and Dion.

Aelia was determined to get to the bottom of the mystery, and so when Dion drifted out onto the patio, she followed him purposefully.

"It will be dark soon. Aren't you afraid of the demon?"

Dion shrugged. "Death comes for us all, sooner or later."

Aelia pushed into his thoughts. This time, she was prepared for the misery and grief that permeated everything. Bracing herself, she forced her way through the barrier of pain and into Dion's memories.

Running into the forest while Adamo shouted after him to stop, to come back, to spare himself the sight of—

Lies. Lies. Lies. A mistake. A terrible, dreadful, mistake—and nothing more! Nothing more! The guards who brought him the news would be sacked at once for frightening him so! And he would savor every moment of it!

He followed the footpath through the trees, where the other children were still gathered. They gazed up at him with tear-stained faces as he shoved past them to the place where several town guards were huddled.

"You don't want to see this, sir," said Celio, turning so that his broad shoulders blocked Dion's view of what lay ahead. "Come. I'll escort you home. We've already sent for a priest."

"No!" screamed Dion. "You're wrong!" He beat his fists against Celio's chest, but he might as well have attacked a stone wall for all the good it did. "Let me see him! Let me see my son!"

Aelia pulled away from the memory. Dion continued to stare out toward the river, and the forests beyond.

"No children, then?" she asked.

Dion did not reply.

"I think you're lying," she said.

"You may leave," Dion retorted curtly. "Or you may be escorted to your room by the guards. It makes very little difference to me."

"This house should be in mourning," pressed Aelia. "Why have you not been allowed to grieve?"

"You have no idea what you speak of," Dion said flatly.

"Tell me, then! I want to understand. Especially since I think it's tied to whatever is manifesting in your woods."

Dion continued to stare at the distant trees for so long that Aelia was afraid he had decided to ignore her once again. But finally, he said, "My son was named Efisio."

Aelia nodded, even though Dion was not looking at her.

"Two weeks ago, he went into the woods to play with his friends. They were climbing trees. The branch he was standing on was rotted, and gave way under his weight."

"I am sorry," said Aelia.

"It would have been easier if he'd been murdered," whispered Dion. "At least then I could have my revenge, see the killer sentenced."

"And the apparition in the forest? What do you make of that?"

"I have seen it. It is not Efisio." Dion turned to look her in the eyes. "Not unless he has been warped beyond all recognition. And besides, why wouldn't he have gone to Iestil?" Dion named the plane in Asterium that belonged to Adranus, God of Death and Tenth of the Ten. Most Men who did not serve any one particular God went there after they died.

"I don't know," Aelia admitted.

"I know some of our townspeople are speculating," said Dion. "But Adamo will not hear it. 'My son is not a monster,' he says. But seven days after Efisio died, that thing began appearing in the forest."

"How long was your house in mourning?" asked Aelia.

"We had planned for a month. But Adamo told the servants to put the shrouds away the morning after the monster manifested for the first time," Dion admitted. "I think...no. I don't know what Adamo thought. I feel as though I hardly know him anymore."

Aelia tried to remember what she knew about Adranus and Iestil. It was rare, but not impossible for a spirit to refuse to move on from Inthya. If the apparition was Dion's son, being destroyed by the town guards every single night might cause him to become more distraught and confused—and more dangerous.

"I need to go," said Aelia, lurching to her feet. Dion said nothing as she jumped over the low stone divider and ran toward the street.

The forest was on the other side of the stream, but Aelia could not see a bridge anywhere in the gathering dusk. So she gave herself a good distance for a running start and very nearly cleared the stream.

Staggering onto the opposite banks, her wet and muddy skirts weighing her down, Aelia followed the treeline until she found the path into the forest. Orsina and a few guards were waiting just inside, holding heavy ceramic mugs of tea and talking quietly amongst themselves as they waited for sundown.

"Orsina!" cried Aelia, stumbling on her wet skirts. A look of horror came across Orsina's face as she looked at Aelia.

"Elyne!?" Orsina cried. "What do you think you're doing! Are you *mad?* You promised me—there's going to be a malevolent apparition here in a matter of minutes—"

"I know!" cried Aelia. "But listen. I've discovered something important. Is this the place where you're expecting the specter to materialize?"

"It is," said Orsina. "And that is why you must leave, immediately."

"Did Adamo tell you that his son died on this spot?" demanded Aelia.

Orsina dropped her mug in the dirt. *"What?"*

"It's Catorisci all over again. Keeping up appearances is more important than the truth, I suppose," said Aelia. "Dion and Adamo's son was killed two weeks ago."

Orsina looked around at the town guards, who all refused to look her in the face.

"Is this true?" she demanded.

Nobody spoke immediately. Finally, one said, "Yes. It is true."

"But...how?" asked Orsina.

"An accident, I think," said Aelia. "At least, that's what it sounded like. He was climbing trees with his friends and..."

Orsina frowned heavily, thinking. "Then this apparition... if it is the child...it needs a priest of Adranus to guide it into Asterium, not soldiers to kill it every night. Destroying it time and time again might very well make things worse!"

"Where are we going to get a priest of Adranus at this hour?" asked Aelia.

"We're not. We'll have to send for one in the morning." Orsina chewed her lower lip. "If they'd only told me the truth to start with!"

"Do you think he can be reasoned with?"

"Maybe once, we might have been able to," said Orsina. "But if he's been slain every night for a week, I doubt he'll be in any state to listen. Still, I will try my best. Now get out of here before he arrives."

Aelia had no intention of leaving now. Still, for Orsina's peace of mind, she moved back behind the line of guards so that she was at least not in immediate danger. Orsina turned her face to the darkening woods as the last traces of sunlight slipped below the horizon.

"Wait for it," advised one of the guards. "You'll hear it before you see it."

Aelia strained, but she could not hear anything beyond the ordinary sounds of the forest. She reached out with her mind, brushing past birds and rabbits and foxes...

And she found it.

It was dark and malevolent, and it reeked of grief and rage. Aelia took a step backward just as an anguished howl echoed through the woods.

Orsina murmured a prayer, and her sword began to glow golden. Something was moving through the trees, a looming, shadowy figure wrapped in tattered gray robes. It seemed to glide as silently as mist, not rustling a single blade of grass in its path. As it reached the edge of the trees, it raised its shrouded head and howled once again, the agonized cry echoing to the night sky.

And in that moment, Aelia knew that the apparition was not a lost soul that had failed to make its way to Asterium after death. It was nothing of the kind. Nor was it a demon spawned from a careless god's magic.

It was a wraith.

Orsina was already moving, preparing for the fight. Aelia turned and ran without looking back. She sprinted all the way back to Dion and Adamo's home and pounded on the front door until a fearful servant answered.

"Where are Adamo and Dion?" she demanded.

"Mistress, come inside!" said the servant, pulling at her arms. "The demon will be here soon!"

"I have seen your demon. I must speak with Adamo and Dion."

"What is the meaning of this?" Adamo was striding toward them, his mouth turned downward in a heavy frown. "Shut the door! We don't—"

"Why didn't you tell Orsina that your son died in the same place the wraith is manifesting?" Aelia interrupted.

Adamo's eyes went cold. "If you are implying that my son had anything to do with this, you may find alternate accommodations tonight."

Aelia pressed a hand to her forehead. Maybe a few decades spent regenerating would be relaxing.

"The monster out there is a wraith, a physical manifestation of grief," said Aelia, fighting to keep her temper. “I am certain that it first spawned from Dion. Then you took your house out of mourning, hoping that would weaken it, but you only made it stronger. You can’t cover it up. That thing is going to keep appearing until you and Dion release it.”

There was a subtle change in Adamo’s face. “The paladin cannot destroy it?”

“No,” said Aelia. “But you and Dion can. Together.”

Adamo stared at her helplessly, and she could see his distress. He was worried about what people would think if they learned the monster originated from his household. Would they ever trust his leadership again?

“Listen to me,” said Aelia. “This is not entirely your fault. I have reason to believe that there is a chaos goddess named Xara nearby. She may not have targeted you directly, but her presence amplifies grief and sorrow. If not for her, I do not believe things would have come to this.”

“What must we do?” That was Dion, standing in the far doorway. For the first time, his eyes were focused and bright. He walked forward to stand beside Adamo and took his hands.

“Come with me,” said Aelia. “If we hurry, we might be able to finish this tonight.”

When they finally arrived back at the forest, the area surrounding the wraith was blazing golden with the light of every failed banishing circle that Orsina had tried. It seemed she was desperate and had inscribed every ritual she knew into the dirt. But none of them were doing any good.

The wraith continued to howl, striking out toward Orsina and the soldiers with long arms. Orsina gestured for the soldiers to remain back as she attempted another useless prayer.

One of the guards caught sight of Adamo and Dion. "Sirs!" he protested. "You must return home immediately, there is—"

"That's enough," said Dion, pressing past the armed guards and approaching Orsina. "Dame Paladin. If you would?"

Orsina glanced back. "What are you doing here?" she shouted.

"It's all right, Orsina," said Aelia. "Look."

The wraith had stopped screaming, or even lashing out. It sank closer to the earth as Dion approached it with his arms outstretched.

"I've missed you," said Dion, his voice calm and clear. "So much that sometimes I think I might die from it."

Orsina's mouth fell open, but she did not move or speak.

"I keep replaying that day in my mind, what I could have done differently. If I'd only kept you inside. But I didn't. I didn't even think that something might happen to you. It seemed impossible."

The wraith continued to hover there. Aelia wasn't sure if it could even hear Dion's words. But it was not attacking.

"I think about everything you'll never do and I..." Dion's voice broke, and tears spilled down his face. "It's not fair. You'd just barely started. It's not fair."

Then Dion turned partway to face Adamo, an accusation in his tearstained face. "And you. Did you even care?"

"Dion!" Adamo looked stricken. "How can you ask that?"

"Because you did not mourn him!" Dion gestured to the wraith. "I think I saw you shed tears once, at the funeral. And then you never spoke his name again. You act as though he never lived."

"Dion, I..." Adamo shook his head. "I. I didn't want them to think I was weak. To question my leadership. Of course I loved our son. How could I not?" He covered his face with his shaking hands. "There is so much darkness in the world, so much evil. Why would the gods take him?"

Dion moved toward his husband, pulling him into an embrace. Aelia looked back at the wraith, still drifting, but visibly smaller than it had been only a few minutes ago. It was weakening.

"I'm sorry," murmured Adamo, his voice slightly muffled by Dion's shoulder. "I knew how much this was hurting you and I did nothing. I cared more about my position than your pain."

Dion said nothing, but Aelia could see some of the darkness around his heart shake loose. After a long moment, Dion pulled away from Adamo and went back to the wraith.

"I'll always miss you," said Dion. "And I'll always love you."

What little remained of the wraith drifted nearer to Dion, near enough to touch. Dion reached out and pushed its hood back, revealing its face for the first time.

It was Dion.

The real Dion looked at Aelia, his face questioning.

"I told you," she said. "It's not your son. It's your grief."

Dion nodded and clasped the wraith's spectral hands.

"It's all right," he told it. "You can go now."

The wraith tilted its head back and began to glow from within. Within moments, it was blazing with white light. Dion covered his eyes with his arm and stumbled backward into Adamo's arms.

When Aelia's vision cleared, the wraith was gone.

In the silence of the woods, with the moon slowly rising, Orsina grabbed Aelia by the arm.

“What was *that*?” she yelled. Aelia flinched. She had never seen Orsina truly angry before, and now she never wanted to again.

“I, I, it’s not—” Aelia babbled, as memories of Orsina’s sword slicing through her midsection overtook all rational thought. “I’m sorry! I’m *sorry!* I know I promised, but there was no time to explain! Please...”

Orsina’s eyes softened. “Elyne,” she began.

“I can explain. I promise, just...please don’t be mad at me. Please.”

Orsina looked at Dion and Adamo, and the gathered guards of Aola.

“Is it really gone?” asked one of the guards.

“It should be.” Aelia looked at Orsina. “But we can stay one more night, to be certain.”

Orsina shook her head. “I’ve never seen anything like that before. I couldn’t even begin to guess...I may have to write to Bergavenna.”

“It was a wraith,” said Aelia.

“And how did you know that, when I didn’t?” asked Orsina.

Aelia licked her lips and swallowed. “I...” she began.

Running through the olive grove.

Heavy footsteps behind her.

A sword through her stomach.

All the guards, as well as Adamo and Dion, were watching her closely.

“When I was a girl, one of them struck near our family home,” Aelia said. “The priest said they were rare but could become powerful if not dealt with properly. When this one manifested, I recognized it immediately.”

Aelia could see the suspicion in Orsina's face, like maybe, finally, the gears in her head had started to turn. But she knew she wasn't going to start an interrogation in front of an audience.

Aelia only hoped that she'd be able to talk her way out of this once they were alone.

THE SILENCE WAS almost painful. Aelia chewed on her lower lip and waited, waited, waited for Orsina to speak.

But instead, Orsina removed her armor, piece by piece, and began sorting through her bags for her night-shirt. Aelia turned away.

"Before we departed Catorisci, I spoke to Vissente," came Orsina's voice from behind her.

"You what? Why?" Aelia spun around, unable to hide her panic. "What did he say to you?"

"Why don't you tell me what you think he might have said to me?"

Orsina's face and voice were unreadable. Aelia forced herself to think, but it was difficult when her first impulse had always been to run. Orsina was bluffing, she had to be. There was no way she would have spent so many days with Aelia if she'd known the truth all along.

"I never spoke to Vissente. He wouldn't have any way of knowing a single thing about me! Whatever he said to you was a lie!"

"*Someone* is lying to me, I will grant that."

"You'd take the word of a man who stood by and let his mother feed his fiancée to a shark over mine?" Tears were beginning to swell up in her eyes, and Aelia hoped Orsina interpreted them as tears of pain, rather than fear. "Do you think so little of me?"

"No, I..." Orsina seemed taken aback. "I just want the truth."

"And I just want to leave my past behind!" The tears weren't stopping. Aelia sniffed and wiped at her face with her sleeve. "Why does it matter? Why does it even matter?"

"Because I'm trying to understand you, Elyne."

"I never asked you to! It's not any of your concern!"

"It's my concern when you act like you want a courtship, and it's *certainly* my concern when it involves chaos cults!"

"You think I'm a cultist?" Aelia's voice broke on the last word, and something in Orsina's face softened.

"You were, once," said Orsina. "That's why you fled Otradosa, isn't it?"

Aelia was not sure how to respond. She was still reluctant to tell any outright lies that she might get caught in later. But if she denied it, Orsina might start looking for other explanations. So she just bit her lower lip and wiped at her eyes again.

"Are you refusing to talk about it because you're afraid of your family? Or do you think I'll abandon you if I learn the truth?"

"Won't you?"

"You left, didn't you?" Orsina gave her a searching look. "That's something to be proud of. Especially if you were born into it. Plenty of people never manage to break free. Vissente never did."

"What did he say about me?"

"That you weren't what you seemed to be. I...I will admit I didn't pay much attention to it at the time. I thought he was just saying whatever he could to distract from his own guilt. Did your family also worship Iius?"

Aelia shook her head vigorously. "No! I had no idea he was even in Catorisci."

"Then how did Vissente identify you?"

"I don't know!"

She could tell Orsina did not quite believe her, but the paladin seemed placated for now. Maybe it would be enough.

FROM THE WAY Orsina held her close as they lay side by side, Aelia supposed she had been forgiven.

Aelia turned her face to the window and gazed up at the moon, guilt gnawing at her stomach.

What's happening to me?

Aelia shifted her gaze to the tattoos on Orsina's shoulder. Upon closer inspection, Aelia realized that the lines of the design were actually Asterial runes for order and protection. Cautiously, she pressed a fingertip to the marks, half expecting Orsina's eyes to snap open immediately.

But Orsina merely sighed and continued to dream.

"I want to tell you the truth," she whispered in Asterial. *"But I'm having so much fun. I love being with you. I know it can't last forever, but...I'm not ready to end it yet."*

Aelia waited a little longer, then pulled free of Orsina's arms. She left the room silently, hurrying barefoot across the cold floor.

Adamo and Dion's home was silent. Even the servants would not rise for several hours. She crept out to the front of the house, unlatched the door, and slipped outside.

Wrapping her arms around herself for warmth, Aelia raised her face to the night sky and reached out with her mind.

Xara? she called.

No response came. Aelia reached deeper into her reserve of power, which seemed fuller than last she'd checked. Were Riana's prayers really having such an influence on her?

Xara? Aelia repeated. *Xara, I know you're near.*

After another long, awkward moment of stillness, something began to gather on the lawn. Vapors, black, gathering into a woman-shaped cloud. Aelia stepped toward it just as it solidified.

Xara was dressed in the same tattered gray robes that the wraith had worn, but her hood was lowered, revealing a gaunt, tearstained face and moon-white hair. She stared at Aelia with sunken eyes.

"Aelia..." she said, drifting closer. "Is that...you?"

"Yes, it's me! I'm just...having a difficult time."

Xara's eyes narrowed. "I see."

"I had a run-in with a paladin. I need the Unbinding Stone. Do you know where I might find it?"

"The Unbinding Stone?" Xara repeated. She shrugged. "Ask Edan."

"That's what Iius said. He thought Edan might be somewhere in Xytae."

"He was correct," confirmed Xara. "Years ago, he requested I meet him on the border. I was curious, so I went. Only days later, the Order of the Sun was expelled from Xytae."

"What? How could he have known that would happen?"

"I do not know. I suspect he is allied with one far more powerful than himself. But I wanted no part in it. I made the right choice, I think. I will not be found within Xytae's borders when Iolar finally decides it has fallen too far into darkness. And that moment is coming, believe me."

"Do you know what city he is in?" asked Aelia.

"Kynith is where he asked me to meet him. Will you seek him out?"

"It's between that and throwing myself off a cliff, and I don't wish to spend the next decade regenerating. Nor do I care much for pain."

"Pain can be a release. Though seldom so...literally." Her thin lips twisted into a smile. "You say a paladin did this to you?"

"I've managed to pass fairly well, I think." Aelia looked down at her body. "You wouldn't believe how much fluid a mortal body excretes."

Xara shuddered. "I believe I may actually feel sorry for you. How curious. I have not felt pity in a millennium."

Aelia rolled her eyes. "Glad to be of service."

Xara was already beginning to retreat back into mist. "Is that all?" she asked, her voice little more than a whisper.

"Yes," said Aelia. Normally, she would want to take advantage of being able to converse with one of her siblings, but for some reason she wanted Xara gone as quickly as possible.

Xara gave her a final nod and vanished into mist.

Behind Aelia, the door slammed open.

"Elyne!" cried Orsina. Aelia turned to look at her. Orsina's hair was wild, and her face was panicked. She hurried out to Aelia and grasped her by the arms.

"What's wrong?" asked Aelia.

"I sensed..." Orsina looked around. "...and you were gone...I thought..."

"I couldn't sleep," said Aelia. "I went out to get some air. I didn't mean to worry you." She pressed into Orsina's arms.

“I thought I sensed something,” murmured Orsina, but she sounded uncertain already.

“Probably just a dream,” Aelia whispered back, her hand rubbing Orsina’s back soothingly. “Nothing but a dream.”

Chapter Seven

ORSINA

When Orsina rose the next morning, the servants were putting the mourning shrouds back out over all the furniture and decorations. They would remain, Adamo said, for another two weeks.

After the events of the previous night, Orsina was fairly confident that there would be no more nighttime apparitions. But they were going to spend a second night in Aola, just to be certain.

All the servants appeared to be in good spirits, and even Dion flashed a smile once or twice during breakfast. It was not in Orsina's nature to eavesdrop, but she overheard two of the servants whispering that they were so relieved that the monster had not been Efisio after all, that his memory was unsullied.

Orsina composed a brief report to send to her Knight-Commander in Bergavenna, describing what she had seen and recommending that wraiths be added to the curriculum for initiates. By the time she was done, Elyne had gone missing once again. Orsina sighed and decided to go looking for her before she got into trouble.

She was barely off Adamo's property when the first few children came over to ask her about the wraith. After assuring them that it was very unlikely that they'd ever see a creature like that ever again, she asked them if they'd seen Elyne. They all nodded and said that she'd wanted to go swimming and that their stream ended in a lake if one followed it a few miles down.

Orsina still wasn't sure if Elyne knew how to swim, so she set off immediately. Outside of Aola, the trees grew more densely, and it was a little colder in temperature, though not unpleasantly so. Eventually, the stream did empty into a small lake. On the banks, Orsina could see Elyne's familiar dress had been rolled into a ball and thrown aside, along with her shoes and stockings. She picked the dress up, shaking the dirt off, and draped it over a tree branch.

"Elyne!" she called. She could see Elyne's head bobbing in the water, but she did not appear to be drowning.

"Oh!" cried Elyne, smiling brightly and paddling closer. "Orsina! This water is *cold.*"

"If you wanted a bath, the maids could have drawn you one."

"I didn't want a bath. I wanted to swim! It's harder than it looks." Elyne rolled over onto her back and pulled one of her own bare feet close to her face for examination. "I think something bit me."

"Come out of there at once. There's no telling what's in there."

"It's far too small for a shark," Elyne asserted. "I think it was a turtle. It served me right, I stepped on him first. That's justice, isn't it?"

"Elyne."

"Why should I come out? I'll only be cold. You should come in."

"You're going to ruin your undergarments."

"More incentive to stay, then!" Elyne ran her fingers through her hair. "Though, to be honest, this water is not terribly clean. I might need a bath afterward. And also. We need to go to Xytae."

Orsina gave a little start. "We—what? Why?"

"That's where my brother is."

Orsina frowned. "You said he was in Sabarra?"

"I was wrong. He's in Xytae, in Kynith."

Elyne's tone was light and casual, but Orsina's frown only deepened. "When did you learn this?"

"Recently," said Elyne. "Very recently. Will you go with me?"

That was not at all a satisfying answer, and Orsina was more determined than ever to get to the bottom of this. She'd thought she'd get answers from Elyne last night, but it seemed she only had more questions.

But pressing Elyne for more details would not yield fruitful results, she knew that from her own experiences. She would have to keep her temper, and be patient, and pretend like she did not really care about what was going on. One way or another, she would uncover the truth.

"I would like to, but I cannot go to Xytae," Orsina said. "The entire Order was explicitly told to withdraw."

"Is it really that important?" Elyne pleaded. "Nobody will ever know. It's only Kynith. That's practically on the border, isn't it?"

"Elyne..."

"Besides, you were only told to withdraw. Nobody ever said you can't *enter,* did they?"

"Elyne."

"Fine!" Elyne laid her head on a rock as though it were a pillow. "I'll just go alone."

"Don't be ridiculous, you need protection. Especially in Xytae. Just give me some time to think. I'll come up with something."

Elyne pouted at her but picked her head up again. She began walking toward the banks, squeezing the water from her long hair and shaking her limbs. Then she flopped down in the long grass to dry in the sun. Orsina came and sat down beside her, trying to keep her eyes to Elyne's face.

"I know it's a lot to ask," said Orsina. "But...could I take you to Melidrie instead? My fathers are very kind men. They would be happy to house you until my quest is done. And we could find you work in the manor, or elsewhere in town. It might be nice."

Elyne looked torn. "That does sound nice," she whispered. "But I don't know."

"I understand." Orsina hugged her knees. "Truthfully, I think the Order would understand our circumstances if I wrote to them. The real danger in Xytae would be from the Emperor's soldiers. They would arrest me on sight."

"Just get rid of your cloak and tabard and claim you're a mercenary," suggested Elyne. Her fingers plucked aimlessly at the strands of grass. "Or, if you can't lie, at least imply it."

"Perhaps," murmured Orsina.

"And besides, what if the evil you're meant to defeat is in Xytae after all, not Vesolda?"

Orsina looked at Elyne in surprise. "You think it might be?"

"I don't know, but it seems logical, especially since all the other paladins have been gone for years. Who knows what kind of evil has been brewing in the meantime?"

"You're not just saying that so I'll agree to take you, are you?"

"I was at first," Elyne admitted. "But the more I think about it, the more sense it makes. You've had no luck at all in Vesolda, and why should there be some task here that only you can complete when there's thousands of paladins who are just as capable? But Xytae is a different story, isn't it? Nobody from the Order has had a reason to go there until now."

Orsina tried to calm herself, but she could not help but be filled with renewed hope. Could Elyne be correct? Was her quest nearly at an end? She swallowed, forcing herself to be calm. No. She had to be rational. Her quest would not be over until Iolar gave her a sign.

"Alright," said Orsina. "We'll go to Kynith and call upon your brother. You are certain he can be trusted?"

Elyne nodded. "Yes. But...I do not know if he would welcome me for long. He might be unhappy for the reminder of our family. He might be afraid that I will lead them to him."

"I will reassure him," said Orsina. Even if Elyne's brother did not welcome them, he might be a source of information about their family. And Orsina needed as much as she could get to bring them to justice for what they had done to Elyne.

Still, Elyne looked at her hands, uncomfortable.

"What is it?" asked Orsina.

"Maybe we shouldn't go to Xytae," she mumbled. "Maybe we should forget the whole thing and just go to Melidrie and I'll learn to be a milkmaid or, or..."

"Is that what you want?" asked Orsina.

"I don't know what I want," Elyne said.

"Well, we're closer to Kynith than we are Melidrie. I think it won't hurt to meet with your brother and see if there's any obvious evil that needs cleansing. And besides, if I finish my quest in Xytae, I won't have to leave you alone at Melidrie."

Elyne reached up and touched Orsina's face. Orsina bent in to kiss her lips, resting one hand on the grass to balance herself.

"I'm sorry I'm so difficult," Elyne whispered. Orsina could feel her soft, warm breath on her own lips.

"You've been through a lot," Orsina replied.

"Most of it was my own stupid fault."

Orsina tilted her head to the side curiously and opened her mouth to ask a question just as her tattoos pricked in warning. She frowned, her other hand going idly to the markings across her chest. Was the wraith manifesting again after all?

"How sweet," purred a cold voice from somewhere very close to Orsina's ear. A look of horror came over Elyne's face, and Orsina turned. A woman with a gaunt, terrifying face was standing over her. She was dressed in a tattered gray robe, and her white hair was almost luminescent in the daytime sun.

Orsina yelped in surprise and spread her arms wide to protect Elyne.

"How utterly adorable," drawled the gray woman. She looked at Elyne. "You almost got away with it, didn't you? You thought I wouldn't learn it was you breaking my things?"

"Get back!" demanded Orsina, stumbling to her feet. She drew her blade, and the woman gave her a contemptuous look.

"Ah yes, the pet," she said cryptically. "I'll deal with you first. Let me see. *She never loved you.*"

Pain shot through Orsina's body, and she nearly dropped her sword. She was not injured, not exactly. But it was as though all the hurt and rejection of the last few years suddenly struck her all at once. Perlita did not love her. Perlita had never loved her. If Perlita loved her, she would have written. She would have called Orsina home, quest or no quest. Perlita did not love her, *nobody* loved her, and Orsina was going to die alone—

Elyne rushed forward and punched the gray woman in the mouth. The spell over Orsina's mind broke, and she gasped heavily.

"Ow!" cried Elyne, staring down at her own bloodied fist in dismay. Then she punched the woman again for good measure.

"Elyne! Get away from her!" cried Orsina, wiping the tears from her eyes.

The gray woman spat out a mouthful of blood and laughed.

"Who are you?" demanded Orsina.

"My name is Xara," said the gray woman. "Put your weapon down. There's something I think you ought to know."

But Orsina recognized the name from her studies, and she had no interest in anything a chaos goddess had to say. She began to recite the prayer to trap the goddess in her body.

Xara hissed in outrage when she realized what was happening, but she did not attack. Instead, she backed out of range of Orsina's sword and called, "I'd reconsider that if I were you."

"Don't listen to her," said Elyne, desperation in her face. "Don't listen to anything she says!"

Xara laughed contemptuously.

"Foolish little girl," she said to Orsina. "How can you be so blind? Surely you must have realized by now."

"Shut up," snapped Orsina. "You don't know anything about Perlita."

"I'm not talking about your empty-headed noblewoman." Xara raised a spindly hand and pointed to Elyne. "I mean *her*."

Elyne lunged at the goddess, screaming wordlessly. They hit the ground together, landing in the long grass. Orsina ran after them, feeling a little dazed, like perhaps this was all just an exceptionally vivid dream.

Elyne had Xara pinned to the ground, but Xara reached up and struck Elyne in the face with silver light. Elyne seemed to not feel the blow as she clawed at Xara's face with her bare hands. Then the goddess whispered something that Orsina couldn't hear and Elyne crumpled, sobbing.

Orsina grabbed Elyne around the waist and pulled her off Xara, dropping her on the ground a safe distance away so she could recover from the mental assault. Then she turned back to the goddess, her blade readied.

Xara was halfway to her feet when Orsina struck, her blade sinking deep into that thin, bony chest. She screamed in agony and outrage as she died, her hands grabbing desperately at Orsina's blade. But Orsina did not withdraw it until all the life went out of Xara's avatar.

Elyne was still laying where Orsina had dropped her, sobbing piteously into the dirt. Orsina crouched down beside her and rested her hand against Elyne's back.

"It's all right," she murmured. "She's gone. It's over."

Elyne sat up and wrapped her arms around Orsina's neck. Her eyes were wide with fear.

"You're all right," Orsina soothed. "It's all right."

"I'm sorry," sobbed Elyne. "I'm sorry, I'm sorry, I'm sorry!"

"Shh," Orsina held Elyne closer. "It's all right. You're all right." After a pause, she added, "Were you planning on punching her to death?"

"Maybe," warbled Elyne. Fresh tears spilled from her eyes. "I'm sorry!"

"For what?"

Elyne pressed her face into Orsina's chest and did not respond.

"Where did she come from?" murmured Orsina. "Why did she attack us? Was it the wraith?"

Elyne said nothing while Orsina continued to think. Xara, Goddess of Melancholy. It made sense that a wraith, all misery and remorse, spawned from her presence. Perhaps they had been lucky to be attacked. If they'd left without encountering her, she would only target more people.

Orsina remembered the wave of despair that Xara attacked her with, far worse than any weapon. Its effects were beginning to fade, but slowly. She looked down at Elyne again, and her heart filled with guilt. She'd replaced Perlita so easily...

No. Perlita had rejected her, and she hadn't even had the decency to do it with words. Orsina owed her nothing anymore.

Logically, it made sense, but Orsina still felt sick and anxious and disloyal. She tried to tell herself that it was only chaos magic, designed to weaken her resolve. But it seemed the effects of the magic would not go as quickly as they came.

"Come on, let's find your dress," Orsina told Elyne, forcing a weak smile. "Not many ladies can say they fought a chaos goddess in their underwear, now can they?"

"I don't want to. I want to *die*."

"What did she say to you?" asked Orsina. Elyne shook her head, which she probably should have expected. More secrets. What would it take to finally win Elyne's complete trust, to learn the story she was hiding?

Orsina shifted into a more comfortable position and continued to rub Elyne's back until she was calm again.

THE ROADS TO Xytae were ancient, whispering memories of a time long past when the empire controlled the entire continent, and lands beyond. They passed old shrines where depictions of the gods had Xytan facial features and wore traditional Xytan garb. Orsina knew that all Men depicted the gods as being of their own nation, but it was still a bit strange to see it in practice. She always visualized the gods as Vesoldan.

Orsina had still not pried an acceptable answer out of Elyne regarding how she learned that her brother was in Kynith, but she would admit she had not pressed very hard. She had more or less given up on getting direct answers from her.

But a paladin was patient. There was no need to alienate Elyne any further when the truth was waiting for them in Kynith.

The journey to the border was uneventful. When they arrived at the outpost, the guards who interviewed them seemed more bored than suspicious. There were only three of them, and one was not even pretending to be awake. The other two sat at a large table with a heavy, leather-bound book between them. All three wore the crest that marked them as soldiers of Reygmadra.

The first guard said something in Xytan that Orsina only barely understood.

"Elyne Vigneta," said Elyne in response. "*Ta Otradosa.*"

The guard said something else, gesturing to Orsina. Elyne responded too quickly for Orsina to make out any individual words, but the guard seemed satisfied as he made notes in his book.

After a few more questions, none of which Orsina understood more than a few words of, the guards led them back outside to search their bags. They would find nothing objectionable, for Orsina had left her cloak and tabard in Aola with Dion and Adamo for safekeeping during their excursion. She planned to recover them upon returning home.

"I didn't know you spoke Xytan," commented Orsina as they rode away from the guard-post half an hour later.

"Oh!" Elyne looked embarrassed. "It is not so different from Vesoldan, really."

"How many other languages do you speak?" Orsina asked.

"A...few," said Elyne. She stared at Lavender's mane. "It's not that impressive."

"That's not true at all. You could probably find work as a translator, if you wanted. It pays much better than milking cows."

"But I couldn't do that in Melidrie, could I?"

"Well..." It was true that the Baron didn't have much need for a translator, Melidrie being so far inland. "Perhaps not. But elsewhere, certainly. What languages do you speak?"

"Oh just...just the usual ones," Elyne looked around, as if frantic to change the subject. "Look. More ruins."

Orsina made an appreciative noise at the pile of crumbling white marble that had once been some sort of wayside temple. She wanted to ask Elyne more questions but forced herself to be content with the knowledge that soon everything would become clear.

It was still a few days to Kynith, so they stopped that night at an inn. Being so close to the border, most of the residents spoke both Xytan and Vesoldan fluently, but Orsina tried not to make conversation for fear that her inherent truthfulness might lead her to reveal her religious affiliation.

That night, with Elyne in her arms as usual, she whispered, "There's nothing wrong with knowing languages, you know."

Elyne tensed. "I know," she whispered back. "I'm sorry."

"For what?"

Elyne went quiet. "Everything," she said at last.

KYNITH WAS A medium-sized city, bustling and colorful, though not as colorful as Antocoso had been. They arrived at midday, and Orsina knew in an instant that it would not be an easy task to locate Elyne's brother.

The inn did not take Vesoldan coins, so Orsina went to get her money changed and left Elyne to begin pursuing leads, under the strict condition that she return no later than six in the evening.

Elyne returned by five, saying that she had a few leads but needed to be careful pursuing them. It seemed that her brother had taken steps to conceal his identity when he came to Xytae. Orsina was not surprised to hear this, given what she knew of Elyne's family, and asked what she could do to help.

"If you don't speak the language, I don't know how much you can do," Elyne said. "But maybe it's for the best. If he sees I've come with some kind of mercenary, it will be far more difficult to gain his trust. He may even flee Kynith altogether if he thinks I've come to drag him back home."

"Perhaps so. But I dislike the idea of you running around Kynith alone."

"There are guards everywhere. I am not in any danger."

Orsina was not sure if she agreed. But then, she might have been biased, for all the guards were affiliated with the Temple of Reygmadra. Nevertheless, she wondered if she ought to follow Elyne in secret to make sure she did not get into any trouble. But that struck her as deceitful, and a violation of Elyne's privacy and trust.

No, her time would be better spent trying to track down signs of evil activity.

"I think I'm going to go to bed," announced Elyne, getting up.

"Are you certain? The musicians will be here for a few hours yet," said Orsina.

Elyne shook her head. "I'm too tired to stay up tonight."

Orsina was a little concerned and followed Elyne up to their room. The rented bedroom was large, and well lit, and far nicer than the inns they had stayed at as they'd approached the Xytan border.

Orsina sat by the fire, wrapped in a blanket, and watched as Elyne changed into her night-dress.

"You seem distracted," said Orsina.

"It's nothing," said Elyne. "Just...exhausted, I suppose."

"Come sit with me. It's warmer over here."

Elyne seemed hesitant but approached Orsina and slid into her lap. Orsina kissed her neck and drew her closer.

"I have a confession. I'm almost hoping that you won't find your brother at all, so you'll have to stay with me."

Elyne shook her head. "I think I might be as well," she said, resting the back of her hand against Orsina's face. "But..."

"What's the matter?" asked Orsina.

"I don't know how to explain. I just...I don't want to hurt you."

"Hurt me?" Orsina smiled. "How in the world would you hurt me?"

Elyne shook her head again.

Orsina shifted Elyne off her lap and slid to the floor. Then, kneeling, she wrapped one arm around Elyne's waist and began to push the skirt of her night-dress upward.

"Orsina—" Elyne's voice hitched.

"Just relax," Orsina murmured. "I promise you'll like this."

"Wait!"

Orsina released Elyne's waist immediately. "What's wrong?"

Elyne seemed to struggle with words. Finally, she said, "I don't want you to do anything you'll regret."

Orsina had to bite back a laugh. "Why in the world would I regret this?"

"I'm not who you think I am," said Elyne. "I...I've been lying to you. If you knew the truth, you'd leave me in an instant."

"I highly doubt that."

But Elyne only shook her head and brought her hands to her face.

"Elyne," said Orsina. "You don't need to come up with excuses if you don't want my attention. If you tell me you don't want to, that's reason enough for me to stop."

"I do want to!" cried Elyne. "I think I want this more than I've ever wanted anything. But I can't. I'm sorry."

Orsina stood back up. “You don’t owe me anything, Elyne. You never will.”

“Stop.” Elyne’s voice was muffled by her hands. “You’re so good I can’t stand it.”

“Elyne...” Orsina took her hands and pulled them away from her face. “Please. Just tell me what’s going on. Whatever it is, I can help you.”

“Nobody can help me,” said Elyne.

“There is nobody on Inthya who is beyond redemption,” Orsina reminded her. But the words did not seem to reassure Elyne.

Orsina did not really believe that Elyne had done anything to warrant such guilt. Or if she had, her family was to blame, and an investigation would show that she was coerced. But that hardly mattered now when Elyne was so distressed.

“I will tell you everything,” Elyne promised, setting her hands back in her lap. “But not tonight. Not until I’ve finished what I came here to do.”

Orsina shifted closer. “You came here to find your brother, did you not?”

“I have reason to believe that he knows the location of a sacred ritual object that I need,” said Elyne in a low voice. “That is the true reason I am seeking him out.”

The smile fell from Orsina’s face. “What?”

“See?” Elyne rose, so abruptly that she almost knocked Orsina to the floor. “You don’t know anything about me. I’ve been lying to you!”

“But...” Orsina suddenly felt ill. “What—how—”

“See?” repeated Elyne, but her voice broke on the word. “I hate lying to you, but I can’t tell you the truth!”

“What is it?” demanded Orsina, her mind going back to endless lessons on cursed relics, gems that brought pestilence, chalices that poisoned, harps that struck the listeners dead. "What is the relic?"

"I'll tell you when I recover it," said Elyne. "In fact, you can have it when I'm done. Take it to Bergavenna, to your knight-commander. He can decide whether he wants to put it in a vault or have it destroyed."

"But what if you fail?" asked Orsina. "What if your brother refuses to give the relic up? What if he kills you?"

Elyne shrugged.

"You cannot be serious. Do you care nothing for your own safety?"

"I can handle my siblings. They expect me to be subservient and obedient. If I play at loyalty, they do not watch me too closely and I can do as I please."

Orsina shook her head. "I don't like this, Elyne."

"I know. That's why I have kept it from you until now. But I couldn't go on lying to you. Not when you've been so good to me."

"I don't know what to say," whispered Orsina.

"You make me wish I was someone else. Someone better."

"You can be," Orsina insisted. "Whatever you have done, I feel certain that you are not beyond redemption."

"You say that now," sighed Elyne. "But never mind. I've already said too much."

Orsina fell silent, playing through countless scenarios in her mind. Was Elyne's family affiliated with a chaos god's cult? It seemed the most likely thing. What foul rituals had she been forced to perform in their name?

And what was the purpose of the relic she had gone to such pains to recover? What was she hoping to accomplish once she had it in hand? Perhaps use it as evidence of the abuse she had suffered, the pain she had been forced to inflict? Was this all a roundabout way of bringing her siblings to justice?

That night, in the silent stillness of the bedroom, Elyne pressed her face into Orsina's chest and whispered, "Promise you won't follow me?"

"What?"

"Promise me." Elyne pulled back, her eyes bright and determined. "I have to face my brother alone. If you come, it'll all go wrong. Alright?"

"Alright," Orsina whispered.

"Promise!"

"I promise," said Orsina.

Elyne looked at her searchingly for a long, long moment, then nodded.

Chapter Eight

AELIA

Aelia had officially lost all control over the situation.

It had happened so quickly that it still felt unreal. What had Orsina done to her? What had she done to herself? Who was she anymore?

She had no idea.

Aelia moved quickly through the streets of Kynith, determined to have this finished by sundown. She still wasn't sure how she'd get the location of the Unbinding Stone out of Edan without first swearing loyalty to him, but she'd come up with something.

"Guess what I made!" Riana called happily.

Go back to bed, Aelia commanded. The sun was not even up yet, and the first merchants were only now just beginning to set out their wares.

"I didn't sleep at all! I was inspired!" Riana's giddy happiness was warm and comforting, melting through Aelia's cold panic like firelight. *"It's another painting. I hope you're not tired of paintings."*

Aelia supposed she could spare a few minutes for her only worshipper. She stepped off the main road and onto a quiet side street. *What is it?*

Again, Aelia's mind was filled with an image, this one of a dark forest made of glittering crystal trees. In striking contrast, the sky was bright and colorful, as were the tiny, meticulously-detailed flowers that grew around the roots.

Aelia found herself smiling for a brief moment, despite everything.

Your friends must all think you've gone mad, Aelia observed.

"They might! And maybe I have!" Miles and miles away, Riana yawned. *"I don't mind, though."*

Go to sleep, Aelia commanded. *You're no good to me if you work yourself to death.*

Riana went, and Aelia sighed. It had been nice to forget her problems for a moment. Once this was over, once she had the Unbinding Stone and was free of her body, she would do nothing but come up with ideas for Riana and get prayers and gratitude in return.

But what about Orsina?

Aelia paused to consider this. She did not think Orsina would turn on her, as long as she was careful. She had meant what she'd said last night; she wanted to tell Orsina the truth. And she thought that maybe Orsina might at least be curious enough to at least hear her out.

But if Orsina did turn on her...

...well, it wouldn't matter, because Aelia would have the Unbinding Stone by then. If the worst happened, she'd just use the Stone on herself and go back to Aethitide before Orsina even had a chance to draw her blade. Orsina would go back to her stupid quest and Aelia would spend the next few decades hovering around Catorisci.

It was a satisfactory plan, at least when held to the standard of all Aelia's previous plans.

Still, the thought of Orsina rejecting her was...unsettling. Orsina had spoken of going to Melidrie, of introducing Aelia to her fathers, of finding her work in town so she could have an ordinary life, free of fear and the influence of chaos cults. And when her quest was over, Orsina would join her, and they would be together...

Why was a pathetic, unremarkable life as a milkmaid so appealing to her? It defied all reason.

Aelia forced herself to remember that Orsina had not offered any of that to Aelia. Those promises had been for Elyne.

Maybe if she got a few more prayers from Riana, Aelia would have enough power stored up to erase Orsina's memories of the previous night, when Aelia had come so close to confessing what she was.

But even as she thought of it, Aelia knew she could never do such a thing to Orsina. Even without Dayluue's warning weighing on her like a rucksack full of stones. Orsina wasn't a thrall, and she wasn't a toy. She was, at the very least, Aelia's equal. Perhaps even her better.

Almost certainly her better.

She wanted to tell Orsina the truth. Deep down, she knew it was the only way to ever be free of this awful torment. But with the truth came the potential for rejection.

But then, maybe rejection was what Aelia deserved.

Xara had certainly believed so.

Aelia shook herself. She was not going to think about Xara. Xara was gone, off regenerating in Asterium, and all of Inthya was better for it. Xara was a liar—she always knew just what to say to cause the most hurt, no matter how absurd, and Aelia was not going to waste any more of her time thinking about it!

Today she would find Edan.

She shoved aside her dread and tried to muster up some semblance of her old self, carefree and impulsive and oblivious to the world around her. She would skip right into Edan's lair, do a little spin to admire the decorations, and tell him she'd already forgotten why she'd come. Then he would insult her, and she'd nod agreeably and knock a few things over. After about fifteen minutes, she would suddenly remember that she needed the Unbinding Stone, by which point Edan would be so disgusted with her that he'd tell her the location just to get her out of his city.

It would work. It had to work.

She could send out a call for him, just as she had with Xara, but she decided that she wanted to surprise him. She needed every advantage she could get, after all.

Yesterday, she had identified a few people that she thought might be affiliated with Edan, but none of them had led her anywhere useful. They just appeared to be going about their lives with little touches of his spiteful magic woven through their souls, like spots of black mold. But today she would try harder. She already had a plan.

One of the people she'd noted yesterday was a young man who worked as an apprentice to a cobbler. She made her way to the shop, knowing that he had no reason to be elsewhere.

She arrived just as the shop was opening. Just as she'd expected, the apprentice was there, trying his very best to look busy.

To a mortal's eyes, there was nothing wrong with the young man. But Aelia knew the moment he came around the corner that she had been correct about him. He served Edan, and in return, he had been given magic. Aelia did not want to think about what he had already used it for.

Aelia glanced around, but nobody else was in the shop, not even the apprentice's master. He opened his mouth, probably to ask her what she wanted, and that was when Aelia pushed into his mind.

She had not done this in a while, but she had not forgotten just how chaotic and confusing mortal minds were. She could sense the young man's alarm and confusion, and decided that this would go more quickly if he aided her.

I am looking for my brother, she said. *You know him. You serve him.*

A flurry of memories struck her, all relating to Edan. Aelia ignored the ones that didn't seem relevant and shoved away the ones that sickened her to look at.

Where is he hiding? Aelia asked the young man.

He did not want to answer her, but he had no control over his own mind. The mere act of asking the question raised the answer in his memories. Aelia smiled and withdrew.

"Thank you for your help," she said brightly. "I hope I never see you again."

THE YOUNG MAN'S memories led Aelia to a quieter area of the city, where ruins seemed to outnumber the buildings that were still in use. When she spotted the house that he'd unwillingly shown her, she went inside. The door was not locked.

The interior looked ordinary: dusty, lightless, and containing a few pieces of furniture too badly damaged to be of use to anyone. But Aelia knew what to do. She stepped forward and lifted the threadbare carpet, revealing the trapdoor beneath.

A ladder went downward into the darkness, and Aelia told herself that she was not afraid. She climbed down and, once she was safely on the ground, she called up a little bubble of violet magic to light her way.

It smelled terrible down in the cellar, but that was because it was not really a cellar at all. Someone had made an opening in the wall, and Aelia could see stone tunnels ahead. She peered into them, but even with the light of her magic, she could see nothing but plain stone walls. With no other options ahead of her, Aelia began to walk.

It did not take long for Aelia to grow bored. There was nothing to look at in the tunnels except ancient stones, and nothing to do except try to breathe exclusively through her mouth. She tried not to contemplate what exactly she was breathing in, and what prolonged exposure would do to her mortal body.

The tunnels sloped downward, guiding her deeper into Kynith's ruins. Gradually, Aelia realized that she could see something unpleasant-looking growing on the walls, and she shuddered. Why were mortals so disgusting? Adranus had to give official mandates just to get them to wash their hands!

Over the centuries, Aelia had heard Men argue that there was no need for such rituals because Adranus protected them from disease. They did not seem to realize that these 'rituals' were *how* he sought to protect them from disease, not just something he made everyone do because he really liked water.

And then whenever a plague did strike, those same people claimed it was Adranus' will or punishment for their own sins. It was as though they'd never met him!

Edan's presence hung heavy in the air, overpowering even the awful smell. Aelia paused, knowing she must be near. The tunnel split, just ahead, but Aelia did not need directions to follow the source of the magic. She banished all thoughts of Orsina from her mind and tried to focus on something that Edan would have no interest in.

She remembered the skipping-game that she'd learned from the children in Antocoso. That had been fun. Aelia liked children. It was never hard to coax them away from their chores, they came up with good ideas all on their own, and they always told the truth when it mattered.

Maybe next time around, she'd manifest as a child. Nobody ever suspected children of anything.

The tunnel came to an end, and just ahead, Aelia could see a large, open room. The magic was strongest there, too. Edan must be in there, waiting for her. No doubt he already sensed her approach. She was a little surprised he hadn't already shown himself and demanded to know why she was in Kynith.

Skipping games. Counting games. Playing dice for soft, smooth pebbles. What else existed in the life of the goddess of uselessness?

She emerged from the tunnels and found herself in an unexpectedly large chamber with a high, distant ceiling. Remembering that she was supposed to be thoughtless and silly, Aelia did not even bother to look around. Instead, she gazed up at the ceiling, craning her neck uncomfortably to contemplate it.

"I was wondering when I would hear from you," said a voice from behind her. Aelia forced a bland, empty smile across her face and turned around, her skirts fanning around her as she spun.

Edan looked just as terrible as Aelia remembered. He was painfully thin, with unnaturally long limbs. His skin was stretched over his bones so tightly that she could see the individual muscles and sinews in his body. His cheeks were sunken in, as were his dark eyes, and he had no lips at all, only a set of bared teeth. He had no nose, either, only an eerie triangular void where one might be. Aelia smiled up at him—and it was a long way up because his body was at least seven feet tall.

"Oh," she said in a light, cheerful voice. "There you are! It's terrible down here, isn't it?"

His hands were abnormal, too. Each finger ended in a long, ivory claw. Aelia tried not to stare.

"Such interesting stories I've heard about you, Aelia," said Edan. His voice was a low purr. "Why don't you tell me what you've been up to?"

"Me?" Aelia laughed. "I don't do anything. You know that."

Edan laughed as well, and for a moment Aelia thought everything would be all right.

Then, before she even had time to blink, he'd wrapped his awful clawed hand around her neck and slammed her to the floor. Her vision blurred, and she screamed, struggling to get those claws away from the delicate flesh of her throat, but Edan was so much stronger than her. He did not even appear to be exerting himself as he knelt beside her, watching her struggle with clinical indifference.

"Let's try this again," said Edan.

"Wait!" gasped Aelia. "Stop! I—I can—"

"Shh." Edan raised one claw to his lipless mouth. "I'm talking now. It will be your turn soon enough. I want to tell you a story. I heard it from a mortal woman. Her name is Sousana of Catorisci. I think you know her?"

"I can explain," Aelia managed. She was having difficulty breathing. "Edan—stop—listen—"

"You can explain why you've spent the last few weeks allied with the Order of the Sun?"

"I'm not allied with them!"

"That is not what I've heard, Aelia. I heard that only a few days ago, you rode into a Vesoldan town with one of them and destroyed Xara's avatar."

"Xara attacked us! I was going to leave her in peace!" objected Aelia. "And it was the same with Iius! If he hadn't tried to eat me, we'd have just left and he'd still be on Inthya! It's not my fault!"

Edan's grip on Aelia's throat relaxed enough for her to breathe easily.

"I'm *not* allied with the Order of the Sun. I found one paladin, and she thinks I'm a mortal woman who needs protecting. If she knew what I was, she'd destroy me. If I wasn't trapped in this body, I'd never have bothered with her! But I can't get rid of her until I find the Unbinding Stone!"

Edan released her throat. Aelia sat up and raised her hands to her neck, pressing healing magic into her wounds. Edan stood and watched her, his expression unreadable.

"I'll go, then," said Aelia. "Forget it. I'll find the Unbinding Stone myself."

"You are welcome to try, but you will not find it. I have it in my possession."

Aelia could not keep the hope from her face. "You have it?"

"Of course I do. How do you think I've been avoiding the priests here?"

"Then what do you want for it?"

Edan paused, and for a moment Aelia was afraid that he would say there was nothing she could offer to match the value of the Unbinding Stone. But then he said, "I told you that I had plans in Xytae. If you aid me with them, you will have the Unbinding Stone."

"Very well," said Aelia. "But...what are your plans?"

"You have come at the right time," said Edan. "After all these years of waiting, it is only a few weeks away now. I am going to kill Emperor Ionnes' heir, the Crown Princess Ioanna."

Chapter Nine

ORSINA

Orsina woke to find Elyne gone. Either she was eager to be finished with her quest, or she did not completely believe that Orsina did not intend to follow her, vow or not.

But Orsina had not lied when she told Elyne that she would not follow her. She intended to spend that day trying to track down any signs of evil that might lead her to the completion of her own quest.

Not speaking the local language would be a setback, but Orsina was used to dealing with uncommunicative people. In fact, she had no idea how Elyne managed to so frequently coax detailed explanations from near-strangers. Normally, she relied on the training she'd received as an initiate, and her ability to detect chaos.

The largest and most obvious source of chaos magic in Kynith was located not in a hidden shrine or mysterious ruins in a forgotten area of the city, but the Temple of Talcia. Whether one believed that Talcia ought to be classified as a chaos goddess or not (and people far wiser than Orsina had spent *centuries* arguing over the point), the fact remained that paladins were constantly alerted to the presence of Talcia's magic, no matter how benevolent the practitioners.

In this case, the practitioners were two priestesses and two acolytes. Nobody was in robes today, they were all dressed like ordinary women, and working the flowerbeds outside the temple. Orsina could sense Talcia's uniquely multi-hued magic on all four of them, but nothing beyond that.

Next she went to the temple of Iolar, more out of habit than any real hope that she'd find useful information there. The temple was ancient, the architecture marking it as a remnant of the days when the Xytan Empire ruled the known world. But unlike the ruins that dotted the area, the temple was in fine condition, looking no different than it might have one thousand years ago.

Orsina entered the chapel and sat down to reflect. If she were a chaos god, where in Kynith might she hide? The old ruins looked like the sort of place that one might be drawn to, but they were open and exposed. Any illicit activity would be nearly impossible to conceal.

A young boy dressed as an acolyte was replacing burned-down candles with fresh white tapers, but Orsina saw no sign of the Temple's priests until about fifteen minutes later, when a yellow-robed man of about forty came striding down the center aisle.

He passed Orsina, but then hesitated and backtracked his last few steps so that he was beside her once more.

She looked up at him and saw the shocked realization in his face. He had sensed the deception on her, the lack of her identifying cloak and tabard. He said something in Xytan.

"I only speak Vesoldan," said Orsina. "I'm sorry."

"Why are you here?" he asked. "How are you here?"

"Are you going to call the guards?" asked Orsina.

The priest glanced around, confirming the temple was empty before he spoke. "Why have you come here?"

"I have reason to believe there is evil activity in this city. Possibly even a chaos cult. Do you know anything about that?"

The priest was not sworn to truthfulness like Orsina was, but the surprise in his face seemed genuine enough. "A cult? In Kynith?"

"It is a possibility," Orsina said.

"I hope you don't think that we've been helpless in the Order's absence. In fact, we've found that investigating quietly is more prudent than charging in waving a sword—"

"Sir," said Orsina. "I know that the Temple is equipped to deal with any situations that might arise, and I would like very much to leave it in your hands. But I cannot return home until my task is complete. It has been mandated to me."

The priest frowned. "If there is something amiss, why would Iolar send a paladin to Kynith, instead of merely entrusting a priest with the task instead?"

"I've been wondering that myself," said Orsina. "I can only guess that there's something here that needs slaying."

The priest seemed to consider this. "I won't deny that we have more chaos gods in Xytae since the Order's departure. But we've had no trouble binding and slaying them. If there is a cult in Kynith, they have the sense to stay hidden."

"If one were to hide, where do you think I would find it?" asked Orsina.

The priest hesitated. "The ruins. The old city. Kynith has been built over itself time and again. There's no telling how far down it goes. But it is extremely dangerous. Parts have been known to collapse without warning. Sometimes in the night, we hear it happen."

Orsina rubbed her chin. "How do I get down there?"

"I'm serious, Dame Paladin," said the priest. "If you go down there, one misstep could bring a thousand years of architecture down on your head. That is, if you do not become lost and starve to death."

"That is a risk I am willing to take," said Orsina. "My quest must be completed, at any cost."

The priest shook his head. "Sometimes I wonder why our organizations parted ways, and then something reminds me. Very well, you're in luck. The Temple has some old passageways that will get you at least partway to your goal, though they may very well have collapsed by now."

"I appreciate your aid," said Orsina.

The priest still looked extremely reluctant, and Orsina did not really blame him. He thought he was sending her to her death. And perhaps she was being a bit more reckless than usual. She would blame Elyne's influence for that.

But perhaps some recklessness could be excused. What if this truly was the end of her quest?

Followed by acolytes bearing lanterns, the priest led Orsina down into the depths of the temple, the rooms becoming darker and quieter as they proceeded. The acolytes shouted in surprise whenever they walked through a cobweb.

Finally, they reached a place where the priest said he would go no further, a shadowy corridor filled with fallen beams and heavy with the scent of something musty. Orsina accepted a lantern from one of the acolytes and a stick of white chalk from the other. Then she bid them all farewell.

Orsina moved slowly, taking care to disturb as little as possible. The warnings about collapses had seemed so abstract when they had been above ground. But now, surrounded by nothing but stone and memories, the danger felt significantly more real.

Orsina wondered how many paladins had died inglorious deaths, killed by decrepit falling ceilings in forgotten shrines to forbidden gods. Her teachers had never mentioned. She supposed nobody wanted to write about that when there were so many tales of glory and honor to document instead.

She had thought she might find the ruins interesting, from a historical perspective, but she was wrong. One chunk of limestone didn't look significantly different from the other six hundred, and she could not read any of the ancient inscriptions that might have given her clues as to their long-forgotten purpose. Perhaps a Justice or a scribe might be interested in the ruins, but to Orsina it was just an exceptionally old basement.

She supposed anything important would have been saved and brought upstairs to safety centuries ago. Besides, Kynith was a small border town. It was not as though she was exploring the ruins beneath Xyuluthe, the capital city. There probably had not been anything of significant interest here even during Xytae's golden age.

The only noise in the ruins was Orsina's own footsteps and the distant drip of water. She expected to find rats, or even spiders, but it seemed the only thing living down here was the unpleasantly moist green-black mold that grew over the walls.

As she went along, Orsina dotted the path behind her with white chalk stars so that she would be able to find her way back. Nevertheless, she found herself wishing that she had a map of Kynith. Not that she had many options regarding where to go, nor did she trust herself to be able to accurately gauge her location on a map, but it might have been nice for moral support.

After a while, Orsina grew hungry, so she set her lantern down on the floor and found a mostly-dry marble slab to sit on while she ate some dried meat and hard cheese. Despite the priest's warnings, it seemed that the only thing she was in danger of dying from was boredom.

Orsina could not guess how long she had walked for when she finally caught sight of something interesting. It felt like it had been hours. Up ahead, she could see the orange light of torches, just beyond a narrow, partially-collapsed hallway. And her tattoos were finally beginning to warm.

Orsina set her lantern down on the floor carefully and made her way forward, stepping as lightly as she could manage in her chainmail. As she entered the hall, the sound of distant voices met her ears. She put a hand to her sword.

Orsina edged further and further into the dark hall, squinting into the large, open room up ahead. She could not see anyone, but she could hear people speaking in an unfamiliar language. It was not Xytan. It was unlike anything Orsina had ever heard before, except...

The night Elyne was drunk. She had said something to Orsina just before falling asleep, something in a language that Orsina could not identify. Orsina felt certain that it was the same language that she was hearing now.

The voices fell silent, and she heard footsteps moving away. Orsina came to the edge of the hall just as a figure walked past the doorway. Orsina reached out and grabbed her by the arm.

The woman gave a cry of shock, but when Orsina pulled her closer, she realized that she knew her.

It was Sousana of Catorisci, the runaway priestess who had killed her son's fiancée.

They stared at each other, equally incredulous, for a long moment. Then Sousana opened her mouth, hatred in her eyes, and lunged for Orsina's throat with her teeth.

She was significantly stronger than she looked, just as Vasia had been. Even though Iius was gone from Inthya, she retained the blessings he gave her. They slammed into the floor together, Sousana's fingers scrabbling for Orsina's neck.

But Orsina had the advantage now. There was no lake for Sousana to drown her in, no giant shark waiting to rip her apart. And Sousana was no true fighter. Like the God she worshipped, she was all mindless brutality and muscle and teeth. And that had been enough to terrorize the civilian residents of Catorisci, but Orsina had been trained with a sword since childhood.

Orsina kicked Sousana away from her and drew her sword. Sousana was back up on her feet in a moment, but Orsina was ready for her. When Sousana threw herself at Orsina's neck again, teeth-first, she impaled herself on Orsina's blade.

As Orsina wiped her blade clean, she found herself wishing she'd paid more attention to whatever Vissente had been trying to tell her.

At the sound of footsteps hurrying near, Orsina turned and readied her blade once more. A figure appeared in the doorway, one hand held aloft and a little bubble of purple light gathered there like a makeshift lantern, and Orsina realized that she knew this woman, too.

"Orsina?" gasped Elyne. "What—how—what are you doing here?"

"This dungeon is structurally unsound," said Orsina. "Also there's a chaos cult operating out of it. But you already knew that, didn't you?"

Elyne's eyes flicked from Sousana's corpse to the blade in Orsina's hand. A look of panic came over her face. "You need to get out of here, now!"

"I could say the same to you," said Orsina, replacing her blade in its scabbard. "Now, what are we fighting today?"

Elyne gaped at her. "Orsina! This isn't a joke! You swore you wouldn't follow me! You promised!"

"I didn't follow you," said Orsina. "I was doing an entirely separate investigation of my own. Weren't you the one who suggested the evil I am destined to defeat might be in Kynith?"

"Why aren't you taking this seriously?" Elyne cried. Her voice echoed up to the ceiling, and she winced.

"Aelia?" called a male voice.

Elyne gave Orsina a furious look. "Go. Now. You're going to ruin everything. I can't believe you. You promised that you'd leave this to me, and now you turn up here like you think you're going to be some sort of hero."

"Whose cult is this?" asked Orsina.

Orsina's protective tattoos burned in warning at the same instant that a clawed hand wrapped itself around her neck and slammed her head into the wall with supernatural strength.

"Mine," said a smooth voice from just behind her.

Orsina tried to break free, but she was still disoriented from the blow. As her vision swam, she could make out the dark stones of the floor and the sound of Elyne screaming.

A second set of claws dug into her arm, and she was dragged out of the hallway and into the larger room. Orsina caught a glimpse of a high, distant ceiling and walls smeared with something dark. She tried to reach her scabbard, but the hands that held her were utterly unyielding.

"Edan, stop it!" yelled Elyne, running after them. "I told you, she's not part of this!"

"Shut up," said Edan. He looked down at Orsina, and Orsina looked up into a gaunt, skeletal face that made her heart stutter. *Edan,* said the memory of one of Orsina's teachers. *God of Wrath. His plane is called Aratha, and it is there that evil souls are forced to spend eternity.*

"If I kill you," said Edan in a low purr, "you'll just go to Solarium, and the fun will be over. So let's see how long we can make the game last."

"No!" yelled Elyne. "Let her go and I'll stay with you!"

"Oh, but this is far more amusing," said Edan, his claws digging into Orsina's throat. Orsina struggled to pull them off her, but his grip was like iron. "Such a pretty pet you've found, Aelia. I think breaking her will be a better punishment than anything I could do to you."

"Aelia?" murmured Orsina. Wasn't that the goddess she had driven out of Soria only a few weeks ago? The one who had...

...kissed her.

"So, she really didn't know?" Edan laughed. "Either you're more cunning than I gave you credit for, or she's just exceptionally stupid. Tell me, Aelia, how exactly were you planning to avoid catching Iolar's attention for the rest of her natural life? Did you think he'd tolerate your hands all over one of his precious paladins?"

"You're so pretty," Aelia whispered to her from the darkened glass windows of Soria's neglected temple. "Do you really wish to destroy me? We can have such fun together."

"Elyne?" whispered Orsina. She could feel the tears threatening to overtake her.

Elyne shook her head helplessly. "Please, listen," she begged. "I love you, I'm sorry!"

Edan slammed his fist into the side of Orsina's head, and the world blurred again. Elyne moved to run to her, but Edan wrenched her away by the hair.

"Is *this* the reason you destroyed Iius and Xara?" he demanded. "This pathetic, whimpering girl? I can hardly believe it. Or did you think it was funny? I might forgive you if you tell me it was all meant to be a joke."

Elyne said nothing.

"If you want her back so badly, perhaps I can be generous," said Edan. "In return for your loyalty, of course."

"Yes!" Elyne nodded vigorously.

"Then here are my terms. I'll keep your pet here, in my temple. In return, you will help me as I finish my task in Kynith. If I am satisfied with your service, I'll let you visit her."

"Alright," said Elyne. "Just. Just. Let go of her. Please."

The claws around Orsina's throat loosened. Orsina slumped to the ground, too stunned to move just yet.

She did not see exactly what Elyne did, but she did see a wide beam of violet light strike Edan in the chest, blasting him backward into the wall. Then Elyne's arms were around her, pulling her near.

Elyne said something that made Orsina's ears ring, and the world vanished into blackness.

There was a sickening jolt, and light returned. As Orsina's vision cleared, she realized that she and Elyne were now sitting in the outer courtyard of the temple. The sun was lowering across the horizon. And Elyne was still holding her.

Orsina wrenched herself free of Elyne's arms, still not able to speak. Elyne watched her with worried eyes, hands glowing with the violet light of magic. Not Talcia's magic. Aelia's magic.

Orsina raised herself up onto her knees and drew her sword.

"Stay back!" she screamed, the same way she had screamed at so many monsters before.

Elyne lowered her hands slowly. "Orsina, you need healing. The wounds on your throat look bad. And if you have bleeding inside your skull—"

"Stop it!" Orsina screamed, fresh tears spilling from her eyes.

Elyne fell silent. For a time, the only sound was Orsina's wrenching sobs.

"I am sorry," whispered Elyne.

"You expect me to believe that? I have to turn myself in to the Justices now!"

"If they punish you, they are fools," Elyne said. "You had no way of knowing. I led you to believe you were protecting a defenseless traveler. You *were* protecting a defenseless traveler. None of this was your fault."

Orsina rubbed her eyes. It seemed she had run out of tears.

"I need to heal you," Elyne insisted. Orsina did not acknowledge this. Instead, she got up and began stumbling toward the street. Elyne ran after her, but when Orsina reached the place where she had left Star to wait, she slung herself into the saddle and rode away without her.

ORSINA STOPPED AT the inn only long enough to bandage her throat, pay her bill, and collect up her possessions. As soon as that was settled, she was on the road, riding as fast as she could for the Vesoldan border, desperate to leave Xytae behind.

She could not think. She could barely speak. Was this all just a dream? Would she wake up in her bedroll? Or her room at her fathers' house in Melidrie? It felt unreal.

She had *defeated* Aelia! She'd struck her head off, and the villagers burned her avatar. Hadn't they? Yes. She'd seen them build the fire. Had she seen them throw the body onto it? She couldn't remember now. But even if they hadn't, Aelia wasn't powerful enough to reattach a head. Was she?

And then the very next day, Orsina had encountered Elyne...

Don't think about it.

A mercenary, Elyne had said. Sent by her brother.

Orsina's vision fogged with tears, and she wiped them away rapidly.

How old are you? Twenty-five?

Fourteen billion.

And Orsina had laughed. Elyne had practically come right out and told her what she was, and Orsina had laughed at her.

Orsina pushed the memory away. She would go to Bergavenna and tell her superiors everything. It was out of her hands, now. All that was left to do was report in and await judgment.

But first, she would go to Melidrie. Some of the pain in her heart lifted at the thought. Yes, she would go to Melidrie to see her fathers and perhaps even Perlita. She wouldn't stay long, not more than the few days she needed to recover, and then travel onward to Bergavenna. It was not even as though it was more than a day's detour.

Orsina crossed the border back into Vesolda without incident the next day. She had planned to go to Aola to recover her cloak and tabard, for she felt incomplete without them. But as she approached the little town, she realized that this would mean answering questions about Elyne's whereabouts, and she was not ready to speak of that.

She remained on the main road and did not stop in Aola at all.

When she slept, it was in makeshift campsites rather than inns or taverns. She ate very little, for her appetite was gone and the few things she did consume tasted like dry ash in her mouth. She conversed with no one she encountered.

The only thing that really concerned her was Star's well-being. She had a responsibility to her mount, after all. She forced herself to stay attuned to the mare's needs, to feed and water her frequently, to stop and allow her some rest, even if Orsina knew she herself would not be able to sleep at all.

Most nights were spent staring at the eastern sky, anticipating a dawn that was hours away. She rarely dreamed, but when she did, it was of Elyne's happy laughter and Edan's claws around her neck.

Without her identifying uniform, she did not get as much attention as she usually did. People saw an ordinary warrior, rather than a paladin. Nevertheless, she avoided all the towns that she and Elyne had stopped in, even adding an additional day to her journey in order to give Catorisci a wide berth.

The days blurred together so much that Orsina was never completely certain of their exact number. Guilt and shame tore at her spirit every waking minute. How had she been so oblivious? How had she been so *stupid?* She'd become complacent, that much was clear. After two years of continuous victories, she'd grown careless and confident and been a prime target for a clever chaos god...

Stop thinking.

There would be time enough for reflection once she got to Bergavenna.

She allowed herself a brief but vivid fantasy of the day she'd first encountered Elyne, asleep in the woods. But this time, instead of reaching a hand out to wake the sleeping woman, she drew her sword and...

No. Her own mind rebelled against her, and she was unable to complete the thought. Even now, the idea of hurting Elyne was repugnant.

What was wrong with her?

Then, finally, after what felt like a lifetime, the roads began to look more familiar. Suddenly signs were inscribed with the names of towns that Orsina had known since childhood, and the local guards wore the baron's uniforms.

She had not realized just how terribly homesick she had been.

Orsina sped past green fields and through Melidrie's village without stopping. Her destination was the Baron's manor, up on the hill. And as she approached the familiar old place, her heart felt light, even happy. She could think of nothing other than seeing Perlita again.

She did feel guilty about ceasing her letters now. Perlita was learning to become a baroness. It wasn't unreasonable for her to be too busy to respond.

The Baron's manor looked no different than it ever had, as though Orsina hadn't been gone for more than a few days. Miri and Rodger were on duty when she approached the manor. They were not paladins, only ordinary guards trained by the Temple of Reygmadra. It took them a moment to recognize her, but when they did, they both rushed forward.

"Orsina!" cried Miri. "You're back!"

Orsina dismounted and rubbed at her eyes, forcing a smile. "Is Lady Perlita here?" she asked, only to pause at how strange her voice sounded. She had not uttered a word in days.

Rodger and Miri looked at each other, and Orsina feared they were about to say Perlita had gone to a party at a neighboring noble's home, but finally Miri spoke up.

"Yes, she is here," began Miri. "But—"

Orsina needed to hear no more than that and immediately pushed past them toward the manor.

"Orsina, wait." Rodger grabbed her arm. "Come to the barracks. You cannot see the Baroness without changing first. Besides, we have important news for you."

"The barracks can wait, and so can your news," retorted Orsina, pulling herself free. But then, the meaning of his words struck her. "The Baroness?"

"Baron Casimiro died last spring," said Miri softly. "Had you not heard?"

Orsina shook her head. "But how? He wasn't ill."

"His heart failed him suddenly," said Rodger. "By the time the healer arrived, he was already dead. There was nothing anyone could do."

"I had no idea," said Orsina. "The news never reached me. But I must speak to Perlita."

Rodger started to say something else, but Orsina pushed past him, uninterested in anything other than seeing Perlita again.

She made her way down familiar halls, marveling at how almost nothing had changed in her absence. She truly could pretend she hadn't been gone for more than a few days. A servant passed her—Zita. Orsina grabbed her by the shoulders, surprising the woman so badly that she dropped the folded towels she'd been carrying.

"Dame Orsina!" cried the woman. "But—when did you arrive?"

"Not five minutes ago," said Orsina, laughing. She was so glad to be home; the events of the last weeks felt like a dream compared to the familiar faces and sturdy gray stones of Melidrie. "Where can I find Perlita?"

A horrified look crossed Zita's face.

"Don't worry," said Orsina. "I already know that Baron Casmiro is no longer with us. The guards outside informed me."

"But—" Zita looked deeply uncomfortable.

"Zita, it's me. I don't need a formal invitation to see Perlita."

Zita began collecting up her towels, refusing to meet Orsina's eyes. "If you really wish to see her...the Baroness is in the central gardens."

"Thank you!" said Orsina. She took off again, feeling guilty for not helping with the towels but promising herself she'd make it up to Zita later.

The central garden was part of the manor, located at the roofless heart of the structure. It was filled with brightly-colored plants from all over the continent, and a small pond housed a few colorful fish. Orsina had spent much time here, with Perlita, both in childhood and as young women.

As she made her way down the familiar path, she could hear the sound of a young woman laughing and quickened her step. She rounded a rosebush that was not yet in bloom and there, sitting on a stone bench, dressed in a light green brocade, was Perlita.

Perlita's golden eyes met Orsina's and her mouth, painted coral, slowly fell open. One gloved hand reached out and gripped the arm of the other figure on the bench.

Slowly, very slowly, Orsina moved her gaze from Perlita's beautiful face to the tall man who sat just beside her. Perlita's fingers tightened around his arm.

"Orsina?" she said.

Orsina swallowed. "Lady—Baroness—I am sorry I was not announced," she said. "I, I just, I only..."

"Perlita," said the man, tilting his head curiously. "Who is this?"

"This is Dame Orsina, of the Order of the Sun," said Perlita. "Dame Orsina, this is my husband, the Baron Leofric of Melidrie."

The ground under Orsina's feet seemed to be shifting, churning like the sea. She expected to find herself falling, but when she glanced down, the stones were still and unmoving.

"Lady Perlita," she said, keeping her voice so soft that she could barely hear it over the ringing in her own ears. "I...I had no idea that you had been married in my absence."

Perlita looked at her with cold eyes, as if daring her to say more. Orsina had the sensation that some manner of monster was trying to rip through her own chest. Finally, the new Baroness looked at her husband.

"Dame Orsina was my personal bodyguard before she began her mission." The Baron seemed to accept this without question and continued to regard Orsina with boredom. "But my father believed Iolar had need of her and sent her out into the world. Have you accomplished his task, Dame Orsina?"

"I... I do not know." Orsina could feel her hands trembling and hoped that her armor covered it. "I have slain many monsters, but never did Iolar come to me. It would have been easier if only he said what he wished me to do."

“Well, the gods are mysterious,” Leofric didn’t seem particularly concerned. “But you’re here now, so I see no reason to send you on another pilgrimage when I need knights to keep our lands safe.”

Orsina felt herself frown a little. “My lord, though I should like nothing more than to remain, my vows to Iolar must be upheld. I have come only to rest on my journey to the capitol. I must depart tomorrow.” Though, in truth, she was reconsidering staying even that long now.

“Nonsense,” said Leofric. “You’ve served Iolar well, and now you will serve Melidrie. Report to the barracks, we’ll find a place for you.”

She would not be staying in Melidrie, or at the barracks, but Orsina was far too emotionally exhausted to argue the point. If Leofric was offended by her departure tomorrow, he could take it up with Sir Biagio. He’d set the nobleman right.

Orsina looked back at Perlita. The woman was still regarding her coolly, but she might as well have been throwing knives into Orsina’s chest.

“Thank you, my lord,” said Orsina. She gave a short bow. “By your leave?”

The new baron waved a hand dismissively, and Orsina fled.

THE GUARDS OF Melidrie were waiting just outside when Orsina burst from the manor as if pursued by a demon. She pushed past their outstretched hands, their pitying faces, and ran until she reached the place where she had tied Star.

When her trembling hands failed to undo the knot, Orsina drew her sword and sliced through it. Then she all but flung herself onto Star’s back and rode off.

Until that moment, Orsina had never understood how people could lose their faith in the gods. It would be like losing faith in the seasons, or the tides.

Until that moment, she had never understood what could drive someone to walk into the sea with no intention of ever reemerging.

The orchards were empty and would be until midsummer when their fruits ripened. So there was no one there to see as Orsina fell to her knees and screamed as though she had been stabbed.

After a while, she ran out of tears, though not from lack of grief. She pulled herself upward and leaned heavily against Star, reaching into her saddlebags for the waterskin there.

She thought, again, of the ocean. Of the jagged cliffs that she'd explored while hunting the manticore-that-wasn't. She thought of her own sword, how easy it would be to just fall on the blade.

And what would Iolar say when she met him?

Orsina found that she cared less about that and more about how badly her death would hurt her fathers. Perhaps, if only for their sakes, she would try to struggle through.

She thought of her childhood home, her childhood room, and suddenly could think of no place she'd rather be. She mounted Star again and slowly, very slowly, set off in the direction of home.

Her fathers lived in town, not too far from the manor. When she approached the house, there was a light in the window. Her heart lifted at the sight, and she knocked at the door. A moment later, it opened and a familiar man with silvering hair stood before her with a look of shock on his face.

"Orsina!"

"Papa!" she yelled, throwing her arms around his neck. Tedoro laughed and hugged her back. Together, they took a few staggering steps backward into the house. When Tedoro pulled away, Orsina had tears in her eyes.

"Have you been to the manor?" he asked.

Orsina nodded, her lower lip trembling. Her father hugged her again.

"I'm sorry, love," he said. "We...we were going to write to you. But Sir Biagio thought it would be best not to distract you from your quest."

Orsina swiped at her eyes with her hand, wanting to say any number of things: that she didn't care, that she was fine, that it didn't matter because she had never loved Perlita anyway. But she still could not lie, not even for her father's peace of mind.

"I'm so glad you're home," he said. "Your father won't be much longer. Go sit down. We'll eat as soon as he arrives."

Orsina could smell something roasting in the oven and went over to sit at the fire. Tedoro continued to watch her with worried eyes.

"How was your journey?" he asked.

Orsina shook her head, not ready to talk about it yet. Tedoro looked even more concerned at that.

"I'm not done," she said. "I'm only stopping here on my way to Bergavenna."

"Not done?" repeated Tedoro. "How long does Iolar mean for you to wander, then?"

"I don't know. He has not spoken to me."

Her father frowned but did not say anything. Orsina just stared at her hands, thinking of Bergavenna. She did not really want to go, but she could not stay in Melidrie, either. Not after what Perlita had done.

The fire was warm, and Orsina was exhausted from crying. She lay down in front of the hearth and soon fell asleep on the old, rugged stones.

A while later, someone shook her awake. Orsina opened her eyes and realized that someone was crouched next to her. Her other father, Dario.

Orsina pulled herself upright and hugged him. He embraced her back, and she could see the sadness in his face. She forced a smile for him.

"It's almost ready," called Tedoro from the kitchen. "Orsina, come sit down."

Still groggy, Orsina shuffled over to the old wooden table and sat down in her usual spot, or at least what had been her usual spot two years ago. She felt like she ought to help Tedoro with the meal, but for some reason, she couldn't bring herself to do much more than stare at the surface of the table.

Orsina had not thought she would be very hungry, and indeed the thought of eating wasn't very appealing. But when Tedoro sat half a chicken and an entire bowl of roasted vegetables in front of her, it was as though the past week's hunger finally caught up with her all at once.

She tried to pace herself, to make sure her fathers would not go hungry on her account, but they kept encouraging her to take more, and if she gazed too long at one of the serving-dishes, Tedoro reached over and added more to her plate. They spoke very little, though. It was as though they were afraid to ask her any questions.

Orsina hated to see them so sad, especially on her behalf. Part of her wondered if it would have been kinder to sleep in the orchard. But no. They would have been hurt if they'd learned she'd come to Melidrie and never visited them.

When the meal was finished, Orsina helped them clean up while they asked her cautious questions about who else she had seen today. Orsina did not want to talk about the way she had embarrassed herself in front of Rodger and Miri and Zita, so she just said, "I have not spoken to many people yet. I should probably report to Sir Biagio tomorrow morning." Should, but would not. She didn't think she'd be able to stop herself from telling him the entire story. And then, once told, she wasn't sure that she'd have the strength to tell it again to the Justices."Are you really going to Bergavenna?" asked Dario. Orsina nodded. "That's a shame. We were hoping you were home to stay."

"Perhaps they will send me home after this," said Orsina.

"You think your quest is in Bergavenna?" asked Tedoro.

The question had been innocent, but tears sprang to her eyes again. "No," she said, her voice breaking. "I do not."

Tedoro was beside her in an instant, one comforting arm around her shoulders. "It's all right, love," he soothed, stroking her hair. "It's all right. Whatever happened, it's going to be all right."

"It's not!" sobbed Orsina. "Nothing is ever going to be all right again." And she could say that because, in that moment, it was true.

Tedoro hugged her to his chest but did not try to refute her claim. Perhaps he sensed that it was not what she wanted.

Dario came to her with an earthenware mug filled with hot tea. Orsina accepted it and took a few sips, burning her tongue.

"Here, stop crying or you'll have salt water in your

tea," he teased. Orsina giggled despite herself. Even if everything in the world was going wrong, she could at least count on her fathers.

The tea did help, and she was feeling a little calmer by the time she finished the cup. But her head was aching again.

"I need some air," said Orsina. "I won't be too long."

Behind the house was a very small garden, with a crumbling stone bench beneath an old oak. This was where Orsina sat now, tilting her head back to breathe in the night air. She closed her eyes and thought of nothing.

After a while, she heard footsteps approaching and opened her eyes, expecting to see one or both of her fathers. But instead, it was Perlita standing there in the garden, her green brocade gown at odds with their common surroundings.

At first, Orsina thought she might be hallucinating from grief, because there was no reason for the Baroness of Melidrie to come to the house of two common guards and their daughter, even if that Baroness was also Perlita.

But no, Perlita was here, standing before her as though no time had passed at all. Orsina lurched to her feet.

"I was afraid you might have left already," said Perlita. She looked around. "Strange. I've never actually come here before. Is this where you grew up?"

"More the manor than here," said Orsina. "Perlita..."

"I know. I know." Perlita sighed and walked closer. "I should have told you. But I didn't know how."

"I don't blame you. I realize that you didn't want to distract me from my quest."

"Your...?" Perlita rubbed at her eyes. "Oh, for the love of—Orsina, please. Do you still believe in all that?"

Orsina paused to turn over the words in her mind, but

could not understand what Perlita was trying to imply. "What do you mean?"

"Iolar never spoke to my father, Orsina! Iolar cares nothing for ones as insignificant as us! My father sent you away so that I could be married!"

Are you certain, Elyne had asked, *that they were not just looking for an excuse to send you away?*

Orsina's vision swam with tears. "That's not true! He would never claim a vision if—"

"He would claim whatever he needed to in order to protect Melidrie!"

Orsina was stunned into silence for a long moment.

"You speak as though I am an invading force," whispered Orsina at last.

Perlita sighed heavily. "I do not mean to." She sat down beside Orsina, one lacy glove resting itself over Orsina's hand.

"If you knew it was a lie," Orsina began, "why didn't you—"

"Because my father was right. I realize that now. Melidrie is my responsibility. Even if you can make the Change long enough to give me heirs, you're still just a soldier. Leofric is the second son of the Baron of Deinder, in Ieflaria. Both of our lands are safer thanks to this union."

"You could have told me," whispered Orsina. "You could have told me the truth. I would have—I would have—"

"You would have accepted it?"

Orsina said nothing.

"No." In the dim light, Perlita's eyes were pools of blackness. "Even now, you cannot lie to me. Tell me this, then. Do you love me?"

"I *hate* you."

Perlita laughed, very softly, and raised her other hand to brush the side of Orsina's face. "Do you want me?" she whispered.

"I…"

Perlita leaned in closer. Orsina could feel her breath on her throat.

"You will love me again, I promise. It won't be so bad. I am the baroness of Melidrie; nobody tells me what to do or how to behave. As long as you keep your hands to yourself when Leo is around, he'll never suspect a thing."

Orsina ripped away from Perlita. "What?" she cried. "You can't be serious! He's your husband!"

"So?" Perlita's eyes glimmered with disdain. "I don't want him anymore. I want you."

"If you didn't want him, you shouldn't have married him!"

"I did want him," said Perlita. "But now I've changed my mind. I'd forgotten how much fun we used to have together."

"I said no!" screamed Orsina. "Why should I love someone who ignored my letters for two years? Who knew I was on a fool's errand, yet let me wander the country aimlessly? You could have called me home at any moment, but you never did!" She choked on her sob. "You planned to let me die of old age in the Vesoldan wilderness! How can you believe I feel anything but contempt when I look at you?"

"This is why I never summoned you back," said Perlita coldly. "You throw these melodramatic, self-righteous fits. If you could just learn when to remain silent, we wouldn't have had to send you away in the first place!"

"Don't you dare blame me for what you've done! I can't

believe I've been so blind. I can't believe you don't realize how unforgivable your actions are!"

"Orsina—"

"No." Orsina felt hatred coil inside her like a serpent. "I will not help you betray your husband, now or ever. And if you try to change my mind, I will go to my Knight-Commander and tell him that you knew your father forged a prophecy. See if the Order of the Sun is so willing to protect your lands after that!"

Perlita's eyes flashed with fury, but she seemed to realize she could not win.

"Fine, then," she said. "Your quest is finished. Report for duty tomorrow morning."

"No. I discovered something terrible in my travels, and I am going to Bergavenna to report it."

She could see the suspicion in Perlita's face.

"I will not tell them anything about your father's actions unless you force my hand. I do not wish for Melidrie's people to be punished for the sins of one man. What I have discovered is far more sinister than a false prophecy."

"But, after that," said Perlita. "After that, you'll come back."

"If I am allowed," Orsina agreed.

"Why wouldn't you be allowed?" demanded Perlita.

Orsina stood up. "Good night, Baroness. I trust you know the way home."

Perlita's lips pressed together in a pout that Orsina had once found irresistible, but now only struck her as pathetic. When Orsina did not react, she spun on her heel and stormed off into the dusk.

Orsina watched her go, then went back to the bench to

ruminate.

Elyne had been right all along. The quest that had become a part of her very identity was nothing more than the lie of a man desperate to see her gone. Had Elyne known the truth all along?

You make me wish I was someone else, Elyne had said. *Someone better.*

Another lie, surely?

But it did not feel like a lie.

I think you might be the kindest person I've ever met.

Orsina rested her hand over her heart.

I don't want you to do anything you'll regret.

What sort of thing was that for a chaos goddess to say?

I love you.

I'm sorry.

Orsina got up again, suddenly restless. She went around to the front of the house and was relieved to see that there was no sign of Perlita. Satisfied she would not be waylaid again tonight, Orsina began to walk in the direction of the barley fields.

The darkness was no issue; Orsina could have walked through Melidrie's streets blindfolded and not stumbled once. The barley fields were silver in the moonlight, rustling softly in the slight breeze. Orsina continued to walk along the familiar stone fence in the direction of the main road that eventually led to Bergavenna.

She moved at a meandering pace, with no real destination in mind. She tried not to think about the future and the report that she would give at Bergavenna. Had any paladin ever, in the history of the Order, been so thoroughly fooled?

Would they use her story as a humorous-but-grim

example for initiates? Would her life become nothing but a parable for other, more competent paladins? Would they throw her out of the Order entirely?

As a girl, Orsina had been certain that she would never commit any of the crimes that might cause one's paladin status to be revoked: murder, theft, extortion, kidnapping. She did not know if kissing a chaos goddess was on that list. Perhaps the Justices had not foreseen a need to state it explicitly. It was certainly in violation of the spirit of the code, if not the letter.

Orsina leaned her back against the stone fence and rubbed her eyes. They'd have to write new rules just for her.

Someone was approaching on horseback, from the direction of the main road. Orsina watched as the figure came nearer, only mildly curious. But then the figure dismounted, taking their pony by the reins to walk the remainder of the way.

Orsina squinted, and only then did she recognize Lavender's dappled coat. The traveler walking toward her was Elyne. Orsina froze, unable to decide whether to reach for her sword. After a moment, she decided she didn't have the energy.

When she was near enough that Orsina could see her face clearly, Elyne laced her fingers together and scuffed at the dirt with her shoe.

"I was wondering if you wanted to kill Edan with me?" she said.

Chapter Ten

AELIA

Orsina did not react immediately, but Aelia could sense the despair and exhaustion radiating from her in waves. Finally, Orsina leaned back against the primitive stone wall and crossed her arms.

"Your parents aren't vintners," said Orsina.

Aelia could not help but laugh, though she was not certain if it was from amusement or relief. "No," she agreed. "They're not."

"Do I even want to know what they are?"

"You wouldn't have ever heard of them, but their names are Chrona and Aethia." Aelia fiddled awkwardly with Lavender's reins. "I. I'm sorry. I wanted to tell you, but I was afraid you'd turn on me. And I liked being with you. I've never been able to trust anyone before the way I trusted you. I didn't mean for it to end the way it did."

"How did you mean for it to end?" asked Orsina.

Aelia looked down at her feet. "I was going to stay with you and love you for the rest of your life."

"You thought a relationship built on lies could last that long?"

"Well, I'd hoped," said Aelia. "Orsina, I'm sorry. I didn't mean to ever fall in love with you. When you found me in that forest, I thought I could use you as protection until I got out of this body. That's all. I never intended for it to go as far as it did."

Orsina rubbed at her eyes.

"And if you want me to leave and never bother you again, I will. But if you just let me explain everything from the start, we might be able to fix this."

"*This*?" repeated Orsina, with more than a hint of incredulity in her tone. "You think we just had a lover's quarrel? I am a paladin of the Order of the Sun. I took a vow to drive out disorder and corruption wherever I found it. And you are the personification of making terrible decisions! How could there possibly be anything here to fix, Aelia?"

It was the first time Orsina had ever addressed her by her true name, and Aelia hugged her sides and looked away.

"I love you," said Aelia, not taking her eyes off the silver fields in the distance. "Do with that what you will."

"What does that even mean, coming from you?" asked Orsina.

"More than it did from Perlita," Aelia replied.

Orsina set her jaw.

"I take it I was correct, then?"

Orsina pressed her lips together and did not respond immediately. Finally, she said, "She's married."

Aelia's face twisted with disgust. "Dayluue's teeth! Here, tell me where she lives. I want to break her nose."

"It doesn't matter," said Orsina. After another pause, she added, "I don't think I was ever really in love with her. I was in love with the woman I thought she was. But that woman never existed, except in my mind. I was so blind to her true nature, and it wasn't as though she made any effort to hide it from me. I have no excuse."

Orsina slid to the ground, her back still pressed against the stone wall. Aelia went and settled beside her, and Orsina did nothing to stop her.

"I mean it, though," said Aelia after a long silence. "If you don't want me to hurt her, I can go to her room in the middle of the night and give her a scare she'll never forget."

"No!"

Aelia groaned and rested her head against the wall as well.

"How did you know?" asked Orsina.

"Know what?"

"About Perlita?"

Aelia glanced over at her. "Because if she loved you half as much as you loved her, you'd be with her right now."

Orsina swallowed. "Did you know my quest was fake, too?"

"She told you that?"

Orsina nodded.

"I suspected, but...I wasn't certain. You had such conviction. And I know how Iolar is. I could see him giving you as little information as he could get away with for the sake of reserving his power."

"Why didn't he tell me?" whispered Orsina. "I might have wandered forever if..."

"I don't think he knew," said Aelia. "I don't think he even noticed."

Orsina looked at her, and the hurt in those brown eyes made Aelia's heart ache.

"I mean, I'm probably not the one to ask. We don't get along very well, when he remembers I exist. He's so..." Aelia shook her head. "You have no idea how powerful he is. He has worshippers on almost every continent. And maybe I'm a little jealous, but I think it's been bad for him. He's forgotten what it's like to be weak, and unimportant, and scared."

She expected Orsina to yell at her for her disrespect, but Orsina only said, “Are you scared?”

“All the time,” said Aelia. “I have no worshippers. Well, almost no worshippers. There’s mortal women blessed by Talcia that have more magic than I do, and my siblings like Edan are always looking for someone to enslave. The only place I’m ever really safe is Aethitide, and it’s so lonely there.”

Orsina was quiet for a little longer. Then she said, “People might worship you if you didn’t take over their minds.”

“I’m starting to realize that. And...the strange thing is, I’m starting to get prayers. From the artists we met in Catorisci.”

“What?”

“I know. I don’t know why! Riana was the first one, do you remember her? She was praying, though not to anyone in particular, I think. And the prayer went to me.”

“Did you answer her?”

“I gave her some ideas for a painting. She liked it.” Aelia shrugged. “And she must have told the others because now I’ve started hearing from them as well.”

“Aren’t those prayers meant for Ridon?” asked Orsina.

“Not exactly,” said Aelia. “Though I think they would have gone to him if I hadn’t been so near. But Ridon grants skill, and talent. Riana wanted inspiration. That is not his domain.”

Orsina was quiet for a little while. Then she said, “I still don’t understand how I wasn’t able to sense what you were. You don’t even set off my tattoos.”

“I know. That was a surprise for me as well. I think it’s because I’m trapped in a flesh body. Or it might be because I have hardly any magic to sense. I’m not sure, honestly.”

"And I suppose you really are fourteen billion years old?"

"What? Oh." Aelia chewed her lower lip. "No. That's just how old Inthya is. I'm actually much older. But it's not like you're thinking. Most of that time was spent staring at nothing. Just waiting and hoping."

"It must have been boring," said Orsina.

"I was not as I am now. I had no self and very little identity. It is...difficult to explain, especially in this language, but I was barely aware of my own existence. Only when Men became complex enough to understand me did I become like this." Aelia gestured to her face. "It's actually only been a few thousand years."

"That is still rather old," said Orsina. "Though I'll admit you don't seem it."

"I'm not terribly different than I was ten thousand years ago." Though, she reflected, that wasn't completely true anymore, after the events of the last few weeks. "Men are constantly changing throughout their lifetimes. Not like the gods. We are stagnant, compared to you."

Orsina did not say anything immediately. Then she asked, "What did you do before Inthya?"

Aelia swallowed and gazed up at the stars.

"Building a universe is hard," she whispered. "Getting everyone to agree how energy and time will work. Then gathering up enough power to trigger creation. Monitoring conditions for billions of years, hoping the entire thing won't be wiped out by a few bad weather patterns...it's difficult, and tedious. But even that is nothing compared to the task of keeping sentient creatures with free will from finding stupid reasons to kill each other."

Orsina leaned forward. "You had other worlds before Inthya?"

"We don't generally brag about our failures. Don't tell anyone I told you?"

"I don't think anyone would believe me if I did," said Orsina.

"They might, if it was coming from you."

Orsina glanced down at her boots. "And in those other worlds, did you ever love a mortal?"

Aelia shook her head. "Never once. You remember how I was when we first met? I saw mortals as toys or sources of power. That is how I was for all eternity before I met you. I was in no state to love anyone."

"You've seen so much, compared to me," observed Orsina. "I can barely comprehend how long you've been alive, let alone all that you've experienced. I don't see how you could possibly love me. I don't see how you can view me as anything other than an insect."

"I'm not nearly as powerful as you think I am," said Aelia. "And though I've lived a long time, I've learned very little from it. Besides...don't you remember what I told you before? In Catorisci? You've been kind to me. Kinder than anyone I've ever encountered."

"There must be more to it than that," said Orsina.

"There really isn't," Aelia replied, resting her hands behind her head. Orsina fell silent once more, and Aelia gazed up at the stars.

"Edan is planning something terrible," said Aelia after a while. "And I'm not nearly strong enough to stop him on my own. I know Xytae isn't your problem, but he won't be expecting an attack from both of us. I can get us back into his shrine. Protect you from the worst of his magic. You can bind him into his body and kill him. Then..."

"I'll think about it," said Orsina. "Tomorrow. I'll give you an answer tomorrow."

Aelia nodded.

"What's the relic you were searching for?" asked Orsina.

"Oh, that. The Unbinding Stone. It's a sort of magical dagger. If I stab myself with it, I can get rid of my mortal body and not have to wait for my consciousness to regenerate."

"You were going to stab yourself?"

"I'm not sure, at this point," said Aelia. "I wanted to tell you the truth. Remember the last night, in the inn? I wanted to tell you so badly. I thought maybe I'd tell you after I found the Stone. And if you'd accepted me, I'd have given you the dagger to turn in to your commander. If you'd rejected me, I'd have used it on myself and gone back to Aethitide."

"And do you have it now?"

"No. I'm certain Edan has it. It's how he's been avoiding the priests. The last handful of chaos gods they've detected have been him. He fakes his death after they trap him in his body, just as I did in Soria. Then he uses the stone to free himself once they're gone."

Orsina rubbed at the marks on her throat where Edan had grabbed at her with his claws. Aelia frowned.

"Did you ever visit a healer after you left Kynith?" she asked.

"I'm fine."

"That wasn't the question." Aelia squinted at the marks in the dark. "Is this the worst of it? How is your head?"

"I'm fine. I mean it."

That, at least, seemed true. Orsina was no longer radiating grief or despair, but Aelia could tell she was exhausted. She reached out to caress Orsina's face, but drew her hand back at the last moment, realizing that this might be an unwanted display of affection.

"You should rest," said Aelia. "I'll come find you again in the morning, and then we can decide what we want to do."

Orsina nodded. Aelia reached for her again, and this time Orsina leaned in to her hand. Aelia cupped Orsina's face.

"I only want you to be happy," Aelia said in Asterial. She knew Orsina could not understand the words, but her tone was gentle and affectionate. She pressed a soft kiss to Orsina's lips. *"I love you."*

To her surprise, Orsina returned the kiss, shifting forward and running her hands through Aelia's hair. Aelia's arms instinctively pulled Orsina closer, and a moment later she was flat on her back, staring up at Orsina's face and admiring the way the starlight illuminated her hair.

Aelia was vulnerable like this, but she could not muster up any fear as she gazed up at Orsina. Could she kill Aelia right now? Perhaps. Her hands were so strong. But Aelia was not afraid. She would never be afraid of Orsina again.

Orsina leaned down and kissed Aelia's forehead, then the bridge of her nose, and then her lips again. Aelia reciprocated immediately, eager to please, but Orsina pulled away to kiss her chin, her throat, the base of her neck...

"Wait," said Aelia.

Orsina lifted her mouth from Aelia's warm skin, a question in her eyes.

"You should go before you do something you'll regret," Aelia whispered.

Orsina hesitated, then pulled away. Aelia watched as she rose to her feet.

"Tomorrow, then?" Orsina asked.

Aelia nodded.

THE NEXT DAY, Aelia and Orsina met at one of Melidrie's taverns. It was early in the day, so there were only a few patrons, and nobody was interested in the conversation of two young women.

"What do you know of Emperor Ionnes' daughters?" asked Aelia.

"Not very much," said Orsina, looking surprised. "Why?"

"His heir, Ioanna, is seven years old and she's going to be arriving in Kynith today. She might even be there already."

"Why is the heir to the Xytan Empire going to Kynith?"

"Officially, she's visiting an aunt," said Aelia. "But that aunt is one of Edan's followers."

Orsina's brow knotted in a frown.

"Edan has been storing more power than I realized," said Aelia. "He plans to put all of Kynith in thrall tonight, at midnight. Ioanna will be killed and the city will destroy itself."

Orsina shook her head helplessly. "We'll never make it in time."

"We won't. Not on horseback, in any case. But I have another way. I have enough power to transport us there instantly. It is the same thing I did to get us away from Edan."

"Are you sure you have enough power?"

"Only barely. But I can do it. If you agree to help me fight."

"I will not leave a child to die at Edan's hands, no matter who her father is," said Orsina. "I only wish to understand what he hopes to accomplish. Surely killing Ioanna will only inconvenience Ionnes, if he has two other children to become his heirs."

"I don't know. I don't even know how he expects Iolar will let his actions go unpunished," said Aelia. "The chaos gods in Xytae have been careful to never go too far, for fear that Iolar would intercede directly. This contradicts everything I have been told."

"What is your plan?" asked Orsina.

"I know where Princess Ioanna is staying, but we can't just go charging in. We'll have every soldier in Xytae after us," said Aelia. "I've got enough power to trick her guards into thinking I'm a maid. I'll get to the princess and tell her whatever I need to in order to make her trust me. She's young, it shouldn't be difficult."

"How are you planning to get her to safety and then be back in Kynith in time to defeat Edan before he puts the entire city under thrall?"

"I..." Aelia realized she had not thought about that. "Oh."

"Aelia."

"Stop it, don't be mean to me. I'm not used to planning things out." Aelia pressed her hand to her forehead. "I should have known I'd forget something!"

"Calm down," soothed Orsina. "Maybe the Temple of Iolar can help us. I already warned them that something's happening in Kynith. Maybe they can take her away while we confront Edan."

Aelia had her doubts about the competence of a few small-town priests, but she would admit that she cared less about saving Ioanna and more about ripping Edan's face off with her teeth.

"And how are we going to defeat Edan?" Orsina pressed. "He got the better of us so quickly. I am not too proud to admit he might be too powerful for us to defeat alone."

Aelia reached into her skirt and pulled out her sketchbook, where she had written a series of runes, followed by their pronunciation in Vesoldan letters. She passed it over to Orsina.

"What is this?"

"This is the prayer that you say that activates the magic on your blade. Except it's in Asterial, not Vesoldan. You'll find it significantly more powerful."

Orsina frowned. "I don't think Iolar meant for—"

"You're right, he didn't. But I doubt he'll notice. And if he does, you can tell him it was my doing. We need every advantage we can get."

"I'm surprised," said Orsina. "I'd have thought you wouldn't want to fight Edan directly."

Aelia pressed her lips together and stared at the tabletop. "He hurt you. I want to hurt him back."

"Paladins do not deal in revenge."

"Revenge is just another word for justice," said Aelia.

"It certainly is not."

"It comes out the same in the end, doesn't it?" asked Aelia. "Either way, he needs to be stopped, and we're the only ones who can do it."

Orsina did not respond immediately. Then she said, "Give me half an hour to gather all I need, and we will be on our way."

Aelia nodded. “I have more prayers to answer in the meantime,” she said.

Orsina’s lips quirked in a smile. “How respectable of you.”

“I’ve been keeping respectable company,” said Aelia. “And it seems that I may be becoming respectable in turn.”

Orsina stood. “I will return quickly,” she said. She hesitated a moment longer, as though she wanted to say something more, but walked away without another word.

Aelia watched her leave, then rested her head against the back of her chair and turned her thoughts to the most recent prayers she had received. There was another request for inspiration, this time from Claretta. And there was a prayer of gratitude from Lucil for showing them an ancient memory of Inthi teaching early Men how to forge.

The gratitude was invigorating, enough that Aelia knew she could get Orsina and herself to Kynith without trouble. As the power washed over her, she giggled in delight. This was like being drunk, but better.

She turned her attention to Claretta’s prayer. What sort of thing might Claretta enjoy seeing? She was fairly domestic, and most of her drawings were of birds and flowers. She probably wouldn’t appreciate anything too unusual.

Aelia thought of Cyne’s cats, the ones that sometimes wandered into Aethitide. She had once seen one curled high up in the branches of a crystal tree, which looked dreadfully uncomfortable to Aelia’s eyes, but the cat did not seem to mind.

Aelia sent the memory along, which was greeted immediately with joy and gratitude. She was still smiling when Orsina returned.

"Do you know a place I can transport us from where we will not be seen?" asked Aelia.

Orsina led Aelia down one of Melidrie's side streets. Aelia looked around, satisfied that the only witnesses were a stray dog and some hanging laundry.

"Alright," said Aelia. "Hold very still. This might feel a little strange."

Transporting herself and Orsina out of Edan's temple had been difficult. With Star and Lavender added to the group, it would take even more out of her. Without the prayers that were coming from Catorisci, she would not have had a chance of accomplishing something like this.

She closed her eyes and focused, selecting a spot just outside of Kynith for their landing place.

There was a jolt, and Aelia opened her eyes. They were standing in the middle of some ruins. Next to her, Orsina groaned like she might be about to throw up.

"Oh, good," said Aelia, looking around. In the distance, she could see Kynith's high walls. "I didn't miss."

"Good," echoed Orsina, holding onto Star for balance.

"Edan is planning to act tonight. You need to be ready to run as soon as I return with Ioanna."

"Can't you just transport us again?"

Aelia shook her head. "Not after that. I only have a little bit of power left. It will be enough to get to Ioanna, but not much more than that."

They re-entered Kynith together, but when they reached the temple, Orsina went in alone. Aelia waited just outside with the horses, watching people come and go.

It was nearly an hour before Orsina arrived back with good news. "They were surprised to see me again," she reported. "I think they thought I was still in their basement. But they agreed to help. They can get Ioanna out of the city and somewhere safe."

Ioanna's aunt, Livia, lived in one of the largest homes in Kynith. Aelia had walked past it a few times, but not noticed anything unusual. She had reached out with her mind, searching for some hint of Edan in the residence, but the place did not seem to have any chaos magic in it at all. It was almost suspiciously clear.

Livia herself seemed to be an ordinary woman, and Aelia had seen her about town twice. She did not behave suspiciously at all, but there was no missing Edan's spiteful magic in her heart.

"I'll go in at dusk," said Aelia. "You wait for me around the back, near the servant's entrance. And be ready to go once I come out."

They spent the rest of the afternoon in a quiet tavern, with Orsina studying the prayer that Aelia had transcribed for her and Aelia attempting clumsy sketches with charcoal. Art, she decided, was even more difficult than she'd imagined. It was incredible to her that anyone possessed the patience to practice long enough to develop any real skill.

When Orsina asked to see what she was working on, Aelia threw the pages into the fireplace.

"You're never going to improve that way," said Orsina disapprovingly.

"I'm never going to improve *any*way," Aelia retorted. "I told you, I'm stagnant."

Orsina's lips quirked. "You know, I'm not entirely sure about that."

Aelia huffed and hunched her shoulders, using her own knees as a barrier so that Orsina could not see the page.

"I mean it," said Orsina. "I wonder if...maybe that's why I'm not sensing you as a threat. Maybe you're not chaotic anymore."

"I'll never not be chaotic."

Orsina did not reply, but there was the tiniest smile on her lips.

Dusk finally arrived, and Aelia approached Livia's house alone. When she came in sight of the servant's entrance, she called up what little magic she had left. There was a single guard in the back garden, but when he looked at her, she pressed the words *familiar serving-maid* into his mind. He gave her a friendly wave as she passed by.

The door led her into the kitchen, where the family servants were all cleaning up from the evening meal. Aelia slipped past them in a cloud of *unimportant-ignore* and went out into the main area of the house.

In contrast to the bright, noisy kitchen, the rest of the house was quiet and dim, almost eerily so. Aelia moved very slowly and peered around each corner before she rounded it, hating the way her footsteps echoed on the limestone floors.

Up ahead, she could see two guards posted at one door. She approached them openly, and when they looked at her, she pressed *nursemaid-familiar* into their minds. They relaxed, and one of them even opened the door for her.

The room was a bedroom, filled with expensive-looking furniture. By the golden light of the oil lamp, she could see a little figure sitting at a writing desk with her back to the door.

The girl turned in her chair and stared up at Aelia without moving. Aelia froze, the breath catching in her throat. In that moment, she suddenly understood why there was no trace of chaos magic in the house, and why Edan wanted the young princess dead.

Ioanna was all but radiant with the light of Iolar's magic, crowned with an invisible halo of warm golden light. Orsina's weak blessing was like distant starlight in comparison. It almost hurt Aelia to look directly at her.

The little princess lifted her chin, and Aelia realized there was magic in her eyes, too.

She was a truthsayer.

"Hello," said Ioanna mildly. "You're not supposed to be here."

Aelia swallowed. There was no point in lying. "You're right," she agreed. "But I'm here to help you."

Ioanna paused, as though considering, then nodded.

"There's a chaos god named Edan who is trying to hurt you," said Aelia. "He doesn't want you to become Empress. He's going to turn everyone in this city against you very soon. My friend and I want to get you to safety before that happens."

Ioanna stood up and examined Aelia closely. She turned her head from side to side, looking at Aelia with one eye, and the other, then both. She frowned, and squinted, and shook her head around as though she had something in her eyes. It was clear that her truthsayer magic didn't know what to make of Aelia.

"Are you Talcia?" asked Ioanna at last.

"No," said Aelia, flattered despite the urgency of the situation. "My name is Aelia. You wouldn't have heard of me; I'm not very important. Will you come with me?"

Ioanna took Aelia's hand. "How will we get past the guards?" she asked.

"I can make them sleep. As long as we're both very quiet, they won't wake until we're gone. Promise me you'll stay quiet?"

Ioanna nodded solemnly. Aelia closed her eyes, reaching out with her mind until she found the guards.

Sleep, she suggested, pressing the order into their minds with just enough force that they would not be inclined to resist. Outside the door, she heard something heavy collapse, followed by the clatter of swords on the stone floor.

"Come on," said Aelia. "We don't have too much time."

They slipped past the guards, but the kitchen was still filled with people. Aelia hesitated, wondering what the best way to approach the situation would be. She wasn't powerful enough to convince the servants to ignore her if she was accompanied by Ioanna. Nor did she know if she had enough magic remaining to put them all to sleep.

But Ioanna released her hand and ran right into the kitchen. She grabbed a fruit tart off one of the countertops, in plain view of the servants.

"Oh, princess," scolded the head cook half-heartedly. "You know you're not supposed to be eating sweets at this hour."

Ioanna jammed the rest of the tart in her mouth, as though she was afraid someone might take it away from her, though Aelia was certain that no servant in Xytae was going to do that to Ionnes' daughter. The servants all turned back to their cleaning, and Ioanna raced right out the back door, unnoticed. After a minute or two, Aelia followed her in another cloud of *unimportant-ignore.*

It still wasn't as dark out as Aelia liked, but she supposed it would have to do. She could see Orsina at the end of the street, with Star and Lavender behind her. Aelia picked up Ioanna and then immediately regretted it. Little girls, apparently, were heavier than they looked.

"Is this her?" asked Orsina in a low whisper, once they were near enough to speak. Aelia nodded, and Orsina placed Ioanna on Star's back. "You'll be all right," she promised the young princess. "We're going to get you to safety."

Orsina could not see the magic on Ioanna. To her, the princess was no different than any other child. Aelia decided it wasn't worth raising the subject, and turned her attention to getting back on Lavender.

Orsina climbed onto Star's back behind Ioanna. "Hold on," she said. "We don't have too far to go."

They set off in the direction of the temple. Aelia wanted to get there as quickly as possible, but Orsina convinced her to move at a normal pace so they would not attract attention.

"I think Papa knew this would happen," said Ioanna to nobody in particular.

"What?" asked Orsina.

"I think he knew Aunt Livia was going to do something bad. I think he wanted it." Ioanna frowned at her hands. "He doesn't want me to be Empress. And neither does Grandmother. They'd have been happy if I never came home."

"That's horrific," said Orsina.

"It's okay," said Ioanna. "You saved me."

"Still, it's not right," said Orsina. "Your family should love you."

Ioanna shrugged, and Aelia wondered at how different the princess's life must be from Orsina's own idyllic childhood. Aelia did not share Orsina's idealistic view of family relations, but she also felt a little sorry for Ioanna.

"Are you a paladin?" Ioanna asked.

"I am," confirmed Orsina.

Ioanna nodded. "When I'm Empress, I'll let you all come back. And when I do, you should come visit me. You can work for me."

In the dim light, Aelia could see Orsina smile. "I'd have to get permission from my knight-commander to leave Vesolda," she said.

"He won't say no to me," said Ioanna confidently. "And your wife can be one of my waiting-ladies."

Orsina sputtered, and Aelia burst out laughing.

"Oh, you're not married?" Ioanna frowned. "I thought you were."

"What in the world made you think that?" asked Orsina.

Ioanna nodded at Aelia. "She said you were friends, but she was lying. And you're not enemies. So I thought maybe you were married."

"No," said Orsina.

"Engaged?"

"No."

"Just in love, then?"

Orsina seemed to be struggling with an answer. Aelia said, "It's complicated, Ioanna."

"Lying *again*!" Ioanna proclaimed. She craned her neck to look at Orsina. "She loves you."

"What makes you so sure of that?" asked Orsina with a frown.

"When someone lies, their words hit me in the head." Ioanna reached up and poked her forehead a few times to demonstrate. "Sometimes they hit me so hard that my head opens up and I can see what they meant to say instead."

Orsina's eyes narrowed. "You're a truthsayer?"

"Maybe. Papa won't let the priests test me for it."

"But you are," said Orsina. "Aren't you?"

"I think I am. But I think lots of things that turn out not to be true after all. So maybe yes. But maybe no."

"You are," said Aelia with complete conviction.

"Oh, all right," Ioanna looked relieved. "Good. Finally. Thank you."

"Glad to help," Aelia laughed.

Ioanna turned her head and looked up at Orsina.

"Do you think...if something bad happened...do you think the Order of the Sun would help me?"

"How do you mean?" asked Orsina.

"Like if..." Ioanna chewed her lower lip. "If when it comes time for me to be Empress. If someone was trying to stop me. Or if they tried to make someone else Papa's heir."

"You think that's going to happen?"

Ioanna hugged her sides. "Maybe. Maybe not. Yes."

"Well, I can't speak for a Knight-Commander or a Justice, but you are the rightful heir to the throne. The Order of the Sun might very well be compelled to back you, especially once they learn about your blessing. If you're serious about it, the one you want to speak to is Knight-Commander Livius. I believe he is currently in Birsgen."

Ioanna brightened up. "Thank you," she said. "I know it's probably not going to happen for a long time. But I think about it. A lot."

Two riders were waiting at the temple when they arrived. Orsina dismounted and approached them to verify that these were the same men that she had spoken to earlier. But even before Orsina called back that all was well, Aelia could see Iolar's magic on them. It was not nearly as radiant as Ioanna's blessing, but it would be enough to protect her on the journey.

"Will you still be in danger when you get home?" Orsina asked Ioanna as she removed the princess from Star's back and set her down on the ground.

Ioanna shook her head. "There's people who like me at home," she said. "Especially Iolar's Archpriest. If something happens to me, they'll turn on Papa. They know it and he knows it. It'll be all right."

"If you're certain." Orsina sounded dubious.

"And I meant what I said," added Ioanna. "When I'm Empress, I'll let the Order of the Sun come back, and you can be my personal guard."

"You don't think you might change your mind in the meantime?" asked Orsina.

Ioanna shook her head solemnly.

"In that case, I'll keep it in mind," said Orsina. "Though I can't make any promises. I don't know what my future holds."

"Do I still get to be a waiting-lady?" asked Aelia.

"If you want." Then Ioanna clasped her hands together, glancing in the direction of the two priests, but did not move. "Do either of you have any paper?"

"Paper?" repeated Orsina. "Whatever for?"

"I need to write a letter."

"What?"

"Here," said Aelia, taking her sketchbook from a saddle-bag. "You can use this."

"Don't—we don't have time for this!" Orsina looked from Aelia to Ioanna helplessly. "Both of you! Stop!"

"D'you have a pen?" asked Ioanna.

Orsina covered her eyes with her hands and groaned. Aelia decided to be helpful and fish a pen and some ink out of her bags.

"Don't worry," Ioanna asserted, settling down by the side of the road. "I'll be fast. Promise. Just wait."

Orsina went over to speak with the priests, while Aelia waited with Ioanna. She could not make out exactly what Ioanna was writing, but her handwriting was painfully neat, even without a desk to write on. After a few minutes, Ioanna read the letter over, nodded once, and blew on the ink.

"Are you finished?" asked Orsina.

"Yes. Can you give this to Knight-Commander Livius?" Ioanna folded the page in half and handed it over to Orsina. "If I sent it from home, I know someone would open it. But I trust you."

Orsina tucked the letter away in her bags without reading it. "I will do my best to see that he gets it," she said.

Ioanna smiled. "Thank you. And also, thank you for saving me tonight. I won't forget you, ever."

"It's no trouble," said Orsina.

Ioanna gave her one last smile and ran to the priests. One of them set her on his own horse, and then the two took off in the direction of Kynith's western gate. Aelia and Orsina watched them ride away until they disappeared into the dusk.

"I think that went pretty well," Aelia observed.

"We can get into Edan's shrine from the temple of Iolar," suggested Orsina. "I marked the way last time I was down there."

"I know a faster way," Aelia said. "There's an entrance in an abandoned house that the cultists use. It's a direct path, but also more dangerous. There will be guards."

"Are they in thrall?"

Aelia shook her head. "They serve willingly."

There was nobody in the house when Aelia and Orsina arrived. Down in the tunnels, the air was clammy and moist. The passageways were occasionally lit by torches, but Aelia remembered the way even without them. And even if she had not, she could sense Edan's magic in the air, growing stronger as they approached and filling her with dread.

It seemed Orsina could sense it, too, for she drew her blade and moved more slowly down the tunnels. It was not long before they encountered their first cultist, a man in a hooded black robe. Aelia wondered if she would try to reason with him, like she had with Vasia in Catorisci, but Orsina did not waste a moment. She ran him through before he was completely aware of what was happening.

"Come on," said Orsina in a low voice, stepping over the corpse.

"I sense two more up ahead," warned Aelia. "They're coming toward us."

Orsina nodded. "Stay back. I'll take care of them."

She made swift work of the two, but Aelia noted that there was no malice in her actions. Orsina was swift and impersonal and, unlike Aelia's siblings, she did not gloat over her victories. But she did not mourn, either. She simply stepped over the fallen bodies and continued down the passageways.

They encountered three more cultists on their way to the shrine, one individual and one pair. All were taken by surprise by Orsina, their few, quick shouts heard by nobody.

The passageway came to an end and Aelia knew from experience that it would let out in the large, open room that served as the heart of Edan's shrine, the same one that their last disastrous confrontation with him had taken place in. As they approached, they could hear voices speaking.

Aelia peered around the doorway and saw that Edan was standing in the middle of the room, facing a strange woman. She was dressed in leather armor, with feathers woven through her messy hair, and a long smear of rust-colored paint across her eyes.

"Is it done?" the woman asked. Bitter red-brown magic emanated from her lips and eyes, reeking of dried blood and wrought iron.

"Mistress..." Edan wrung his hands anxiously. "Not yet. It will be done at midnight."

"More excuses?" The woman did not sound amused. "I did not think that killing a little girl would be such a difficult task. Perhaps I should enlist another. Cytha would have had it done before sundown—"

"Mistress, no!" Edan protested. "It will be done! I only—"

"Who is that woman?" Orsina whispered as Edan continued to make excuses. Aelia said nothing, horror slowly curdling in her stomach as she realized the scope of what was happening in Kynith.

"We need to leave." Aelia turned around and pushed Orsina ahead of her. "We need to leave *now.*"

"Who is she? Is she a chaos goddess?"

Aelia glanced back over her shoulder just in time to see the woman give Edan a dismissive wave of her hand and then vanish into thin air, leaving Edan standing alone in the middle of the room with his fists clenched.

"Aelia?"

"No. Come on, we're leaving, this is so far over our heads that I can't even think up a proper metaphor." Aelia broke into a run, pulling Orsina along behind her by the hand.

"Aelia!" Orsina stopped short. "Tell me who that was!"

Aelia sensed that Orsina would not cooperate until she got answers, so she gritted her teeth and growled out, "That was Reygmadra."

Orsina's mouth fell open.

"Still want to fight her?" Aelia asked.

“No,” said Orsina meekly.

“Glad to hear you have some sense.” Aelia continued to pull Orsina along.

“Why does Reygmadra want Ioanna dead?”

“The Isinthi family has always venerated Reygmadra, and she’s always given them her best blessings in return,” Aelia explained. “That’s why they’ve been so obsessed with warfare. There’s no doubt that she planned to grant the same blessings to Ioanna when the princess was born. Reygmadra must have been furious when Iolar beat her to it.”

“She’d murder a child because Iolar blessed her?”

“Someone like Ioanna is a threat to the Xytan Empire’s history of conquest,” said Aelia. “Reygmadra is afraid that Xytae will become peaceful under Ioanna’s reign, and she will lose power. I just don’t know how Iolar managed to put his most powerful blessing on Ioanna before Reygmadra turned up.”

“So what are we going to do?”

Aelia looked back at Orsina. “What? What do you mean?”

“How are we going to stop Reygmadra?”

Aelia groaned. “We’re not! But if you want to try something impossible, we can spend the rest of tonight trying to stop the sun from rising!”

“You can’t expect me to just—”

“Ioanna is safe. We did our part. Don’t try to go up against one of the Ten, you won’t win.”

“But,” Orsina seemed to struggle for words, “that’s not fair.”

“Nothing’s fair.” Aelia sidestepped one of the corpses that Orsina had left behind on their journey down. “I’d have thought you’d worked that out by—”

Without warning, the ancient stones just ahead of them came loose from the ceiling and crashed to the ground, blocking off their exit. Orsina yelped in surprise, and Aelia spun around, violet light blazing at her hands.

"Edan!" screamed Aelia. Orsina raised her sword.

"How cute," his voice sneered. Aelia looked around frantically, but she couldn't see him. "You managed to win her back. Is she in thrall, or are you just that adept at Dayluue's arts?"

"Where are you?" she demanded. But Edan was silent.

After a long moment of nothing, Orsina relaxed her stance and said, "Maybe he—"

Her words ended in a scream as something dropped down from the ceiling and landed on her back. Aelia could see Edan's ivory claws reaching around Orsina's neck, his teeth bared in a hateful grimace.

Orsina spun free, her silver blade flashing in the dim light. He met the sword with his claws, which, eerily held firm against the metal. Orsina looked shocked but did not fall back. Instead, she began chanting the prayer that Aelia had transcribed for her.

Orsina's sword blazed with light, far brighter than Aelia had ever seen before. Aelia flinched and covered her eyes with her arm instinctively, and she heard Edan hiss in pain. He vanished, only to reappear behind her.

Aelia shouted a warning, but Orsina was already reciting the words that would trap Edan in his body. He roared in outrage as he realized what she was doing, and raised both hands to strike. But before he could lunge forward, Aelia gathered up the last few drops of her magic and splashed him in the eyes with violet sparks.

Edan howled in pain and Orsina struck, moving forward boldly. Her blade took off one of his arms, which fell to the ground, still twitching. Edan hissed again and reached out with his remaining arm. This time, he did not miss. His awful claws gouged her throat.

Orsina fell to her knees, her neck an impossible mess of blood and torn flesh. Enraged, and perhaps heartbroken, Aelia flew at Edan, clawing at his face. But it made little difference. His flesh was like carved ivory.

"All out of magic?" taunted Edan, grabbing her by the neck and slamming her against the stone wall. "Really, Aelia, what were you expecting? I'm surprised you managed to last this long."

Aelia kicked outward, but it was like striking a wall. Was Edan's body made of meat or stone? She looked at his shoulder, where his arm used to be. Blood was flowing from the wound, but it was slowing: he was healing himself. Aelia watched in horror as a new arm began to grow from the bloody stump, hideous and twisting.

"You've barely inconvenienced me," said Edan, his fresh arm reaching into his robes. He brought his other hand up, and Aelia could see something glimmering in it: a dagger, with a hilt made of ancient wrought silver and a blade of violet crystal. "Your pet was a fool to believe she could trap me on Inthya."

"Give me—" Purple magic flashed at Aelia's hands, and she fell silent in sheer surprise. She thought she had drained herself.

But no. Her spent magic was returning already, actively refilling her body as though it was being poured in from somewhere else. How was that possible?

Aelia focused on the source of the power, mentally tracing it back across meadows and fields and long, dusty roads until her mind was filled by the sight of a young woman standing before a lake.

Hundreds of miles away, Claretta was singing.

Claretta was singing *to her*.

Hysterical, giddy laughter escaped her, and Edan raised an eyebrow, clearly wondering if she'd gone mad.

Aelia drew up all her renewed power and blasted Edan through the chest with it.

For the briefest moment, his black eyes stared at her in shock and confusion and rage before his body crumbled to ash.

The tunnel was as silent as death. Aelia turned and ran to Orsina, who was still sprawled on the ground. Aelia pulled her into her arms and cradled her against her chest, pouring healing magic into every injury she could find and murmuring soft reassurances.

The wound in Orsina's neck was hideous, and the rasping sound that came from her throat filled Aelia with horror. Even as she pressed her magic into it, she could tell she was fighting a losing battle. Orsina's body was not helping her along, as it had when she'd healed her at Catorisci. It seemed to be in the process of slowing down.

Dion's words to the wraith came back to her: *"It's not fair. You'd just barely started. It's not fair."*

Aelia wiped away her tears with the back of her hand. Orsina was *not* going to die. There was still so much more they had to do on Inthya. They had to bring the Unbinding Stone to Bergavenna and deliver Knight-Commander Livius' letter to Birsgen. They had to help Ioanna take the throne. They had to knock Perlita down a well.

Someone was standing over her. The realization hit her in an instant, and Aelia tightened her grasp on Orsina. When she raised her head, she found herself staring up into a pair of golden eyes.

The man before her was smooth-skinned and ageless. There was something very stern and paternal about him. His hair was dark, his face cleanly shaven, and he wore the white robes of a Justice.

Aelia's eyes darted back down to the half-conscious paladin in her arms.

"This isn't what it looks like," she told her brother.

Iolar knelt down and put his arms out. Aelia allowed him to take Orsina from her and watched as he pressed two fingers to her forehead. Then he cupped one hand over the wound in her throat. When he pulled away, the injury had been replaced by clean, unbroken flesh.

"Is she all right?" asked Aelia. Iolar did not deign to respond, but after a moment Orsina opened her eyes.

"Papa?" she mumbled, gazing up at Iolar blearily. Iolar stroked her hair, but before he could reply, Aelia elbowed her way in, shifting closer so that Orsina could see her.

"Orsina? Are you all right?"

"I'm fine." But her voice was oddly distant. "Just... tired. Is Edan gone?"

"Yes, he won't be back for a while," said Aelia.

"Oh good. Now we can go back to Melidrie," Orsina's voice was strange and slurred, and Aelia had a feeling that Iolar had done something to her mind to suppress her pain. "And we can get married."

Aelia laughed. "That sounds nice. But I don't think I'm the marrying sort."

Orsina looked a little bit hurt. "But I love you. And you love me. Ioanna told me so."

"Yes, that's true," said Aelia. Iolar seemed to have finished his healing, and he got to his feet once more, leaving Orsina sitting there on the ground with Aelia.

"Aelia," said Iolar. "Come."

Aelia nodded and took Orsina's hand. "I need to go now. There's some people who want to ask me questions."

"Oh." Orsina still seemed disoriented, but the disappointment in her voice was obvious. "Are you coming back?"

Aelia rubbed her thumb across Orsina's fingers. "I don't know. But if I don't, it's all right. Don't wait around for me, or anyone else. Live your life the way you were always meant to. Promise me that?"

Orsina nodded weakly, and Aelia realized that she only had a faint idea of what was happening. Whatever Iolar had done to her mind had not completely worn off yet. Aelia shifted forward on her knees and pressed a kiss to Orsina's forehead.

Then she got up and followed Iolar into Solarium.

TO BE BACK in Asterium, free of her flesh body at last, was delightful. But Aelia could not savor the feeling, because Iolar was striding forward purposefully, probably leading her directly to her doom.

Solarium was an endless city, all white and gold. Tall, beautiful structures housed every book that had ever been written. The sky was always blue, and the sun was always at midday. It didn't look too different from Inthya, at first glance.

They passed two long-dead paladins, who were sparring in the middle of a ring. They wore the same armor that they had in life, outdated and archaic, but still bearing a passing resemblance to what Orsina wore.

"It was Reygmadra, you know," said Aelia, deciding that she could not take any more silence. "Edan was taking orders from Reygmadra."

Iolar nodded without looking at her. “I am not surprised.”

“And Ioanna is safe.”

“Yes,” said Iolar.

Aelia said nothing more. She had a feeling that Iolar wasn’t very interested in anything she had to say. He didn’t seem too terribly angry, though. Maybe he’d be merciful and only confine her to Aethitide for a few thousand years.

They came to a white marble fountain done in the Xytan style. Though unlike all the ones on Inthya, this one was gleaming and polished and filled with crystal water. Iolar stopped at its edge.

“Did you write a prayer for Orsina in Asterial?”

“Yes.” Aelia had not been expecting this line of questioning. “It was for—” the words died as she saw the disapproval on his face. “*That’s* what you’re mad about?”

“You know I must preserve my power,” said Iolar. “The Outsiders are a threat. Even now. The Ten are the first line of defense against them. What do you think would become of Inthya if they attacked us while I was drained?”

“You are in no danger of being drained,” said Aelia flatly. “Orsina could perform rituals in Asterial for ten thousand years and still never come close to draining you. Besides, the Elven Gods have no reason to turn on you now. They have their own lands to play in.”

“I am not speaking of the Elven Gods,” said Iolar. “You may have the luxury of forgetting all that exists outside Asterium and Inthya, but I do not. I tell you that we must act as though an attack could come at any time, and it is only through my vigilance that one has not come already.”

“I can’t believe this! You’re upset because I siphoned a few drops of your power? Not because I’m in love with one of your paladins?”

"You believe you love her?" Iolar asked. His voice was heavy with skepticism, and Aelia forgot herself.

"I certainly love her more than you do!" Aelia snapped. "You allowed her to run around the Vesoldan wilderness for two years, waiting for a message that was never coming! You do not deserve her devotion! Did you intend for her to wander Inthya until she *died* just because you're too miserly to expend the morsel of power it would have taken you to warn her that she was being deceived?"

Iolar stared at her in shock. Aelia doubted anyone had spoken to him in such a way in a very, very long time. Despite the terror that shot through her as Iolar stared into the core of her being, she decided that she regretted none of it.

From up ahead, came the musical sound of a woman laughing. Both Iolar and Aelia looked away from one another to see who was approaching them. It was two women, twins, identical in face but not in dress. Iolar frowned.

"What is this?" he asked.

"Now we are not allowed to visit?" asked the one who had been laughing. She wore a simple white dress, cut very low, and deep crimson roses had been threaded through her golden hair. Her beauty was overpowering, even intoxicating. When she drew nearer, Aelia could see her eyes were red.

The woman beside her was dressed far more modestly, with a simple homespun dress and a stained apron. She was beautiful, too, but her hair was pulled up into a motherly bun. The scent of baking bread and fresh herbs wafted around her.

"What interest do you have in this?" asked Iolar.

"I only wish to see justice done," said Dayluue. She bumped her twin sister with her hip. "Pemele is here to be entertained."

"That is an oversimplification of the matter at hand," said Pemele flatly.

"Has something happened that I should know about?" Iolar asked. His meaning was extremely clear, and he suddenly seemed to be very tall as he turned to face Aelia.

"No!" protested Aelia.

"Yes," said Dayluue. "Aelia has done far more for the forces of order than chaos in these last few weeks. I might go so far as to suggest that Orsina's influence on her has altered Aelia's domain."

"What?" said Iolar. Aelia stood rooted to the spot, her eyes on Dayluue.

Among Men, Dayluue had a reputation for being a carefree, lighthearted goddess—a reputation she reveled in. She was known for pleasure, not practicality. But behind her eyes lurked secrets that not even Iolar understood (and here, Aelia's memory supplied her with a memory of an incomprehensible double helix shape, the twisting ladder that was at the heart of Man's existence). It was only by her design that Men had not died off all those thousands of years ago. She was not to be underestimated.

"Can't you see it?" asked Dayluue. "Can't you *feel* it? She's not the same as she used to be."

Iolar turned his golden eyes to Aelia.

"I don't want to keep thralls anymore," said Aelia. "I. I have worshippers. True ones. They sing to me and I give them ideas."

"What kind of ideas?"

"Just—just. Ideas for paintings. They're artists. They paint and sculpt and things like that. There's no harm in it, I swear."

For the first time, Iolar's face appeared to soften.

"Inspiration," said Dayluue with a smile. "How delightful. We haven't had a domain shift in thousands of years."

"Inspiration?" repeated Aelia. *Goddess of Inspiration.* The title sounded so elegant, so important. Could that be her?

"You have done well," Dayluue said warmly.

"I suppose she has," granted Iolar. "Very well. You are dismissed, Aelia."

"But—what about Orsina?" asked Aelia. "Can I—I mean, can we—?"

Iolar did not reply immediately. Then he said, "You wish to stay with her?"

"Yes," said Aelia. "For the rest of her life. If she agrees."

"Aelia."

"You need not be so jealous. She is still devoted to you," said Aelia. Dayluue burst out laughing, but Aelia ignored this. "After she dies, I expect she will come to Solarium."

"Do you?"

"Yes. She loves me as a woman, not a goddess. And I don't think she'd enjoy Aethitide very much." Solarium was the eternal home to thousands of regents and priests and paladins. The only company that Aelia could offer was a few bored cats. "You're not angry at her, are you?"

"No," said Iolar. "I am not angry with her."

She knew that Iolar was not inclined to lie, but she still felt compelled to speak in Orsina's defense. "When she, when she realized who I was, she said she had to turn herself in to the Justices. For the crime of kissing me. If you told her to never see me again, she would obey. Being a paladin, and serving you, is more important to her than being with me."

"I would not be so certain of that," Dayluue commented.

"Stop," said Aelia. "Please."

"I heard someone mention marriage," said Pemele. "Given the circumstances, I am inclined to allow it. Were you planning on having it last only until her death, or beyond that? If it's the latter, there are things I must discuss with both of you."

Aelia covered her eyes with her hands. "We're not getting married!"

"And if you want to raise children, I know plenty of orphans," said Dayluue.

"No! No children!" yelped Aelia. "No weddings and no children!"

"Shouldn't you discuss that with her first?" Pemele sounded a little disapproving. In contrast, Dayluue was grinning broadly, as though she'd just played a hilarious joke.

Aelia turned to Iolar. "Does this mean I can stay with her?"

Iolar gave the smallest of nods. "If that is what she desires."

Before Aelia could come up with a retort, an angered shout echoed across Solarium's peaceful sky.

"Iolar!"

"Reygmadra," said Iolar, looking away. "I will handle this. Aelia, as I said before, you are dismissed—"

He rested his hand lightly on Aelia's shoulder, and a jolt of power shot through her. In an instant, Solarium vanished, and Aelia found herself standing once more in the decrepit ruins of Edan's shrine.

Orsina was still there, sitting on the floor where she'd been left and turning the Unbinding Stone over in her hands.

"Orsina?"

Orsina looked alarmed, dropping the blade and reaching for her sword. "Who are you?"

"Are you serious?" But then Aelia looked down at her body. It was her usual avatar, not the body she had been wearing for the last few weeks. "Oh. Orsina, it's me. It's Aelia."

Orsina leaped to her feet. "Are you all right? What happened?" She moved closer, pulling Aelia to her chest. "I don't remember very much."

"Everything is all right." Aelia paused to collect her thoughts, not sure where to begin. But before she could say any more, Orsina leaned down and picked up the Unbinding Stone.

"Did you still need this?" she asked.

Aelia shook her head. "The binding was undone when I went back to Asterium. You can turn that in to whoever you want." She touched her face. "Do you prefer me like this? Or as Elyne?"

"I'm not sure," Orsina admitted. "I suppose I'm not used to seeing you like this."

Aelia closed her eyes and focused on her avatar. Changing back into Elyne was easier than she'd expected—it seemed her spirit now preferred this new shape. When she was done, she opened her eyes to see Orsina was smiling. She came forward and embraced her again.

"I remember you telling me that you had to leave." Orsina gripped Aelia's hands. "But you're back now, right?"

"Back to stay," confirmed Aelia. "Iolar only wanted to find out what happened. He let me go after I answered his questions."

Orsina's eyes widened. "You met Iolar?"

"Yes, and so did you. Don't you remember? He was here."

"He was *here?*" Orsina repeated. "You mean—*here*? In this shrine?"

"He healed your injuries. He held you. You really don't remember?"

Orsina shook her head.

"I could tell he wasn't delighted, but he said we could stay together for the rest of your mortal life. If. If that's what you want. I know I hurt you. I understand if you don't want me—"

"Don't be ridiculous," Orsina whispered. "Of course I do. I never want to be without you ever again."

Aelia relaxed in her arms. "He said he's not angry with you," she whispered. "He's. He's not so bad. He's not completely unreasonable. Just a little sanctimonious. I think the two of you would get along well."

Orsina burst out laughing and pushed Aelia away. "Alright, let's get out of here. What are we going to do about the rest of the cultists?"

"Iolar knows about them now. I expect he'll tell his priests what he wants done." Aelia shrugged. "But I don't think they'll have the nerve to try anything with Edan gone."

"And what about Reygmadra?"

"There's nothing we can do about her," said Aelia. "I told Iolar that this was all her doing. But I don't know how he'll respond. I hope he'll at least keep a closer eye on Ioanna until she manages to take the throne. I'd like to leave as soon as possible."

Orsina nodded. "Normally I'd argue, but I think I've had my fill of the Xytan Empire."

"I can transport us back to Melidrie. I have the power for it now."

"Well, I still need to go to Aola and get my things. And...I'm not in a terrible hurry to be back home, to be honest. Besides, I need to bring this to Bergavenna." She looked down at the Unbinding Stone in her hand. "I can't believe you were going to stab yourself with this. It doesn't even look that sharp."

"Ten minutes of pain is better than ten years of regenerating," said Aelia. "And don't forget, we need to go to Birsgen as well and deliver Ioanna's letter."

"Oh, yes! I nearly forgot." Orsina smiled. "It seems I won't be going home for a while yet."

"Is that...all right?" asked Aelia cautiously. Orsina had been away from home for a long time, not counting her recent brief interlude. "If you'd rather spend some time there..."

"No," said Orsina firmly. "Melidrie will forever be my home, but I am not ready to return to it just yet. Not after how I was treated by my Baron and his daughter. I have no desire for revenge, but it will be some time before I can forgive Perlita."

Aelia nodded. A peaceful, unhurried journey across Ioshora with Orsina sounded extremely appealing.

As they moved through the ruins in the direction of the surface, something caught Aelia's attention. She frowned and gestured to Orsina, who drew her sword once more. A few minutes later, another cultist rounded the corner and walked into Orsina's blade.

Aelia looked down at the fallen woman and realized her face was familiar.

"What is it?" asked Orsina, turning back when she realized Aelia wasn't moving.

"This is Ioanna's aunt. Livia." Aelia looked up. "Or it was."

"I wonder if she was coming to report Ioanna missing," said Orsina. She pressed her lips together. "Well, I admit I'm glad I ran into *her*, at least."

When they finally emerged from the ruins, the sky was completely dark and the moon was high. Kynith was silent and peaceful, and Aelia could sense most of the residents were all peacefully asleep. They had survived, and most of them would never even know of the disaster that nearly struck their city.

THE NEXT DAY, as they rode toward Aola, Aelia realized she had forgotten to tell Orsina something important. She waited until midday, when they stopped to eat, before she shared her news.

It was a pleasant day, with a clear, bright sky, and so Orsina was easily convinced to pull the horses over and sit. She seemed to sense that there was something Aelia wanted to say, and sat quietly until Aelia found the words.

"When I was in Asterium," began Aelia, "something happened. I forgot to tell you at the time, but..."

Orsina looked at her, openly worried. "What?"

"It's not bad," Aelia said hastily. "It's just. They changed my domain. I'm the Goddess of Inspiration now."

"Really?" The delight on Orsina's face was beautiful to see. "Aelia, that's wonderful."

"I've got a whole five or six followers," she said, picking a little wildflower from the grass and staring at it to hide her embarrassment. "I don't want to oversell myself, but I think I can get to at least ten if I start visiting some larger cities."

"In that case, where do you want to go first?" asked Orsina.

"I don't know. I don't care. Anywhere." Aelia smiled up at her. "As long as you're with me."

"Always," said Orsina, taking her by the hand. She leaned in to kiss Aelia, and Aelia leaned backward, pulling Orsina down onto the grass. Orsina's hair fell around Aelia's face like a curtain, shielding her from the outside world.

"I can't believe I've gone so long without you," Aelia whispered.

Orsina pressed their foreheads together. "And I can't believe you were alone for so long," she whispered back.

"I told you, it wasn't so bad." Aelia hesitated. "At least, it wasn't at the time. I don't think I could go back to it, though."

"You don't have to. I promise. Even after I die—"

"Don't promise that," said Aelia hastily. "You'd hate Aethitide. You'd hate it."

"I wouldn't hate it if you were there," said Orsina.

Aelia shook her head. "Solarium is meant for you. You're meant for Solarium. Trust me. It was designed with someone exactly like you in mind. Besides, I'll visit you whenever I can."

Orsina looked thoughtful. "Could I try them both? And see which one I like better? Or maybe even go back and forth?"

"Well..." Aelia had never considered this. "I don't know. Maybe. That's not usually done, but..."

"You're the one always saying I should ask for special favors," Orsina reminded her.

"Yes, but not from Iolar!" Aelia laughed. "Alright, fine. We'll ask when you get there. But that won't be for a long time."

“I’ve got plenty to do in the meantime,” Orsina leaned in and kissed her again. She tasted like summer, Aelia realized. She tasted like sunlight and forgiveness and hope. “I can wait.”

About the Author

Effie is a librarian living in the Philadelphia area with her cat. She writes science fiction and fantasy.

Email: effiecalvin@gmail.com

Twitter: @effiecalvin

Website: www.effiecalvin.com

Other books by this author

The Queen of Ieflaria

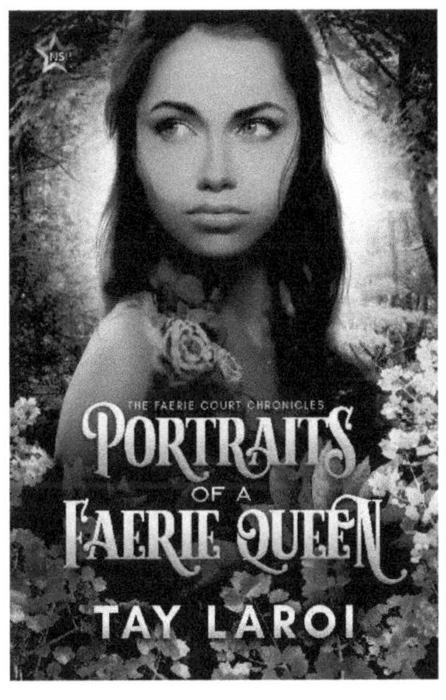

Also Available from NineStar Press

Connect with NineStar Press

Website: NineStarPress.com

Facebook: NineStarPress

Facebook Reader Group: NineStarNiche

Twitter: @ninestarpress

Tumblr: NineStarPress

CPSIA information can be obtained
at www.ICGtesting.com
Printed in the USA
BVHW031921300119
539066BV00001B/23/P

9 781949 909364